THE SHATTERING PEACE

OTHER TOR BOOKS BY JOHN SCALZI

Agent to the Stars
The Android's Dream
Fuzzy Nation
Redshirts
Your Hate Mail Will Be Graded:
A Decade of Whatever, 1998–2008
The Kaiju Preservation Society
Starter Villain
When the Moon Hits Your Eye

THE OLD MAN'S WAR NOVELS

Old Man's War
The Ghost Brigades
The Last Colony
Zoë's Tale
The Human Division
The End of All Things

THE LOCK IN SERIES

Lock In
Head On
Unlocked

THE INTERDEPENDENCY SEQUENCE

The Collapsing Empire
The Consuming Fire
The Last Emperox

EDITED BY JOHN SCALZI

Metatropolis

THE SHATTERING PEACE

John Scalzi

This is a work of fiction. All of the characters, organizations, and events portrayed in this novel are either products of the author's imagination or are used fictitiously.

THE SHATTERING PEACE

Copyright © 2025 by John Scalzi

All rights reserved.

A Tor Book
Published by Tom Doherty Associates / Tor Publishing Group
120 Broadway
New York, NY 10271

www.torpublishinggroup.com

Tor® is a registered trademark of Macmillan Publishing Group, LLC.

EU Representative: Macmillan Publishers Ireland Ltd, 1st Floor, The Liffey Trust Centre, 117–126 Sheriff Street Upper, Dublin 1, DO1 YC43

The Library of Congress Cataloging-in-Publication Data is available upon request.

ISBN 978-0-7653-8919-0 (hardcover)
ISBN 978-0-7653-8920-6 (ebook)

The publisher of this book does not authorize the use or reproduction of any part of this book in any manner for the purpose of training artificial intelligence technologies or systems. The publisher of this book expressly reserves this book from the Text and Data Mining exception in accordance with Article 4(3) of the European Union Digital Single Market Directive 2019/790.

Our books may be purchased in bulk for specialty retail/wholesale, literacy, corporate/premium, educational, and subscription box use. Please contact MacmillanSpecialMarkets@macmillan.com.

First Edition: 2025

Printed in the United States of America

10 9 8 7 6 5 4 3 2 1

For Mal Frazier
I like working with you. I'm sorry I'm such a pain in your ass.

BOOK ONE

ONE

"Hello," I said. "My name is Gretchen Trujillo, and I will be killing you today."

It's always interesting to me to see how this line is taken. Today, in the bare, wrestling-mat-covered multipurpose activity room of the Colonial Union Diplomatic Academy, there were two surprised looks, two smirks, one unreadable expression and one thoughtful expression.

And, well. This is actually a more varied response than I usually get; most of the time the room is evenly split between "surprised" and "smirking." Most of the surprised looks would come from the recruits who weren't aware that murder was part of their orientation session for their Colonial Union Diplomatic Security Force training. The smirking came from the ones who sized me up physically and were pretty sure they could take me in a fight.

A hand went up, from the recruit who had looked thoughtful. "Yes?" I said.

"*Why* will you be killing us today?" the recruit asked.

"What's your name?" I asked the recruit, although I already knew; they give me files, after all.

"Jensen Aguilera," the recruit replied.

"Well, Jensen, that's an excellent question," I said, and then drew the sidearm that had been hidden by my coat and shot him in the face.

The other recruits looked shocked. I shot them all in turn, one also in the face, the rest center mass.

"What have we learned today?" I asked the recruits.

"That you're a good shot," said another of the recruits, who I knew to be named Faiza Vega. She was the one whose expression had been blank. The glowing splotch on her chest, put there by the nanobotic paint round I shot her with, was beginning to fade. The rounds were designed to startle rather than to injure, or (obviously) to kill.

Still, the startle could be significant. No one expects to be shot on their first day of training. Especially not by someone who presents like a midlevel bureaucrat, and who looks like the closest they've ever gotten to a fight was a round of slaps with a frenemy after too many cocktails at a diplomatic mixer.

"You *did* learn I was a good shot," I agreed. "But that wasn't what I wanted you to get out of that."

"We learned that when someone tells you they are going to be killing you, you should believe them," Jensen Aguilera said. His face was now entirely paint free; the nanobotic paint was designed to fall off almost immediately.

I pointed at him. "Closer. What I want to impress on you is that, as a member of the Colonial Union Diplomatic Security Force, you will need to be prepared for threats to yourself, and those you protect, at any time." I motioned around the room. "Even in places where you believe yourself to be perfectly safe."

"All right, but your ambush wasn't exactly fair," began one of the smirkers, a man I knew was named Owais Hartley, and that was as far as he got before I shot him in the face—again—and then shot everyone else in the room as well, for good measure.

"Another thing you should prepare yourself for is the fact this universe is not fair," I said. "Those who mean you harm will not be nice about it. They're not going to give you time to prepare. You will have to work with what you have with you, whatever that is. Starting with your brain."

"That's easy to say when you're the one holding the gun," Hartley said. Being shot in the face twice, even with rounds designed to be (physically) harmless, had not improved his disposition.

"Fair point," I said, and tossed the handgun to him. He reached for it, as much as in surprise as in opportunity, and by the time he'd caught it I was already well within his arm length and slashing at him with a training knife. Its edge was not at all sharp, but it was covered with red nanobotic paint, which streaked his right arm when I slashed down on it, followed by a curving diagonal mark across his abdomen down to his left leg. The two recruits closest to him took a step back, alarmed.

"Now your brachial artery is severed," I said, stepping back from the stunned Hartley, who wasn't expecting more death paint on him. "That probably wouldn't kill you if you applied pressure to it. Unfortunately for you, I also severed your femoral artery, which *would* kill you, and fast. But you probably wouldn't be paying attention to that, because I just disemboweled you. Chances are you would be so preoccupied with keeping your guts off the floor that you wouldn't notice you were bleeding out from the leg."

"Holy shit," said the recruit next to Hartley, named Fatima Ali. She was looking at the bold streaks of red scrawled on her fellow recruit.

"Holy shit indeed," I said, and then slashed at her. She yelped in surprise and took a step back, holding her throat, now covered in red.

"She wasn't expecting that, was she?" I said to the recruit on the other side of Hartley, named Hamisah Meng, and before she could answer I slashed her too, one horizontal and one vertical slash across her torso, which would have opened her up like a box.

I dropped the knife and squared up against the next recruit in the group, a hulking mass with the name of Kostantino Karagkounis. He had been the other smirker, along with Hartley. "Well, come on," I said, to him.

"Ma'am?"

I opened my arms. "No gun, no knife, and you have fifty kilos on me, easy," I said. "Your file says you were a constable back on Erie. You know how to subdue an unruly person. Subdue me."

To his credit, I could see Karagkounis thinking about where the trap might be. He was in fact at least fifty kilos more massive than me, and at least half a meter taller. He had mass on his side, and he knew it, and he knew I knew it too. He was trying to figure out how I would counteract his bulk, whether it would be with speed, with agility, or by using his own mass against him when he attacked. At some point he thought he knew how I was going to get one over on him and made his move.

Ten seconds later he was on the ground, my fingers jammed into his nostrils and the tips hooked into his sinus cavity. This wouldn't kill him, and I wasn't interested in injuring him at this point, but getting my fingers out of his face without my active cooperation would not be pleasant for him.

"Stay down," I advised him.

He exhaled through his mouth and nodded. I extracted my fingers and wiped them on his shirt, and then patted him on the shoulder. "Sorry," I said. He moaned.

I stood up and there was Faiza Vega, my knife in her hand, waiting.

I smiled and pointed at her weapon. "Why not the firearm?" I asked.

"It's probably keyed to your biometrics," Vega said. "Ours were."

I nodded. "You're former Colonial Defense Forces." Which, again, I knew already.

"I got bored with farming," Vega said, and attacked.

She was good, I'll give her that. Her initial thrust was smartly timed, and had I been a tenth of a second less attentive, I would have one less lung, virtually speaking. After that, we both spent a considerable number of seconds sizing each other up for strengths and weaknesses.

I don't know what she thought mine were, but in less than

a minute I knew hers: She thought she was still in the Colonial Defense Forces. Before the current state of affairs, the CDF had been recruited from the ranks of the elderly back on Earth. In exchange for their service, these old people were given new, highly engineered bodies that were super strong, super fast and super resilient.

This was great (well, except for the appallingly low survival rate over just two years), but when you mustered out of the service you were given yet another new body, this one designed within normal human parameters. You became ordinary again, in other words.

Now all your combat skills, honed in a super body, were mapped onto a body far less capable and strong. Unless one had a job regularly involving combat after the switch, it meant that when you went to fight, everything was just a little . . . off.

Vega's job after her service was, as she mentioned, farming. A noble profession. But not one requiring the skills she was currently trying to use on me. Which is why, in another twenty seconds, my knife was out of her hand, and she was on the floor.

"That wasn't supposed to happen," she said, looking up at me.

"I get that a lot," I said, and stood.

I looked over at Jensen Aguilera, who was the only recruit I hadn't killed this round. He put his hands up, clearly not wanting to die for the third time. I nodded and then looked around. "All right, I'm done murdering you for now. Gather round, please."

They did, standing there in various stages of embarrassment as I gathered my knife and handgun and put them away.

"How did I beat you?" I asked. "All of you? Three times?"

"You cheated," Hartley said. His ego was still hurting, poor man.

"There would have to be rules in order for me to cheat," I said.

"You surprised us," Aguilera said.

I nodded here. "Yes, I did," I agreed. "That first time I shot you all was absolutely a surprise. It was meant to be, to shock you out of your complacency. But then I kept killing you. Why?"

"We underestimated you," Vega said.

I pointed. "Yes." I looked at Hartley. "When I shot you, you thought the reason you were dead was the gun." I looked over at Karagkounis. "Then, when I dropped the gun, you thought the reason you were dead was the knife." I brought my attention back to Vega. "And when I had neither, you thought your skills would be superior to mine."

"You've been trained," Vega said.

"Sure."

"CDF?"

"Not exactly," I said. "And not relevant right now. The point was, at every step, you underestimated me, even when I came through that door"—I pointed at the entrance to the multipurpose room—"and *told* you I was going to kill you all. You kept underestimating me as I did it, over and over again. And even as I did it, you never used the advantages you had to stop me."

"What do you mean?" asked Ali.

"There are six of you and one of me," I said. "As we've seen, I can take any one of you down. But more than one at a time? Less likely. If you'd thought to organize and coordinate, you probably could have stopped me. It would have been messy. But you could have done it. As it was, only one of you ever thought to confront me on your own accord." I nodded to Vega here. "The rest of you either didn't put up a fight or had to be goaded into one."

"You don't look like a threat," said Karagkounis.

"I told you I was one."

"Yes, but you . . ." Karagkounis gestured, in lieu of admitting sexism.

I looked over to Vega. "You knew better, at least."

"I was in the CDF," she said. "We fought aliens of all sorts."

"And now we come to it," I said, to the whole group. "The people you'll encounter as part of your job are not all human, or human-sized. Some are vastly larger. Some are smaller. Some are bipedal. Many are not. Some will look cute and harmless to your eyes. Others will look like walking nightmares. What your expectations might be for any of them will be subverted. And any of these species—*any* of them—have a means to be a threat to the people you're assigned to protect. And to you."

"But this is the age of diplomacy," Aguilera said. He nodded toward Vega. "No offense to my colleague here, but there's been détente for a decade now, between the humans and the aliens. We don't need to go into battle every time we see an alien species."

"Who said anything about battle?" I said. I looked around. "We're right in the middle of Phoenix City. Any of you from here?"

Meng raised her hand.

"What parts of the city don't you go into at night?" I asked.

"South Docks and Bedford," she said. "Everybody knows that."

"Every major city on every alien world has a South Docks and a Bedford," I said to Aguilera. "And our diplomats will have reason to go out into those cities every day. As just one example."

"So you want us to kill any alien who tries to mug an attaché," Hartley said.

"We'd prefer it if that wasn't your first impulse," I said. "And if it is, you'll be out of a job. But we want you to get used to the idea that your situational awareness needs to include things and people you might not otherwise view as threats. Détente does not mean no danger."

"When I was in the CDF, we would escort diplomats from time to time," Vega said. "Are we not doing that anymore?"

I smiled. "Believe it or not, the CDF makes our alien colleagues nervous. It's to do with them killing so many of their people over the last couple of centuries."

Vega grimaced. "Fair enough."

I nodded. "By and large other races are doing the same thing with their diplomats, giving them nonmilitary security. Call it a general drawing-down of overt hostilities."

"Until there's a mugging," Hartley muttered.

"Or any other number of events," I concurred. "You're *not* military. But we need you prepared. This exercise was meant to bring that point home to you, before you started your actual training."

"You could have just told us," Aguilera said.

"No," I said. "Just *telling* humans anything has never worked in the entire history of people."

"Are you going to murder us every day to keep the point fresh, then?" Vega asked.

"Me? No," I said. "I'm not one of your instructors." The recruits looked confused. "I'm an analyst. I work the Obin desk."

"You're an *analyst*," Hartley said.

"That's right."

"Un-*fucking*-believable," he muttered again, threw up his hands, and turned away. The idea of having his ass handed to him by someone who was not a professional combat trainer clearly bothered him.

"Are all Colonial Union diplomatic analysts trained like you?" Aguilera asked.

"I'm an unusual case," I admitted. "Which is why they had me come in today and kill you all three times."

"To make the point that you can't ever tell where the danger is coming from," Vega said.

I smiled at her. "That's right. Hopefully you'll all remember it now. We're counting on you to remember it." I nodded to the recruits and left the room the same way I came in.

As I came out, Hector Barber, assistant deputy undersecretary for Diplomatic Affairs, was waiting for me. "Hello, Gretchen," he said. He nodded to the room I just left. "Scaring the children again?"

"Only a little," I said.

"That's a weird little side gig you have there."

"Your boss asks me to do it, so I do it," I said. "Well, her boss, actually. It seems to work. And I get paid extra for it."

"If the recruits knew where you got your training, they might shit themselves."

"And that's why I don't tell them, isn't it?" I said. "Now, is there a reason I'm seeing you, Hector?"

"Maybe it's a social call."

"You don't like me *that* much."

"I like you a little."

I laughed. "I'm delighted," I said. "Tell me what you're actually doing here."

"You're being asked for, and I've come to collect you."

"Being asked for by whom, and for what?"

Hector held out his hands imploringly. "I was just told to come get you. Beyond that, I know only two things."

"What's the first?"

"That whatever it is has got Janine in a fit." Janine was Hector's boss, the deputy undersecretary for Diplomatic Affairs.

"She gets in a fit a lot," I reminded him.

"Yes she does," Hector agreed. "This is more."

I nodded at this. "What's the second thing?" I asked Hector.

"Whatever it is, your father is involved."

TWO

"Where are you going?" Hector asked. At a critical juncture in our walk across the Colonial Union State Department's campus of buildings he started angling toward the deeply impressive Bainburger Tower, where all the important people of the CUSD had their offices. I was heading to the rather less impressive cinderblock construction of the North Annex, where less important people kept their business. Like me.

"I have to check in with Ran," I said, continuing to walk.

"You do not have to check in with Ran," Hector replied, turning to follow, which meant he had already lost the argument, he just didn't know it. "You have a meeting with at least one of my bosses."

"It'll be five minutes at most."

"And your father."

"Maybe ten," I said.

"Gretchen."

"Did they tell you what time this meeting was?" I asked Hector.

"No," he admitted.

"Which means that when we get to your boss's office, I'll probably be sitting there for an hour until they finally get around to me."

"Or it means they are waiting for you *right now*."

"You really believe your boss and my dad are *waiting* for me."

"They *could* be," Hector said.

"How long have you had your job?"

"As long as you've had yours."

"Then you should know better."

"They had me drop what I was doing to get you," Hector pointed out.

"But didn't tell you when the meeting was," I said.

"No."

"Well, then, if I'm late, I'll just blame you."

Hector looked unhappy with that.

Two minutes later we were in the depressing square confines of the North Annex and in an elevator to my office on the sixth floor.

"How long will this take?" Hector asked.

"I told you, five minutes."

"Can you do it faster?"

I looked at Hector. "Are you sweating?"

"No."

I ran a finger across Hector's temple and showed it to him.

"It's hot in this elevator."

"Try again," I said.

Hector sighed. "Fine. Your underling makes me nervous."

"Why, Hector," I said. "You xenophobic monster." The elevator door opened and we exited. I headed to my office, on the far wall of the floor.

"It's not that."

"It's a little bit that."

"He's just a lot."

"It. Ran is hermaphroditic and prefers 'it.'"

"It's a lot," Hector amended.

"I don't know what you're talking about," I said.

From a cubicle in front of my office, a head seemingly attached to a python popped up, spied me and Hector, and made an inhuman squawking sound. Then the head dropped down, and from the cubicle a body emerged, looking like a spider crossed with a giraffe. It galloped down an aisle of cubicles at us.

"Don't run," I whispered to Hector. "You'll engage its prey drive."

"Shut up," Hector said.

The creature stopped roughly two centimeters in front of me and peered down with unblinking eyes. "You have messages," Ran said, to me.

"Of course I do," I said, and motioned to Hector. "You remember Assistant Deputy Undersecretary Barber, of course."

"Yes, hello, Assistant Deputy Undersecretary Barber," Ran said, bobbing its head over to Hector.

"'Hector' is fine," he said, to Ran.

"That is good to hear," Ran said. "Ran is also fine."

"Uh," Hector started, but Ran was looking over to me again.

"I just made a joke," Ran explained to me. "Assistant Deputy Undersecretary Barber wanted me to address him informally, but I pretended to misinterpret his intent, and responded to that feigned misinterpretation."

"No, I got it," I assured Ran.

Ran turned his attention back to Hector. "I have an artificial consciousness," it said, tapping the consciousness harness that was positioned at the base of its neck, and which was in fact the only thing close to apparel that it had on its body. "It is good for many things, but humor is not one of them. I am learning humor."

"Good for you," Hector said.

"Did you like my joke?"

"It surprised me," Hector replied, after a moment.

"I do not think he liked my joke," Ran said, to me.

"I am sure he appreciated the spirit in which it was offered," I replied.

"And now you are attempting to mollify me!" Ran said, triumphantly.

"Yes, that's correct!" I agreed.

"We Obin are also bad at catching the subtle undercurrents of human verbal communication," Ran said to Hector.

"Are you, now," Hector said.

"Yesssssss," Ran replied, looking at Hector suspiciously. Hector suddenly looked nervous again.

"Ran, why don't you give me my messages in my office," I said.

"Of course." Ran motioned me and Hector toward my own office.

"You have had several messages from Deputy Undersecretary Janine Chu-Ward, on the nature of a meeting she wished for you to attend today," Ran said to me, once we were in my office. I had an office by dint of being the lead Obin analyst for State, which would be more impressive if I were not the *only* Obin analyst for State, with exactly one assistant.

An analysis of the thoughts and motivations of the Obin and their government were, how to put this, a lesser concern for the Colonial Union. The Obin were perhaps our closest allies among the hundreds of alien species we knew of, and as Ran hinted, their artificial consciousness, given to them by the Colonial Union in the first place, tended them toward being utterly direct and nondissembling. If we needed them to answer a question, we could just ask them. They were capable of lying, and deceiving, and withholding information, but it stressed them out individually and as a species. Here was an entire nation of exceptionally poor poker players. It made analysis of them an afterthought at best.

Why did I have the job at all? Well, that's a whole story.

"I know about the meeting," I said, and pointed to Hector. "That's why he was sent to retrieve me."

"At one point the deputy undersecretary asked me why you did not have your personal data assistant with you so that she could contact you directly," Ran said.

"What did you tell her?"

"I told her that you regularly abandon your personal data assistant because you don't want to be bothered."

"Ooof," Hector said.

Ran looked over to him. "It's not inaccurate."

"Maybe not," Hector allowed. "But still not something that makes for a great performance review down the line."

"She's not *my* boss," I said. "Anyway, I was doing a thing for her, she knew exactly where I was, and you found me just fine."

"And there's nothing I like more than taking time out of *my* day to haul you from one place to another," Hector said. He motioned to my office. "Not that I have managed even that yet."

"We're going," I promised, and turned back to Ran. "Who else?"

"Representative Trujillo also called, several times," Ran said, referring to my father. "He seemed to become more agitated with every call."

"That's Dad," I said.

"He also questioned your lack of personal data assistant."

"He and I once went for an entire year without using a PDA," I said.

"Why did you do that?" Hector asked.

"We were being hunted."

Hector tilted his head.

"She is talking about when she was part of the founding colony of the planet Roanoke and the Conclave was looking for them," Ran said to Hector, helpfully.

Hector looked back at me. "That happened to *you*?"

"Dad was the administrator for the colony," I said. "The second administrator. Maybe the third one, depending on how you count."

"I thought you two were from Erie."

"We are. We came to Roanoke from there. When the second wave of colonization was completed, we moved back."

"I don't remember any of that from the movie," Hector said.

I narrowed my eyes at him. "You work for the State Department of the Colonial Union, and the only thing you know about a major historical event from your *actual lifetime* is from a movie."

"In my defense, I was eight standard when it happened," Hector said. "And the actual story of it wasn't declassified until I was in college."

"That's a *terrible* excuse," I said, although in fairness it probably wasn't. The Colonial Union kept incredibly tight control of information between its colonies until a decade ago, when the three-way treaty with the alien government called the Conclave, and with Earth, significantly opened up official lines of communication.

Hector was originally from Kourou, one of the smaller and thus frequently forgotten colonies. It's entirely possible that news of the events of Roanoke Colony didn't reach there until fairly recently, and instead of being a monumentally significant moment in Colonial Union history—which it was, thank you very much—it was just another part of a gigantic flood of new information they'd had shoved onto them at the same time. In which case, learning about it mostly from the movie made sense.

But I didn't have to like it. The movie, unimaginatively named *Roanoke*, was about as factually correct as a fairy tale. Historical events were switched around or left out of the story entirely, entire plot points and characters were made up out of thin air, and any real people the filmmakers deemed inessential to the plot were chucked over the side, including my dad and (thus, logically) me.

We went to see the movie when it came out, paying for it like common trolls because why would *we* have been invited to the glitzy premiere, and I nearly murdered Dad because he was derisively snorting through the entire film.

He wasn't wrong to do it. It just got repetitive after a while.

Anyway, it was a huge hit and won a bunch of awards and there was even talk of a sequel, which never went anywhere because they wrote the second administrator (or third, depending) entirely out of the script of the first film, now, didn't they.

"Sorry," Hector said. "I am properly ashamed."

"I think that's sarcasm," Ran said to me.

"I knew that, Ran, thank you," I said. "Any other messages?"

"One more, from Deputy Ambassador Clock," Ran said. "It wishes to reschedule your two p.m. meeting with it into the evening."

I frowned at this. My meeting with Ambassador Clock, who was the rough equivalent of my counterpart with the

Obin diplomatic mission to the Colonial Union, was why I had needed to come back to the office in the first place. Since I didn't have my PDA with me, I needed Ran to ask Clock's office for a reschedule. "Did it say what time?"

"It said any time after six p.m. local would be acceptable."

"Did it give any explanation for the delay?"

"No."

This was unusual. Unusual for Ambassador Clock to want to reschedule a meeting, and unusual for an Obin diplomat of any sort not to offer a reason.

"What time is it now?" I asked.

"It's just after one, local," Ran said. The "local" was important because Phoenix's day was slightly different from the Colonial Union standard day, which was based on Earth's rotational period, and was used for official dates and communications. As a result, an official Colonial Union appointment time and a local appointment time would often have nothing to do with each other as clocks wandered in and out of sync.

"Let's schedule for six thirty local," I said. "If I need to change that I will let you know."

"You may need your personal data assistant for that," Ran noted.

I groaned and reached into my desk and pulled out my PDA. "Fine," I said.

"You will need to turn it on," Ran observed.

I groaned again and turned it on. It immediately blasted through a long series of notification sounds.

"You're popular," Hector observed.

"It's not that," Ran said. "She hasn't turned it on in some time."

"Is that so," Hector said, dryly. "Gretchen. We really have to go now."

I nodded. "Make that schedule change for me, please," I said to Ran.

"I will do it."

I looked at Hector. "Why are you not walking?" I said. "I

thought we were in a rush." I walked past him and out the door of my office.

"She is attempting humor," I heard Ran say to Hector.

"'Attempting' is the word for it, yes," Hector said to Ran, and then followed me out the door.

"You did very well with Ran," I said to Hector several minutes later, as we walked into the atrium of Bainburger Tower.

"When it ran up to us I almost had an incident," Hector confessed.

"I didn't notice."

"This would be where your assistant would tell us you are attempting to mollify me."

"You would be correct about that."

"How did you get Ran as an assistant?"

"I run the Obin desk," I said. "It's useful to have an actual Obin around."

"No, I get that. I mean why . . . it?"

"Your boss suggested having an Obin on staff might be helpful," I said. "The Obin embassy suggested Ran. I interviewed it. I found its enthusiasm charming."

"'Charming,'" Hector said.

"You disagree."

"Like I said, it's a lot."

"Well, I'm a lot, sometimes," I said. "We match."

"Gretchen," someone else said, before Hector could reply. I turned and saw Dia LaBelle, my father's personal assistant, coming up to us.

"Dia," I said, and motioned to Hector. "This is—"

"Assistant Deputy Undersecretary Barber, yes, hello," Dia said, and then turned her attention back to me. "I'm here to take you to your meeting."

"We were just on our way to the deputy undersecretary's office," I said.

"It's not there," Dia said. "Your father booked a conference room on one of the secure floors."

"That feels like overkill," I said. Which was in keeping with my father's way of doing things, to be honest. But I knew what I was working on at the Obin desk and the level of security clearance I needed to do it. Overkill it almost certainly was.

Dia said nothing.

"Seriously?" I replied.

Dia looked over at Hector, pointedly.

"Oh look, I need to be absolutely anywhere else at the moment," Hector said, and then disappeared, hastily.

I turned back to Dia. "You have to be joking."

"By all means, Gretchen, let me explain to you why I am not joking, here in the public atrium of Bainburger Tower, with several dozen people within earshot," Dia said.

I held up a hand. "All right." I looked around the atrium. "Do I at least have time to go to the restroom?"

"Of course," Dia said. "You've already kept your father and the undersecretary waiting for fifteen minutes, what's a few more minutes between friends?"

"Wait, they're already there?" I asked, surprised.

"You were expecting to be waiting for them?"

"Well, yes," I admitted.

Dia shook her head. "The meeting has been going for some time," she said. "They paused it for the sole purpose of bringing you in. They've been waiting for you, Gretchen."

"I think my bladder just locked up," I said to this, after a moment.

Dia nodded. "Smart bladder." She motioned toward a bank of elevators. "Shall we?"

THREE

"At the risk of being insulting, given where we are, I will nevertheless remind you, Gretchen, that this meeting and everything discussed in it are highly confidential," Janine Chu-Ward said to me.

"I understand," I answered. Where we were was a hermetically sealed, glass-encased conference room in a sub-basement level that appeared to be constructed out of concrete and despair. I knew the conference room had to have an air exchange system, if only because the occupants who were in it before me had not passed out from oxygen deprivation. But I couldn't hear it working or see evidence of where it might be. The sound dampening of the room was so complete that even inside the room it felt like voices died the instant they got past the border of the conference table. I found myself leaning in to make sure I could hear and be heard.

I was at the table with Janine; her boss, Zawadi Mbalenhle; my father, Manfred Trujillo; a Colonial Defense Forces officer named Colonel Bridgers, no first name given; and a representative from Earth, Mateu Jordi, no position given although I assumed he was part of Earth's diplomatic service. Earth and the Colonial Union's official mutual position was best described as "frosty," even with the tripartite trade and diplomacy agreement that had been in place for a decade.

And well, who could blame them. If I had been literally farmed for colonists and soldiers for a couple of centuries by an off-world government that directly interfered with my social and technological development to keep that flow of bodies coming, I would be frosty, too.

Jordi seemed to turn that frostiness against me personally when, after I confirmed my understanding of the nature of the meeting, he turned to Mbalenhle and said, "I want to reiterate my strong objection to Ms. Trujillo being in this conversation at all. She is clearly out of her depth, and this is obviously some attempt at nepotism on the part of Representative Trujillo."

"She's been called into the meeting to get her to the correct depth," Mbalenhle said. Then she turned to my dad. "But perhaps you should address the nepotism angle, Manfred."

"That's fair," my dad said, and turned to me. "Gretchen, what is your current position within the State Department?"

"I'm the head of the analysis desk for the Obin," I said.

"And you've been in the role for how long?"

"As head, for six years, and I was under Jervis Hocking for a couple of years before that."

"Do you have any experience with colonization?" Dad asked.

I smiled at this. "Well, yes," I said. "I was part of the first wave of colonists for Roanoke Colony, along with you."

"And when I became colony leader after the departure of John Perry and Jane Sagan, you acted as my unofficial second-in-command, yes?"

"Yes," I said, and then turned to Jordi. "That was definitely nepotism."

Jordi did not seem impressed with this confession.

"Last question," Dad said. "In a fair fight, who at this table could you beat?"

I blinked in surprise at this question, but answered it. "You, and Secretaries Mbalenhle and Chu-Ward for sure. I don't know Mr. Jordi's training history, but if it's similar to most diplomats then him too. Colonel Bridgers is CDF, so he could probably take me in a fair fight."

"What about an unfair fight?" Bridgers asked. I smiled and made a seesaw motion with my hand. He grinned back.

"Why are you so confident about your fighting skill?" Dad asked.

"Back when I was on Roanoke, I was trained for combat by a pair of Obin military commanders, and I've kept up with it since," I said. I turned back to Jordi. "I should be clear that I got this training because they were training my best friend, and she insisted that I get to be trained along with her. Zoë always got her way with the Obin."

There was an about two-second lag while Jordi put together that the "Zoë" in this conversation was Zoë Boutin-Perry, adopted daughter of John Perry and Jane Sagan. I knew when he'd gotten it because his eyes went wide. As I understand it the status of the Perry family on Earth was something between royalty and "actual living saints," even if all of them had expressly chosen not to capitalize on that status. They were all living as quietly as actual living saints could in a small town in Ohio, wherever that was.

I wondered what Zoë thought of her portrayal in that terrible movie about Roanoke. It was so *very* inaccurate.

For his part, Jordi recovered his skepticism. "I don't see how any of that is relevant, especially the last part," he said to my dad.

"It's relevant because every part of Gretchen's resume is relevant," Dad replied. "She's an expert regarding the Obin, and in fact *the* expert for the entire State Department. She has a history regarding colonization both as a colonist and, unofficially, as an administrator. If this situation is as bad as we're worried it is, then we know she can handle herself. And she is a known quantity for us, which adds a measure of security and confidence. Now, *you* might call it nepotism, but if nothing else I'll point out that Gretchen took her State job over my objections."

Jordi turned to me. "That true?"

"Dad wanted me to work for him," I said. "I got enough of that on Roanoke."

"So you think you're qualified for this?"

"I don't know what *this* is," I confessed. "I just now sat down."

"You're being volunteered," Mbalenhle said.

"That much I got, ma'am. Someone please tell me for what."

Mbalenhle nodded to Chu-Ward. "You know that colonization has been on pause," Chu-Ward said.

"Yes," I said. One of the points on the tripartite treaty between the Colonial Union, the Conclave and Earth was that all new colonization by each party would be put on pause for an indefinite period. The reason for this was simple enough: Colonization was the primary cause for conflict between the Conclave and the Colonial Union, and Earth, being only a single planet and farmed as it had been by the Colonial Union, was at a distinct disadvantage in any event. It was a pain point for everyone, so everyone decided to take a time out.

This like many things was great in theory, and less than perfect in practice. Alien species who were not part of the Conclave still attempted to colonize, and the Conclave found itself being the colonization police, which kept it in continual conflict with everyone besides the Colonial Union and Earth. Within the Colonial Union and the Conclave, unsanctioned "wildcat" colonies were still happening, despite the prohibition and despite the fact that most of these colonies were dead within three years because colonizing a new world is hard, especially when you don't have your entire civilization's resources to fall back on.

Beyond all that, the colonization pause was just incredibly unpopular politically. No one likes being kept in a pen, even if that "pen" was dozens of planets, many of which were not even at an ecologically sustainable holding capacity for their particular species. Rabble-rousers of every species railed against the pause, and a lot of those rabble-rousers were in government.

There wasn't any doubt that official colonization would happen again. The question was when, and who would be the first to officially start it up again, and whether a new race for planets and resources would plunge us all back into a continual state of war.

Chu-Ward nodded curtly at this acknowledgment. "Well, we've been colonizing again."

"What?" I said, looking around the table.

"Not only us," Dad said, holding up a hand.

"No, not only us," Chu-Ward agreed. "All three members of the Tripartite Agreement have come to understand that the prohibition on colonizing is unsustainable and that we have to find a way to continue to allow it without all of the . . . negative side effects."

"Like war," Bridgers said. "Which we are not equipped to fight like we once did." He nodded to Jordi. "Our traditional source of recruits has been—rightly—curtailed, and our drive to bring in recruits from within the Colonial Union has been far less successful than we'd like."

"The Colonial Union citizens don't mind aging?" Jordi asked Bridgers.

"They mind aging just as much as anyone else," Bridgers said. "They object to having to join the CDF to get the new, younger bodies. They're demanding all the CDF medical trade secrets get opened up to the public, and eventually they're going to get their way. Which makes colonization even more of a priority."

I nodded at this. It was an open secret that the CDF had been shrinking, first slowly and then more quickly as the years went on. The relative peace brought on by the Tripartite Agreement had done a lot to minimize the issue; if you're not actively fighting as many enemies, you don't need to have as large of a military force. But there's a point at which you can't ignore it any further. We were apparently getting to that point.

Chu-Ward cleared her throat and continued. "To avoid some of these negative issues, and to see whether there could be a peaceful path forward with colonization, the members of the Tripartite Agreement decided to create a test case, where citizens of the Colonial Union, the Conclave and Earth would live together in a single environment to see whether they could successfully mix on a permanent basis."

"The Conclave was already doing that," I said. "The whole point of the Conclave was that any new colonies would have a mix of species."

"Yes," Chu-Ward said. "The innovation here was the addition of humans."

"There was no confidence that we would *mix*," Bridgers said, archly.

"Nor is there any appetite, on any side, for the human governments to merge, or join the Conclave," Mbalenhle said. "The Conclave doesn't want any of us, and we don't want to be part of the Conclave. It makes colonizing together difficult and a special case."

"But you did it," I said.

"We did a *test*," Dad said, emphasizing the word "test." "One colony. Not on a planet. Not even on a moon. On a hollowed-out asteroid space station that we got from the Obin, in a system they intended to colonize but then abandoned. Using the Obin station meant that we could do it discreetly. We call it Unity. A population of fifty thousand. Five thousand humans, three thousand from us, two thousand from Earth, and the rest all other species from the Conclave."

"How long has this test been going on?" I asked.

"Three years," Jordi said. He nodded to Dad. "Your father was the one to negotiate with us and the Conclave about it, and he convinced the Obin to lease their station to us for it. That's why *he's* here."

"And how has it been going?"

"Until two days ago, it was going just fine," Dad said. "The usual problems with any colony, but it turns out that humans integrate just fine. Well, most of them. There are always a few who turn out to be assholes. But overall, it was a positive test."

"You said 'until two days ago,'" I said. "What happened two days ago?"

"It disappeared," Dad said.

"What do you mean, disappeared?" I asked.

"Two days ago the daily skip drone from Unity didn't arrive," Colonel Bridgers said. "We sent an observation drone, and it skipped in and looked for Unity where it should have been in orbit. It wasn't there."

"And it can't be moved," I said. "The space station."

"It's an asteroid. It has an orbit. It can be moved out of that orbit, but it would require effort and planning. Even then it couldn't have been moved that much in the time between the last skip drone we received and when we sent the observation drone."

"And to answer your next question, it hasn't been destroyed," Dad said. "There's nothing that looks like obvious debris. There's nothing natural in the system that would have hit it. Unity tracked anything that would have been a threat. And neither we nor anyone we know could have destroyed Unity so completely that there would be no observable debris."

"If it can't be moved and it's not destroyed, what happened to it?" I asked.

"We're putting together a mission to find out," Chu-Ward said.

"And we need you to go on it," Mbalenhle added.

I gaped at this. "Why me?" I finally said.

"*Thank* you," Jordi said, gesturing toward me.

"We already explained why," Chu-Ward said, glaring at Jordi briefly before turning her attention back to me.

"All right, but there are other people who have those qualifications," I said. "There are other Obin experts. Other people who know about colonization." I pointed to Bridgers. "Other people with combat skills."

"Not all in the same body," Chu-Ward said. "And not with the level of discretion this will need."

"What does *that* mean?"

"It means that just as Unity itself is off the books, so is this mission," Bridgers said. "It needs to stay small and close to the vest, by us and by the other principals of Unity Colony." He nodded to Jordi. "We, the Conclave and Earth are each sending a small group of observers. We'll be traveling in an Obin ship because while they abandoned the system for colonizing, they still claim the system for future use. You will be the deputy lead for our contingent and our liaison to the Obin."

"When?"

Dad looked at his watch. "The ship for this mission departs in twenty-two hours."

"I can't do *that*," I said. "I don't have a cat sitter."

This got a small murmur of laughter. "I can have Hector watch your cat," Chu-Ward said.

"I'll have Ran do it," I said. "It's already met Lucifer. Lucy loves it. I think he thinks Ran is a big weird cat."

I noticed Dad looking at me appraisingly. "You're not reluctant because of your *cat*, Gretchen."

"No, not really," I confessed, and then pointed to Jordi. "But he's not wrong either. This is a job for a field agent, not someone who does analysis. Even if I am proficient in combat."

"So you're refusing to be volunteered," Mbalenhle said.

I shook my head. "No, ma'am. I'll go if you tell me to go. But I need to be sure you understand that if I were in your shoes, I would not be my first choice."

Mbalenhle was about to say something, but my dad spoke up first. "May I have the room for a moment?" he said. "I'd like a word with Gretchen privately."

"Is this really necessary?" Mbalenhle asked.

"If I didn't think it was, I wouldn't ask."

Mbalenhle looked like she was going to say something. Then she nodded, and made a gesture to the others. Thirty seconds later everyone but me and Dad were in the corridor, looking anywhere else but at the conference room.

"Well, this doesn't look like nepotism at all," I said, to Dad.

He ignored this. "There's another reason I want you on this mission," he said to me.

I glanced at the group in the corridor. "Are you keeping secrets from the rest of them?" I asked Dad.

"It's not a secret, and there's nothing I'm going to tell you that they, or you, can't find out just from looking at the files. It's something I figure you would want to know, just not in front of a room of people."

"What is it?"

"The group of colonists who we sent to Unity had to be carefully selected," Dad said. "They had to have certain skills. They had to have a certain psychological makeup. They had to understand the nature of the colony would mean a certain amount of isolation. If they had ever been early-generation colonists before, so much the better."

"All right," I said.

"So it will not surprise you that more than a few of our colonists for Unity came from Roanoke Colony," Dad said.

"You're saying that people I know from Roanoke might be missing right now."

"Yes," Dad said. "And, I'm afraid, one person in particular."

I stared at my dad stupidly for a moment, not getting it. Then it felt like my heart got dropped down a chute.

"Magdy," I said, so quietly it was almost a whisper.

"Magdy," Dad agreed. "Dr. Magdy Metwalli. He signed up to head up the Colonial Union's medical detachment, at my request and on my recommendation. Your old boyfriend went because I asked him to, Gretchen."

"Oh, God. Dad," I began, but he held up a hand.

"Zawadi thought of you for this mission because of all the reasons I told Jordi in the room, and I agreed with her, and so did Janine," Dad said. "All of that is true, and all of those reasons are why you should be on that ship tomorrow.

"But this," Dad said, and shrugged. "One day, one way or another, the story about Unity is going to come out. When it did, you'd find out I was responsible for putting Magdy on that colony. I figure you might forgive me if you knew I sent him out there. But if you knew that you could have done something to save him, and I didn't at least give you a chance to do it, *that* you would not forgive."

"You think he's dead," I said, looking at Dad, trying to read him. "Him and everyone else on that colony."

"I think something's happened we can't explain," Dad said. "And I think you need to be the one to find out how to explain it. If you can save Magdy and everyone else on the colony,

Gretchen, then do that. But if you can't, tell us what happened to them. We need to know. The answer could be what keeps us and the Conclave and Earth from falling back into war. A war that none of us are going to survive."

"Jesus, Dad," I said, after a minute.

"I know it's a lot to put on you."

"You *think*?"

"But am I wrong that you would be angry with me if you found out I sent Magdy to the colony after the fact? Am I wrong that you would find it hard to forgive me?"

"No," I admitted.

"I know you never really did get over Magdy."

"What are you talking about? There was David."

"Obviously you had other relationships."

I narrowed my eyes at Dad. "Dad, we got *engaged*."

Dad nodded. "How is David these days?" he asked.

I pursed my lips at this. I had no idea, and it wouldn't be easy to find out. David and I breaking off our engagement was not why he decided to take a posting on Rus, but it didn't hurt in terms of his decision-making.

Dad caught the thinned lips. "It's not you," he said. "It's both of us. I never got over your mother, you know. We Trujillos are like this. We *imprint*."

"I'm not a baby duck, Dad."

"You're not," he agreed. "But I'm not wrong about Magdy, either."

"No, you're not," I acknowledged, after a minute.

"Go find out what happened to him," Dad said. "Him, and Unity Colony. Do it for the both of us. I'm probably going to have a lot to answer for, Gretchen. All of us who authorized this colony are. I can take the judgment of everyone else who might condemn me. Yours is the only judgment that would break me."

FOUR

"You have messages," Ran said, and I ignored it to stomp into my office and slam the door, collapse into my desk chair and put my head in my hands.

Some indeterminate time later I looked up and saw Ran standing in front of my desk.

"How long have you been there?" I asked.

"Three minutes," Ran said.

"Seems long."

"I didn't want to interrupt your muttering."

I tilted my head at this. "I was muttering?"

Ran bobbed its head. "Yes."

"I don't remember muttering."

"You were muttering quietly," Ran said. "Perhaps you did not hear yourself."

"What was I muttering?" I asked.

"Several variations of 'god damn it, you stupid asshole,'" Ran said.

I nodded. "Yeah, okay. I was thinking that for sure. I wasn't aware I was saying it out loud."

"You were quite emphatic," Ran assured me.

"Sorry. It's not you."

"I did not think you were talking about me," Ran said. "When you are upset with me you do not mutter."

I paused at this. "What . . . do I do?"

"You make a face."

"What face?"

"I cannot show you the face, my face can't make the face."

"I don't get upset with you, Ran," I protested.

"Yes you do," Ran said. "You get upset with me about once a day, mostly when I miss social cues that are obvious to you, or say something you find inappropriate in front of others, and then you have to make excuses for me, or when I say something you do not think is on point and you have to try to bring me back to what you believe is the topic of the discussion, or when I have talked too much and you want me to be quiet." Ran pointed at me. "There. That face."

"That's not my upset face," I said. "That's my 'I'm being patient' face."

Ran looked at me blankly, which honestly didn't look all that much different from its usual face, since Obin faces are not naturally expressive. But I could tell.

"I apologize for getting upset with you," I said to Ran.

"Thank you," Ran said. "However I was not looking for an apology. I have never taken it personally. I understand that for humans being upset is a foundational emotional state."

"I don't really know what to do with that statement," I confessed.

"There is nothing to do with it," Ran said. "It simply is."

"Was there a reason you came in?" I asked Ran, as much to get us off of an increasingly awkward conversational track as to find out what it wanted.

"I do have messages for you," Ran said. "And also I came in because you are in obvious emotional distress and I wanted to see if there was anything I could do to ameliorate it."

"Can you take us back in time so I can punch someone in the face?" I asked.

"I cannot," Ran said.

"A shame, that."

"Would going back in time to punch someone change this particular moment?" Ran asked.

"Probably not," I admitted. "But it might make me feel better anyway."

"I understand," Ran said, and then opened its arms wide, which, if you were not used to such a thing, would look absolutely terrifying. "If you are looking to feel better, I can offer you a healing hug."

I squinted at Ran. "A hug."

"A *healing* hug," Ran said. "I understand that for humans they can be quite therapeutic."

I smiled. "Yes, sometimes they can be," I said. "But I have a better idea."

I was so focused on Ran's knife that I entirely missed its roundhouse kick to my skull. It hit me straight across the temple, and not lightly—Obin are not small in either height or mass, and there was a lot of momentum in that kick. My head snapped at the neck, and I more or less rotated around my center of gravity until my skull smashed into the floor.

If we weren't in the State Department training gym, with me wearing a full protective nanobot mesh fight suit, I would probably have been dead when my head hit the mat, if I hadn't already been snuffed out by the roundhouse kick.

As it was, the fight suit stiffened up my head and neck area almost as quickly as Ran kicked into it. When my head hit the mat, the force of the impact translated through the entire suit, changing a possibly fatal kick into a merely annoying one. The State Department Security fight suits were made of the same nanotech material the Colonial Defense Force combat suits had, and those could absorb the impact of a sniper shot at near point-blank range. A little head contact with an exercise mat wasn't going to stress it.

Didn't mean it didn't *hurt*, though.

"You are dead," Ran said to me, helpfully, as it stood over my putative corpse.

"I'm only mostly dead," I said, from the mat.

"You are fully dead," Ran assured me.

"All right, fine."

"Not for the first time."

"Yes, I know."

"This is not like you," Ran said, and it was right. Ran had mass and height on its side, as well as the standard defense training that all Obin who served in their military or diplomatic service received. But I was the more experienced fighter of the two of us, marginally faster, and typically fought dirtier.

In our usual sparring sessions we were a mostly even match. Today, Ran had seven kills to my two. I was off my game.

"I have a lot on my mind," I said, still on the floor.

"Perhaps you should have gone with the healing hug," Ran said.

"Oh, that's *it*," I said, and grabbed its leg while I was still on the mat. Ran squawked in surprise and tried to avoid my attack, but ten seconds later was dead as hell.

"*There's* your healing hug, you putz," I said, standing over Ran for a change.

"I don't know that word," Ran said.

"It's Yiddish. Literally it means 'penis,' so it wouldn't apply to you. But less literally it means 'fool' or 'jerk,' and *that* applies." I reached down to give Ran a hand up.

It took my hand and stood up. "Thank you. Also, I am happy that you were motivated when I insulted you. You realize that was an intentionally used psychological tactic."

"Yes."

"It's called 'trash talk.'"

"I know what it's called."

"Also, I do have something close to a penis, as well as an ovipositor, so 'putz' could literally apply to me."

I gave Ran a look.

"There's that face again," it said.

"Do you want to go another round?" I asked, pointing to the mat.

Ran shook its head. "We usually go to ten," it said. "And I have won for once and wish to bask in the glory of it."

I smiled at this. "Fair enough."

"As a token of my victory, perhaps you will tell me what it is that got you so distraught," Ran said.

I paused for a moment. "It's about information I was given that I'm not allowed to share," I began.

Ran held up its digits. "I will not ask further," it said.

I held up my own hand. "It's fine. I'm just trying to think of a way to phrase it that doesn't get both of us in trouble." I thought for a moment more while Ran waited.

Finally I said, "Have you ever been in love, Ran?"

"No," Ran said, and touched its consciousness harness. "These latest harnesses improve our ability to handle strong emotions, but they are still very difficult, even pleasant ones like love would be. Also our biology doesn't require it."

"I mean, ours doesn't either, when it comes down to it," I said.

"No. But I understand it can help."

"Well, *that's* true," I said. "But that's not helping me try to explain what I'm thinking about to you." I thought some more. "All right, how about this. You remember how you sometimes think I am annoyed with you, and I make the face."

"Yes, you did it just a few minutes ago," Ran said, helpfully.

"I get annoyed with you, but you don't take it personally because you know that people are like that."

"Humans are like that," Ran said. "Not all people are like that."

"Correction noted," I said. "Humans are like that. But is that the only reason you tolerated it from me?"

"No," Ran said. "We are also colleagues and, I think, friends."

I nodded. "We are both of those things," I agreed. "Which means we can both annoy each other quite a bit before there's a problem."

"That is an interesting definition of what being a friend is," Ran observed.

"There is more to it than that, yes," I allowed. "But the point is, friends care for each other even when there are moments they annoy each other. Or exasperate each other. Or even don't like each other all that much."

"All right," Ran said.

"Well, I have a friend," I said. "More than a friend. Someone who I was in love with and who loved me, too. And now he's gone and done something really really stupid, and I am angry with him for letting himself get talked into it when he should have known better. I'm angry with him, and at the moment I don't know what to do with that anger." I waved at Ran. "Aside from, you know, try to fight you."

"Poorly," Ran said.

I laughed at this.

"I am sorry your friend has made you angry by being stupid," Ran said, after I was done laughing.

"Thank you, Ran," I said. "I am too."

"The offer for a healing hug still stands."

I laughed again, but then stopped. "That reminds me, I need you to watch my cat."

"Lucifer?"

"That's my only cat, yes."

"I will happily watch your cat," Ran said. "For how long?"

"I don't know yet," I said.

"Does this have something to do with your stupid friend?" Ran asked.

"I can't answer that."

"Of course. I will watch Lucifer for as long as it takes for you to deal with whatever it is that may or may not have anything to do with your stupid friend."

"Thank you, Ran," I said. I looked at my watch. "I have a couple of hours before my meeting with Deputy Ambassador Clock. I'm going to shower and take care of some things I need to wrap up. While I'm doing that I need you to check to see what things I might have outstanding so I can deal with them before I leave, or have you deal with while I'm gone. If you can have that for me when I get back from my meeting with Clock, that would be great."

"There is a complication," Ran said.

"What's that?"

"You will recall, before you suggested we spar, that I told you I had messages for you."

"Yes," I said.

"One of the messages was from Deputy Ambassador Clock."

"What is it? Does it want to delay our meeting again? If it does, that meeting is probably not going to happen."

"It does not want to delay your meeting," Ran said. "The meeting will take place at the same time."

"So what is it?"

"It said that it wants me to attend the meeting with you."

"We know of your mission," Deputy Ambassador Clock said to me, after only the barest minimum of diplomatic pleasantries, as I sat down in front of its desk in its office at the Obin embassy to the Colonial Union.

I nodded at this but otherwise said nothing, waiting for Clock to continue.

Clock's office was like every other office in the Obin embassy, entirely bare except for an absolute minimum of brutally functional furniture. This was not because the Obin favored a brutally functional aesthetic; it was because the Obin had no aesthetic at all. To have an aesthetic would require some conscious thought put into it, and the Obin, despite having a civilization at least as old as humanity's, had only had consciousness for three decades. Not nearly enough time to develop aesthetics, or much of an interest in one.

It was my understanding that when the Obin first planned their embassy in Phoenix City, the Colonial Union offered to lend them some interior designers. The offer was declined.

Thus, me sitting in a bare office, in an adequate but boring chair, in front of a standard, unappealing desk, behind which sat Deputy Ambassador Clock. It had a chair and I had a chair. Ran, who was also attending the meeting, stood behind me. It did not seem to mind.

I looked back at my assistant, and then back at Clock. "I am not sure how to respond to that statement," I said. "Except perhaps that the subject you are referring to is not one that should be discussed in front of my colleague."

"I am aware that you were told the mission was classified," Clock said. "However, you must know that inasmuch as we the Obin are supplying you transportation to and from the destination, we are aware of the mission as well."

"That makes sense," I said. "But you will understand that without clearance, I can't discuss or even formally acknowledge that I know anything about that subject."

"I do not need you to either confirm or deny anything about the mission," Clock replied. "What I do request, if you would be so kind, is for you to listen."

I nodded at this and waited for Clock to continue.

"The system that Unity Colony is in we call Karna-Hlaven, or "Sixty-Third," Clock said. "It was the last system the Obin attempted to colonize before the Conclave issued its moratorium on new colonization by any species. The asteroid that Unity is on was never meant to be a formal colony by the Obin, but a forward base to plan future potential colonization of the several moons of Karna-Hlaven's largest planet. However, the Conclave determined that forward base was enough to count as colonization for its purposes. This was important, you see, when Unity was founded. As a *technical* matter, Unity Colony does not run afoul of the Conclave's prohibition on colonization, or the tripartite treaty's pause. It's not a new colony, merely an . . . *expansion* of a previous one. This made it convenient and useful for all parties involved."

"All right," I said. I figured acknowledging I had heard something was not an issue here.

"It may have also created a problem."

I sat quietly for a moment waiting for Clock to continue. It did not. Finally, I said, "How so?"

"Ms. Trujillo, you are aware of the special relationship between the Obin and the Consu," Clock said.

This got my attention. The Consu were the heavyweights in our area of space, a species of intelligent being so far advanced from everyone else in the neighborhood that comparing ourselves to them was like comparing Cro-Magnons to spacefaring humans. They weren't just in a different league than us and every other species in this part of the galaxy; they were playing a different, infinitely more complicated sport.

Which is not to say that they weren't interested in us lesser beings. The Consu were interested in us the way a kid with a magnifying lens was interested in an anthill. They would play with us for their own unknowable purposes and then wander off for a while until they decided to haul out their magnifying lenses again.

No species knew this better than the Obin. Thousands of years ago, the Consu landed on the moon that would be the Obin homeworld, found a species that had the basic intelligence of an armadillo, and uplifted it to into sentience, *without consciousness*, just to see what would happen.

What happened was an entire species that, even without individual consciousness, was so deeply affected by its lack that it dictated nearly everything about them for millennia. The Obin had racial post-traumatic stress disorder from the very moment of their creation.

The Consu, for their part, thought almost nothing of the Obin at all. Imagine if you knew your creator existed, and didn't care about you at all. That's going to mess with your racial psyche.

"I am aware, yes," I said, to Clock.

"Then it may interest you to know that in the last roughly twenty of your years, the Consu have become interested in the Obin again."

I frowned at this. "Why?"

Deputy Ambassador Clock cocked its head at me. "I think you may be aware of a particular event nearly twenty years ago, involving the Obin and the Consu."

I stared at Clock blankly for about three seconds before it hit me. "Roanoke," I said.

"Roanoke," Clock agreed. "And the incident with your friend Zoë Boutin-Perry."

My friend Zoë had been the biological daughter of Charles Boutin, the human scientist who had figured out how to give the Obin an artificial consciousness. She was also the adopted daughter of John Perry and Jane Sagan, the first leaders of Roanoke Colony. As the daughter of the racial hero of the Obin, Zoë was an idol to the whole species. When Roanoke Colony had been threatened with attack, it was Zoë who left to get help, convincing the Obin to get the Consu to give her technology that would defeat the attack on the colony.

How she managed to do that was a hell of a story.

But it did end up requiring a horrendous number of Obin lives.

"Why would Roanoke matter?" I asked.

"Why does anything matter to the Consu?" Clock asked. "The answer is unknowable without asking, and the Consu always exact a heavy price for asking questions. What we know is that after Roanoke, after millennia of neglect, we Obin would spot the Consu surveilling us in our systems. You should understand that if we are seeing the Consu do this, then it is because they want us to see them."

"You haven't tried to contact them?"

"They never communicate with us. If we try to initiate contact with them, they ignore us. If we approach, they retreat. Sometimes they return when we no longer chase them. Sometimes they don't."

"All right," I said. "This relates to Unity Colony how?"

"Because a few of your weeks before the colony's disappearance, we spotted the Consu in the Karna-Hlaven system," Clock said.

I leaned forward in my bland and functional chair. "You think they have something to do with its disappearance?"

"We don't know. I am telling you all we know."

"You have to have told others in the State Department about this," I said. "I'm too far down the chain to be the only one you've told."

"We have informed your State Department," Clock said. "They have asked us to keep this information confidential."

I opened my mouth to ask why, and then immediately clacked it shut.

Ever since the Colonial Union followed up on Charles Boutin's research to give the Obin consciousness, the Obin had a special relationship with us, a relationship they did not have with either the Conclave or Earth. *We* knew something about the disappearance of Unity that the other two participants did not.

What the value of that information might be was unknowable at this point. But apparently it was worth keeping it a secret for now.

Except—

"Why are you telling *me* about it?" I asked Clock. "I can one hundred percent guarantee you that if they told you to keep this a secret, they don't want *me* to know. I was in a meeting with several principals of the State Department earlier today, and my father. There wasn't a peep about it."

"I am not telling *you* about it," Clock responded, and then pointed behind me, at my assistant. "I am telling Ran. You just happen to be in the room."

I goggled at this. This was a level of bureaucratic gobbledygook that I never would have expected from the almost painfully literal Obin. "That makes no sense at all," I told Clock. "Ran is my *assistant*. You have no reason to tell it anything." I turned to Ran. "No offense."

"None taken," Ran said.

"I would have no reason to tell Ran anything if it were not going on the mission with you," Clock said. "But Ran is going on the mission with you. We requested its participation to your State Department this afternoon, and they agreed to it."

I turned back to Ran. "Did you know about this?"

"No," Ran said. "I am just as confused as you are." It turned its attention to Clock. "This is difficult. I have already promised to cat sit."

"If no other solution can be found, I suggest you bring the cat," Clock said, to Ran.

"Forget the cat," I said.

Both of the Obin looked shocked at the statement.

"Lucifer will be fine," I assured both of them. "There was already another cat sitter lined up. I want to know why *Ran* is critical to the mission. That I am not supposed to acknowledge I know anything about," I added, far too late.

"Ran is critical to the mission because you are on the mission," Clock said.

"I don't understand."

"Ms. Trujillo, Ran is your security detail."

I laughed.

"I'm sorry," I said, after a moment. "It's not that I don't appreciate the sentiment. But I can take Ran half the time when we spar."

Clock turned to Ran. "Tell her," it said.

"Tell me what?" I said, looking at Clock and then at Ran.

"I have been holding back," Ran said, to me.

"Holding back?"

"Yes."

"When we fight?"

"Yes."

"How much?"

"A lot," Ran said.

"Ran was part of an Obin military detail that specialized in close-quarter combat," Clock said. "Its training is extensive and its experience using it equally so."

"You never told me that," I said to Ran. "You told me that you had standard Obin defense training."

"I did," Ran said. "Then I had more."

"*Ran.*"

"I apologize," Ran said, and looked in the direction of Clock. "I was told to withhold information."

"You told Ran to keep its experience a secret," I said, to Clock.

"I conveyed the information, which came from above me," Clock said. "We did not wish for you to know that beyond being your assistant, Ran had a second function regarding your person," Clock said.

"I don't need a bodyguard!" I said. "And I didn't ask for one."

"We know you have had combat training, by us," Clock said. "And we are aware that you would have been likely to refuse a formal offer of a security detail. But as the former best friend of Zoë Boutin-Perry during her Roanoke years, you were embedded into our cultural consciousness more than any other person aside from her immediate family. Even though we as a people no longer follow you on a daily basis, you are still significant to us. When you took the Obin desk in the State Department, we assigned Ran, with the permission of your superiors, to be your assistant."

"That's not true," I said. "I interviewed Ran and chose it as my assistant."

"Yes," Clock said. "We trained it to be temperamentally suitable to you."

I turned to Ran. "You're not actually like this?" I asked.

"No, I am exactly like this," Ran said. "Also, I was told to emphasize aspects of my personality it was believed you would like. And now, because you like them, and I like to have your approval, I am even more like this."

"That's charmingly duplicitous," I said to Clock.

"It was important to us that you trust Ran so you would be open with it."

I turned back to Ran. "So you're a spy, too."

"No," Ran said. "I do not report on your daily activities. I do keep an eye on your safety."

"I don't lead a dangerous life," I said.

"No," Ran agreed. "But now you are going on this mission."

I looked back to Clock. "You think it will be dangerous."

"We believe in prudence," Clock said.

"Against the *Consu*," I said, doubtfully.

"With respect, Ms. Trujillo," Clock said. "It's not only the Consu we're worried about."

"What does *that* mean?"

"It means the entire Obin nation will be better assured of your safety with Ran on this mission. If you do not object."

I considered this. "And if I do object?"

"Then we would request that you choose not to be on this mission. But we have reason to believe that you would reject that request."

I understood the implication here. "You know a lot."

"We know enough," Clock said, and then fell silent.

I fell silent too, for a few moments.

Then I turned back to Ran. "So you could have beaten me every single time we sparred."

"Most days, yes," Ran said. "But it would have been counterproductive to the maintenance of your combat skills if I did. Humans need to win occasionally to keep engaged with the training."

"And yet today you were happy to kick my ass," I said.

"Yes," Ran said. "Today you were sloppy. I had no choice."

I laughed despite myself. "I'm going to remember you said that," I said.

"I would be happy if you did," Ran replied. "It might help keep you alive."

I decided. "So, Ran. Do you want to be my bodyguard on this mission?"

"Yes, please," Ran said. "Although I am sad not to cat sit."

FIVE

"I hope you or your assistant will not be offended if I ask to have a private conversation with you," said Caspar Merrin, the head of the Colonial Union mission delegation.

"Of course not," I said, and nodded to Ran, who backed off a few steps from the alcove Merrin and I were standing in on Phoenix Station. As it did so, there was a momentary wave of startlement from the foot traffic behind it. Despite the Obin being a Colonial Union ally of long standing, most humans were still apprehensive about them. An unexpected spider-giraffe-looking creature does bad things to the human limbic system.

I looked back at Merrin, who was still waiting, face blank. I turned back to Ran. "Go to that hamburger place and get us some lunch, Ran," I said.

"Do you actually want food or is this a polite way of asking me to go away?" Ran asked. "I think it's probably the second, but I want to be sure."

"It's mostly the second, yes," I affirmed. "But I would in fact like a cheeseburger and fries."

Ran nodded and headed off, creating a little wave of humans weaving out of his way as he did so.

"Does it always do that?" Merrin asked.

"Get me a burger?"

"Ask for your intent when you say something."

"Frequently, yes," I said. "When your entire consciousness is a prosthesis, it's a lot of work to catch all the subtleties of communication. I encourage Ran to ask."

"That's good of you."

"It's not too much to ask of me," I said. "It doesn't mean I don't get exasperated with it sometimes. But I'm exasperating too, and I don't have the excuse of an artificial consciousness."

"I hope it wasn't offended when I asked it to leave."

"It understands its role, and mine," I said. "Also, I'm unlikely to need its protection here in Phoenix Station."

Merrin nodded at this. "I was told it was going to be acting as your official bodyguard."

"You knew more than I did, then, until yesterday evening."

Another nod from Merrin, and then he looked out the long window of the alcove we were standing in, toward a spaceship built on unfamiliar lines. It was the Obin ship that was going to take us to Unity Station. Me, him, Ran, and the eight other members of the Colonial Union contingent, matched by two equally sized contingents of humans from Earth, and aliens from the Conclave.

"You said you understand your role on this mission," Merrin said, after a minute. "That's good. I'm hoping you might be able to explain it to me."

"Sir?" I said.

Merrin made a dismissive hand gesture. "'Caspar' will do just fine," he said. "And I should probably rephrase that. Ms. Trujillo, I am not questioning your competence or your ability. I've read your file. You're capable. But that doesn't make you an obvious choice for this mission or to serve as my deputy."

"I was told it was because I could act as a liaison to the ship's crew. They're Obin; I run the Obin desk at State."

Merrin smiled. "That's a pleasant enough fiction, but it doesn't hold up to examination. With no disrespect to your field of knowledge, this is not a diplomatic mission to the Obin. They will tell us basic ship protocols, and when we're arriving to and leaving from Unity Colony."

"Maybe they thought I should get out into the field more," I said.

"This is not the mission for an analyst to get a little seasoning, Ms. Trujillo."

"I suppose not," I said. "So how about this. I'm here because my father feels guilty that he might have consigned thousands of Colonial Union citizens to their deaths and is sending me because he can't think of an excuse to put himself on the mission."

Merrin made a motion with his hand. "*That*, I believe."

"I'll understand if the nepotism bothers you."

"It bothers me less than you might think it does," Merrin said. "I read your file. It occurs to me that you serve more purposes on this trip than you might realize."

"How so?"

Merrin turned slightly and pointed at the Obin ship. "This mission doesn't need a diplomatic liaison to the Obin, but the Obin know who you are, thanks to your relationship with Zoë Boutin-Perry. I know the reason your assistant is also your bodyguard is that the Obin are worried something might happen to you."

"It's an overblown worry."

"It might be. It still works to our advantage. There's no doubt the Obin ferrying us know who you are, even when they don't have their consciousnesses on. I can't help but feel that makes us a little bit safer."

"Well, it's good to be useful," I said, only mildly sarcastically.

"It's not just them," Merrin continued. "The delegation from Earth is excited to meet you too."

I thought of Mateu Jordi in the meeting the day before. "That seems unlikely to me."

Merrin shook his head. "You knew John Perry and Jane Sagan," he said. "And their daughter. That's a very big deal. Expect to be asked about them. A lot."

"It's been a while," I said. "Almost twenty years."

"It won't matter. Like it won't matter to the Garvinn that it's been that long since you were on Roanoke."

"The Garvinn?" I asked.

"The Conclave delegation," Merrin replied. "All one species. They thought it would be courteous to the Obin to have the delegation be one species, so their ship quarters could be standardized."

"Huh," I said. "I wouldn't have thought of that."

"You spend most of your time with humans," Merrin pointed out. "Humans and one Obin. My point is, you are a common point of interest for every group on this ship. We can use a common point of interest."

I tilted my head at this. "Do we not have common points of interest? I thought that was what Unity Colony was all about."

This got a grim little smile from Merrin. "The 'unity' in that name is aspirational."

"I was told that most everyone was integrating pretty well in the colony."

"Your father told you that, didn't he."

"Maybe," I said, only a little defensively.

"Your father gets the topline reports on what's going on at Unity," Merrin said. "Those reports are, shall we say, optimistically spun." He tapped his own chest. "I'm lower down the reporting chain, and I've actually been to the colony several times. My own experience has less spin on it."

"That would imply you're the one writing the rosy reports to my dad," I said. "You or someone on your level."

"*My* reports aren't optimistic or pessimistic. I write what I see and am told by the people there. But there are a couple of links in the chain between your father and me."

"Got it."

"It's not even sinister, Ms. Trujillo. Everyone wants Unity Colony to succeed. Being slightly more optimistic in reports means your father finds it easier to get funding and support out of those secret groups he's a part of. Bureaucracy is bureaucracy, whether it's covert or out in the open."

I nodded toward the Obin ship out the window. "Given this

is a covert operation, if anyone asks, what are a bunch of humans and Conclave citizens doing together on an Obin ship?"

"If anyone asks—and they won't—we're a joint scientific mission studying atmospheric anomalies in one of the gas giants in an Obin-claimed system."

"A scientific mission that, for our delegation, includes four security personnel, two diplomats, a doctor and an array technician," I observed. I had read our personnel files as well.

"As I said, no one will ask. We have a number of other joint scientific missions, Ms. Trujillo. No one ever asks about any of *them*, either."

"You can call me Gretchen if you like," I said. "Seeing that I'm meant to call you Caspar."

"Well, then, Gretchen, let me tell you what I think your role will be for this mission," Merrin said. "I think your role is to help us work with the other delegations, and with the Obin."

"You mean, to be a liaison," I said.

Merrin smiled at this, and continued. "In that role I want you to tell me anything you learn about them and their thoughts about the mission. What they think of us, of each other, and what thoughts they have about the possible disappearance of Unity."

"That sounds a little like spying."

"It is a little like spying," Merrin agreed. "But I'm not asking you to do espionage. I just want you to be available for conversation and to keep your eyes and ears open, and let me know your thoughts and observations."

"All right," I said. "But if I'm doing that then it's a good chance the other delegations will have someone like that doing the same thing."

"I'm all right with that. Chat up anyone who talks to you and be as open as you can. These delegations aren't our enemies. If we want this mission to succeed, working together is going to be essential."

"It sounds to me like you're expecting some friction on this mission."

"It's like I said earlier, unity is aspirational. Each delegation comes in with its own expectations and assumptions. Despite each delegation being equally sized, we and the delegation from Earth are the junior partners here. Unity Colony was only ten percent human. The rest are Conclave citizens. The Garvinn are going to want to be in charge."

"How do we feel about that?" I asked.

"If we find our people alive, I won't have a problem with it at all."

"*Do* you think we'll find our people alive?"

Merrin didn't answer this. He looked out the window again.

"Do you have people on Unity Colony?" I asked, after a moment.

"No," Merrin said, and shook his head to negate what he had just said. "Well. People I got to know being a part of the team that connected them to the State Department. Friends. A few colleagues. Not people I knew before."

"I have someone on the colony," I confessed. "An old friend, back from Roanoke."

Merrin nodded. "Another reason you're on the mission."

"Another reason my dad put me on it, yes."

"I'm sorry about that," Merrin said.

"You don't think we'll find our people," I pressed.

"I don't think an entire asteroid of fifty thousand people goes missing just to have everyone on it found safe and sound, Gretchen."

"What do you think is happening?"

"I don't know what's happening," Merrin said. "Which is why I want to know what everyone *else* thinks is happening. Not the official line from each of the delegations. I know that already. I would like the gossip and rumor."

"And you think I can get that out of them."

"I'm hoping you can, yes. We have four days before we get to skip distance. The Obin have given each delegation their own quarters, but there is a common space for all of us. They're calling it a "lounge," but it's really a cargo hold. Apparently the Obin don't have lounges."

"When you don't have consciousness, you don't need to hang out," I said.

"I've been told that the Obin crew all have consciousness harnesses and will use them when they are dealing with us, but they otherwise leave them off."

I nodded. "Ran does the same when it's alone and off the clock. It says being conscious tires it out. It's stressful being cognizant and having emotions."

"Well, that's true enough," Merrin said.

"I'll see what I can find out from the other delegations," I said.

"And ours, too."

"You think one of our people knows something you don't?"

"I'm management here," Merrin said. "Sometimes we're the last to know about anything."

"All right," I said. "That takes us to when we skip to the Karna-Hlaven system. What do you want me to do then?"

"Let's figure it out when it happens," Merrin said. "Are you going to be reporting to your father after all this is done?"

"Excuse me?" I said.

"It's a simple question and I don't mean anything terrible by it. He put you on this mission, and I expect that he expects a report from you directly when we return."

"It didn't come up," I said.

"That's not exactly an answer," Merrin pointed out.

"My direct answer is that I don't intend to go outside the chain of command," I said. "If he or anyone higher up asks me in an official capacity for a report, then I'll give them one. But other than that I'm here to be useful to you. I don't have any plans to undermine you, intentionally or otherwise, Caspar."

Merrin nodded. "All right."

"Do you believe me?" I asked.

"Yes," he said. "Again, I've read your file. You're not the undermining type as far as I can see. But it's nice to have you say out loud." He motioned with his head, past me. "Your bodyguard has returned."

I turned and saw Ran walking up, big paper bag in hand. "I have cheeseburgers for each of us," it said, motioning at Merrin to include him in the statement. "And fries."

"That was considerate of you, Ran," I said. "And quick. They must not have been busy."

"Oh, they were very busy," Ran said. "But when I came up everybody decided to let me go to the head of the line."

"Did they."

"Yes." Ran looked at me, and then Merrin, and then back to me. "Why? Is that unusual?"

SIX

"We would like to probe you," the alien said to me.

"I beg your pardon," I replied.

I was sitting at a table in the ship's common area, which as promised was a mostly bare cargo hold with basic plastic chairs and tables, and had been approached by a quartet of Garvinn who were part of the Conclave delegation to our mission. I had seen them sitting at another table in the common area—their physiology was close enough to humans' that the chairs worked for them, a fact that could not be said for any Obin, which is why Ran was standing behind me—muttering to themselves and occasionally looking over at me.

That was fine; I was there to be approachable, per instruction by Caspar Merrin. I was sitting away from the other humans, in fact, to be less intimidating to approach. But when the Garvinn finally approached me, here on the second day of our mission, this request was not what I was expecting.

"Is 'probe' not the right word?" asked the Garvinn who was speaking to me.

"If it is, there's going to be trouble," I said.

The Garvinn touched the translation medallion that hung on its chest area, which had provided the translation of its clicky words. "I am sorry, we have only recently uploaded our translations for human languages; they are not as precise as they should be." It looked past me to Ran, tapped a chitinous finger on its medallion, and then uttered a long stream of clicks that I assumed were words, which the medallion translated into what I knew would be the standard Obin language.

Ran listened—its own translation circuit was embedded into its consciousness harness—then replied to the Garvinn. The Garvinn suddenly shrank back from me and covered its face, as did its compatriots.

"What's going on?" I asked Ran.

"I explained to them why 'probe' was not the appropriate word for this context," Ran said. "What you are seeing now is a display of contrition and humiliation."

"Tell them they don't—" I stopped because I remembered the Garvinn's translation medallion would translate my words (hopefully) perfectly well. "You didn't do anything wrong," I assured the Garvinn.

The Garvinn clicked and Obin came out, because it had not switched over the translation circuit. "They say they apologize nevertheless," Ran said. "They very much do *not* wish to probe you."

"I believe you," I said, to the Garvinn. I turned back to Ran. "What *did* they want?"

"This one was saying that they had intended to ask to touch you," Ran said. "I understand these four Garvinn are so new to their posting that they had not had time to meet any humans yet, and you are physiologically different enough from them that they were curious, and also, you are small enough that they felt you to be nonthreatening enough to approach. I'm not sure I was meant to translate that last part."

I smiled at this. "It's all right," I said, turned back to the Garvinn, rolled up a sleeve, and held out an arm.

The four Garvinn came out from behind their hands and looked at my arm.

"Go ahead," I encouraged them.

The first Garvinn reached out a rough finger and poked me gently in the forearm, between my radius and ulna. It quickly shrank back and chittered to its friends. The translation medallion gave a translation, still in Obin.

"It has said to its companions that you are squishy," Ran told me.

"Not my first choice of adjective, but okay," I said.

The first Garvinn tapped its translation medallion once more to speak to me directly. "I am sorry if 'squishy' offends you," it said.

"It doesn't," I said. "Tell your friends they are welcome to give me a squish as well."

Two seconds later my arm was being palpated by four different Garvinn. There was much clicking.

In short order I learned the Garvinn's names were Tav, Gil, Eyah and Bertk; they were all male, or close enough to male that it made no difference for pronoun use; and that they were all the Garvinn equivalent of our Diplomatic Security Force. The other six members of their delegation, like ours and the Earth folks, were divided between diplomats and technicians. Being security forces, however, they were most interested in humans and their combat.

Or, as Tav, the squad leader, put it, "Humans fight well despite being squishy."

"Thanks," I said. "We do have some help from technology."

Tav made a motion that I think equated to shaking its head. "It's not the technology, it's the mindset," he said. "A lot of frail species try to make themselves small and unnoticed by others. Not humans. You go out of your way to make nuisances of yourselves."

"I wouldn't have put it that way, but I can't say you're wrong."

"It's not an insult," Tav stressed to me. "You know the first battle of Roanoke."

"I have heard of it, yes," I allowed.

"Yes, of course you have. Four hundred Conclave ships against a colony of two thousand humans with no defenses or weapons, and you humans still managed to defeat them all, decisively."

"To be fair, the colony of Roanoke didn't have much to do

with that battle, other than to be bait," I said. "The Colonial Defense Forces did the rest."

"Until the second battle of Roanoke," Tav pointed out. "That was members of the colony against a trained Conclave battle force."

"That battle force was overconfident," I said, remembering the events of the day.

"Even so," Tav said. And then paused. "Did *you* fight in the second battle?"

"No," I said. "I and most other people in the colony were in a bomb shelter at the time."

"Sensible."

"I thought so at the time."

"Those two battles were the only times humans and the Conclave were officially directly in conflict," Tav said, and then pointed to his squad. "We have often wondered what it would be like to be in battle with humans. We are very good at fighting, and we are built for it." He tapped his hard fingers against his hard head, where it made a flat *tick* sound. "In theory you humans should be no problem. But then—"

I finished his sentence. "But in practice we fight well for being squishy."

"Yes," Tav said.

"Well, I promise to take it easy on you if we ever fight," I said.

From behind me, Ran made a small noise.

Tav looked over to Ran, and then back at me. "What did that mean?"

"So you *actually* knew the Perrys?" asked Feruza Olimova, one of the scientists with the contingent from Earth. She and two other members of that delegation, one other scientist and one of the diplomats, were also sitting with me. They had seen me talking to the Garvinn the day before and had been curious about what we had spoken about. Eventually the conversation led back to Roanoke and from there to John and Jane and Zoë.

"I did," I said.

"You knew them well?"

"Zoë was my best friend."

"You're not in the movie," noted Ong Vannak, the diplomat and head of Earth's delegation.

"Ugh, that *movie*," I said, and then paused. "Wait. You actually saw it?"

"Why wouldn't we have seen it?" Ong asked.

"I didn't know that Colonial Union movies played on Earth."

"Colonial Union pop culture was a fad for a while," Ong said, and there was something in his tone that expressed displeasure about this fact. "*Roanoke* came out in the middle of that. We in the diplomatic corps made a point to see it, to get a better idea of who we were dealing with as a culture."

"And what did you think of it?"

"Eh," Ong said, shrugging.

"The good news here is, we agree on something," I said.

"Well, *I* liked it," said Bethany Young, the other scientist. "And the theme song! Made out of that poem from Zoë's dead boyfriend—" Bethany yelped suddenly and looked at Olimova. "Why did you just kick me?"

Olimova widened her eyes, and then did a little head movement in my general direction.

"What?" Young asked.

"I think your colleague is trying to suggest that I might be sensitive about that poem because I knew the dead boyfriend personally," I said.

"Yes, thank you, that was it precisely," Olimova said, and then muttered something under her breath in a language I didn't immediately understand but, if Merrin's files on the Earth contingent were correct, was probably Uzbek.

Young's hand went to her mouth, and she looked at me. "My God," she said. "I'm so sorry, I didn't mean to be rude."

"It's fine," I said.

"I just really love the theme song."

"I'm glad."

"We played it at our wedding—stop it, Feruza!" Young said, looking back over at Olimova, who had just kicked her under the table again.

"I apologize for my colleague," Olimova said, to me. "She is a very good scientist. But is *very* young."

"It's all right," I assured her. I looked over to Young. "Enzo would have liked that you slow-danced to his poem at your wedding. He would have been embarrassed as heck first. But then he would like it."

"I'm sorry about your friend," Young said, glancing at Olimova as she said it.

"Thank you," I said. "It's nearly twenty years ago now. It's still sad. But I mostly remember the good things now."

"Are you still in contact with your friend Zoë?" Olimova asked.

"A little," I said. "But only recently. Before the Perrys broke the information embargo with Earth and introduced you all to the rest of the universe, there was never any communication between your planet and the Colonial Union. And then after, Earth didn't *want* to speak to the Colonial Union, so there was no communication then, either. It was only after the Tripartite Agreement that there was any way to contact her."

"You lost a lot of years," Olimova said.

I nodded. "And even when communication between Earth and the Colonial Union was established, it was still hard to get in contact. I didn't know where she was on Earth. She didn't know I had moved back to Erie, and then to Phoenix."

"You're in the Colonial Union diplomatic corps, and she's one of the best-known humans on Earth," Ong pointed out.

I motioned at him with my hand. "And in fact that's how we connected again. But even then, it's not easy." I reached for my PDA on the table and held it up. "You can't just make a call." I set the PDA back down. "She'll always be my friend and I will always love her. But the real world keeps us from being close like we once were."

"She and her family are global heroes to us, you know," Ong said.

I smiled at this. "I've been told."

"Liberators, even."

I held up a hand. "You don't need to sell me on the Perrys," I said.

"I don't imagine they were very popular here in the Colonial Union, after what they did."

"It took a while for it to get around," I said. "That whole Colonial Union 'we control the flow of information' thing. And then we had our own problems to deal with. The Perrys were an afterthought to most of that."

"But you all must have thought something," Olimova said. "There *was* the movie."

"Yes, but"—I pointed to Ong—"most of what people know of the Perrys and what happened at Roanoke was from the movie. The vector of knowledge is going the other direction."

"It wasn't that long ago," Ong said.

"We've had a lot of going since then," I replied.

Ong opened his mouth and closed it again, crossing his arms as he did so.

"You will notice Vannak has a chip on his shoulder about the Colonial Union," Olimova said, nodding at the diplomat.

"They have a lot to answer for," Ong said to her, then looked at me. "The last few centuries, for a start."

"I'm not going to defend the Colonial Union for what it did in the past," I said. "Remember, I was part of that past. The Colonial Union almost killed me and everyone I knew trying to get at the Conclave."

Ong motioned at me. "And yet here you are, as part of their diplomatic corps."

"It's a different time," I said. "Or at least, we're trying to make it a different time."

"Vannak is skeptical," Olimova said.

"That's reasonable." I looked at him. "And yet here *you* are, working alongside the Colonial Union."

Ong shrugged. "Well, you know what they say. Know your enemy."

"But *she's* not our enemy," Young said of me, to Ong.

Ong gave me a measured look. "Let's get to Unity and see if that's true or not."

"You know what, I think I could take one of them," Bradley King said to the table, looking over at one of the Garvinn security crew, sitting at another table.

I looked over to the other table and saw Tav sitting by himself, drinking something out of a cup and reading from the Garvinn equivalent of a PDA. He was as nonthreatening as a chitinous sentient being could be at any particular moment of its life.

"What brought this up?" I asked King, suddenly. He and the other three members of the Colonial Union Diplomatic Security Force had sat down with me at my table while I was depressurizing from a slightly disconcerting meeting with the Obin crew of the ship. The meeting had consisted of a couple dozen Obin staring at me mutely in something close to religious epiphany, being that I had been Zoë Boutin-Perry's best friend. This was not as fun as it sounds, and I don't think it sounds very fun.

Ran, who had been with me for the meeting, was several meters away, keeping an eye on me but otherwise being as unobtrusive as a spider giraffe could be. It was the day before we skipped to Karna-Hlaven, and I was ready to be there. When the security cadre had sat down, I had politely ignored most of what they were talking about to gather my own thoughts, but this comment slipped into my consciousness.

"Nothing, really," King said, and motioned to the rest of his team. "We're just talking, ma'am. We don't know what we're skipping into over there, and we're prepping for all options."

"Which includes getting into it with the security team of the Conclave," I said, looking over the team, none of whom I had seen in one of my orientation cameos. Which was not all that unusual—Phoenix was not the only place where Diplomatic Security were trained.

King looked at the rest of his team, and then shrugged. "Sure, why not? I don't think it would come to that, but it doesn't hurt to do threat assessment anyway."

I leaned back in my seat. "And what is your assessment?"

This got a smile. "I mean, I think I just gave it."

"What is that assessment based on?"

"Years of training and diplomatic assignments."

"So, you're eyeballing it," I said.

"I'm comfortable doing that," King said, and smiled again.

I nodded to this, looked back, and waved Ran over. Ran stalked up and loomed, which was what I expected it to do. King's smile did not exactly evaporate, but it got a lot smaller. "Ran, this security operative thinks he could take the Garvinn over there in a fight. What do you think?"

Ran cocked its head and gave King a once-over. "Physical combat?" it asked me.

"Physical combat?" I asked King.

"Yeah, okay, physical combat," King said, after moment, to me, and then looked up at Ran. "What about it?"

"I wouldn't advise it," Ran said.

"Why not?"

"You would lose."

King looked around the table again, and then back at Ran. "And you're an expert."

"Ran is my assistant at the Obin desk back on Phoenix," I said, setting a hand on Ran's arm to quell its desire to offer up any further information.

"I see," King said, to Ran. "Then with all due respect, I'll trust my own judgment."

I nodded, turned and called to Tav.

"Yes?" he clicked, from his seat at the other table.

"I have a human here who thinks he could take you in a fight," I said. "Would you like to let him try?"

Tav held up his cup. "May I finish my drink first? I don't want it to get cold."

"Of course," I said. Tav waved and went back to his drink and PDA.

"Why did you do that?" King said to me.

"You said you thought you could take one of them," I said.

"That doesn't mean I wanted to do it *right now*."

"As a member of the Diplomatic Security detail I'm sure you know that you don't always get to pick your fights," I said. "Sometimes they get picked for you."

Tav finished his drink and ambled over to the table and looked at the security detail there. "Am I fighting all of them? And if I am, is it sequentially or all at once?"

"Just the one," I said, pointing at King.

Tav looked King over. "Weapons?"

"I think the suggestion was hand-to-hand," I said.

Tav looked King over again. "I'd let him have a weapon," he said, after a moment.

"Do you want a weapon?" I asked King.

King's mouth gaped for a second, and then he stood up. "I don't need a weapon," he said, sizing up Tav. "How are we doing this?"

"Ran?" I asked.

"Grappling would be the closest to an equal challenge," Ran said. "I suggest three falls."

"That's acceptable," Tav said.

"Whatever," King said, and nodded to his team, who got up and cleared a space out in the middle of the lounge for grappling, moving tables and chairs. By the time they were done, word had spread, and humans, Garvinn and even a couple of Obin had come in to spectate.

"I'm ready," Tav said to King, who wasted no time in charging in on the Garvinn. Two seconds later King was flat on his back on the floor.

"That's one," Ran said. No one had appointed it the referee, but no one else was offering to do the job, either.

Tav backed off from King, who righted himself and then started circling, treating Tav more warily now. Tav watched King, lightly stepping now and again to keep King in his field of vision, but otherwise appearing to be waiting.

He didn't have to wait too long. King rushed in again, this time forgoing the bum rush to grab at Tav's forearms to restrict his movement and then force him to the ground. This was a fine idea and it didn't work at all, and King was once again on the ground a few seconds later.

"That's two," Ran said. Two out of three, which meant the contest was over.

King yelled angrily and launched himself at Tav, whose back was turned to him. Two seconds later, King was flat on his back a third time and Tav was holding him down with a foot.

"Not very sporting," Tav said to King.

"Man, get off of me," King snarled.

Tav looked over at me, foot still on King. "He called me a man. I'm offended."

"Fair," I said, stood up and walked over to the still-supine King. "I'll take it from here," I said to Tav. Tav took his foot off King and stepped back a couple of meters. I leaned down to look at King.

"Want to know why you lost?" I asked King.

"Not really," King replied, sitting up.

"Ran, tell him why he lost."

"You lost because the Garvinn have faster and more efficient neural and nervous system responses than humans, particularly with regard to their voluntary musculature," Ran said.

"Which is to say you were too slow," I told King. "Everything you did was like walking up to Tav at a leisurely stroll."

"Also you are squishy," Tav said, from two meters away.

King grimaced a sarcastic smile at Tav for that comment and then looked back at me. "You could have told me that before you had me fight him."

"Oh, I'm sorry," I said. "I thought you preferred to trust your own judgment."

King waved a hand. "All right, I get it. Your assistant knows more than I do."

"It is publicly available information," Ran said.

"It doesn't matter if it's *publicly available information* if his brain and muscles run faster than ours do," King said to Ran.

"That's quitter talk," I said.

"Really?" King said, and then motioned at Tav. "Be my guest." King's security squad laughed at this.

I stood up and looked over to Tav. "Mind if I take a shot?" I asked. "One fall."

"Of course," Tav said, and brought himself back into the grappling space.

"Thank you," I said, picked up one of the plastic chairs at the periphery of the cleared space, and threw it at him.

Tav batted it away easily, just in time to see a second one coming for him, one that I threw almost immediately after the first.

Neither of the plastic chairs were a threat, but he had to spend time dealing with them. By the time he had cleared them away, I was too close for him to deal with me like he had dealt with King. Watching Tav throw King told me where his own set of balance points were, and I set to dragging him down.

It took longer than Tav took with King, and the Garvinn almost clawed me off of him a couple of times. But soon enough, Tav was on the floor.

And then he was up, clicking the Garvinn equivalent of laughter. "Was this you going easy on me?" he asked.

"I really wish it was," I said, breathing hard.

Tav click-laughed some more and clapped me on the shoulder.

I turned and saw King and the rest of his crew staring at me.

"I paid attention while you were getting your ass kicked," I said, answering his unspoken question. "To how he was handling you. To how he moved. To where objects were in the environment. And I knew what his innate advantages were, and how I might counter them, because I've read up on Garvinn physiology."

"Also she threw chairs," Tav said, helpfully.

"Yes," I said. "Yes, I did." I looked back to King. "We're going into a situation where we need every single advantage we can get. Every single one of us. It's not too much to ask for you to do a little *reading*."

King stared at me for a moment and then stomped off, followed by his crew.

"I thought that went well," Ran said. Behind it, I noticed Ong Vannak looking at me.

"And you thought it was genuinely necessary to humiliate the head of our security detail," Caspar Merrin said to me, just before the skip to Karna-Hlaven. We were again in the common room cargo hold, watching as the Obin crew brought in a massive screen so all three delegations could assemble and watch the jump together, and then use the screen for any post-jump purpose we might have.

"I didn't humiliate King; he did it to himself," I said.

"Yes, well, and you helped him do that," Merrin noted.

I shook my head. "He expressed a wish; I facilitated it. In the process he learned valuable things about himself and the Garvinn. And about our mission."

"The question is whether *he* actually learned anything, or whether you've just made him more likely to be stubborn."

"We'll find out," I said. "And in the meantime, *we've* learned things. Which is the thing you asked me to do on our way to the skip."

"And what have you learned?"

"That the Garvinn are curious and confident," I said, motioning to the aliens, who were setting up a workstation, as were our team and the delegation from Earth, with their respective workstations. "They think they're ready to face whatever we find after the skip, but they also have a healthy respect for what they don't know, and they're factoring that into their decision-making."

"I told you they think this is their show," Merrin said.

"We could do worse." I motioned to the delegation from

Earth. "The Earthlings are smart and determined to prove they belong on this mission with the rest of us. They also still resent us, even if they recognize the necessity of working with us."

"They have a lot to resent."

"True enough, but it's still something we need to factor in when we're dealing with them. They know they need us, but that doesn't mean they trust us, and that's not great."

Merrin nodded and motioned with his coffee cup at the Obin. "What about them?"

"They're Obin," I said. "They're exactly who they say they are on the label. They're going to do their job brilliantly and without any excitement or emotion, unless we force the latter on them."

"I understand you had a group meeting with them."

"I did. It was basically an exercise of finding out how long they could be in my presence before having to switch off their consciousness collars from overstimulation."

"That sounds . . . uncomfortable for everyone involved."

"That's one way to put it. It wasn't awful, but it was exhausting. And that was for just a few minutes. I don't know how Zoë dealt with it all the time."

"All right," Merrin said, and then pointed at our own team. "And what about us?"

"Well, we're arrogant," I said.

Merrin gave a small smile at this. "All of us?"

"Some more than others," I said, understanding the thought behind the smile. "But yes. King's not an exception, you know. The Garvinn aren't wrong to consider us wild cards. The Earthlings aren't wrong to not entirely trust us. We've shown over and over that if you give us an opening, we'll slide a knife into it."

"Less since the tripartite treaty," Merrin observed.

"I don't know if even that's true," I said. "Whose idea was it for Unity Colony to exist?"

"It was everyone's idea. The Conclave's and both human parties."

I shook my head. "We say that, but I wonder about it. Earth

wasn't in a place to force the colonization issue. It barely has its own military and diplomatic corps, or ships for either. The Conclave has four hundred species in it, each with their own colonies and established planets. Colonization benefits it, but it doesn't hurt the Conclave to put on the brakes for a while and let the connections between its members grow. Meanwhile the Colonial Union's got people like my dad constantly pressing to resume colonization. I'm guessing it was us who forced the issue."

"You're making it sound like your dad's a bad guy here," Merrin said.

"He's not a bad guy," I said. "He *has* always been for colonization. Which means he's useful for the Colonial Union. He pushed for Roanoke Colony, which came in handy when the CU decided they needed a way to take on the Conclave. He gave them cover, whether he meant to or not. If Dad was a prime mover for Unity Colony, the question I'd ask is what the Colonial Union is getting out of it."

Merrin motioned to everyone in the common area. "Maybe this. Maybe peace."

"If you believed that you wouldn't have asked me to pay attention to what every group was doing and report back to you," I said to Merrin. "I think you're feeling what I'm feeling."

"Which is?"

"That just because all three of our groups are working together doesn't mean all three of us are working for the same goal."

Merrin smiled at this and took another sip of his coffee.

"This was what you were seeing on Unity Colony too, wasn't it?" I asked.

"Pretty much."

"And you wanted me to experience it too, rather than just being content with believing what you said."

Merrin looked over to me. "You had King fight the Garvinn for similar reasons, did you not? Experience over opinion."

"I don't know that I like being compared to King here," I admitted.

"It's not exactly the same," Merrin said. "But in my experience you can't tell people things. If they don't experience it, it's not real."

I laughed at this. "Sorry," I said, catching Merrin's expression. "I said pretty much the same thing to a bunch of new security recruits the day before I left on this mission."

"I'm not surprised," Merrin said. "It's good to know. You and I are on the same page now, Gretchen."

"Is that going to matter if we don't find Unity?" I asked.

"I think maybe it's going to matter more," Merrin said. He finished his coffee.

SEVEN

Unity wasn't there when we skipped.

We knew this already. But there is a difference between what we know in our brains and what we feel in hearts. In our hearts, we were hoping for a skip drone malfunction or some other explanation, however far-fetched, that would reveal our worry to have been for nothing, that Unity Colony would be there, hung like a jewel in the darkness, filled with fifty thousand souls who would be confused, and then amused, that we had made the trip to them at all.

We knew exactly where the asteroid that housed Unity Colony should be in its orbit around the Karna-Hlaven star, based on where it was at our last contact. Our ship skipped to within a thousand kilometers of where that was, close enough that we would see it illuminated by its star and by the lights of its inhabitants.

When the skip happened, I and the rest of the Colonial Union delegation, along with the Earth and Conclave delegations, congregated in our common area. We watched an outside view on that large video screen, waiting for the subtle change in star patterns that would let us know we'd moved from one part of the universe to the next.

At the skip, we all searched for the one bright point that we knew Unity Colony would be. We looked and kept looking, until one by one, person by person, you could feel the hope against hope drain from the room.

Our hearts would have to be disappointed.

"All right," said Fris, the leader of the Garvinn diplomatic delegation, to the assembly. Caspar Merrin glanced at me briefly when Fris started speaking; he had been correct that the Garvinn believed they were in charge of the entire mission. "This is not what we hoped for, but this is what we expected. Now it's our job to make this make sense." He motioned to each delegation at their workstations. "I'm open to theories. Start with the most obvious ones."

"The colony was destroyed," said one of the Garvinn scientists.

"If it's been destroyed then there should be evidence of its destruction," Fris said. "Previous scans of the area from skip drones don't show any significant fragments or debris. We'll run new and more detailed scans, obviously, now that we're here. We have between our delegations the equipment to do this. But for now we can assume that destruction by obvious means isn't what's happened here."

"What about by nonobvious means?" asked Feruza Olimova. "This is an extreme long shot, but something like a small black hole wandering through this system."

"It would require pretty much a direct hit," said Keiward Eongen, one of the Colonial Union scientists.

"This is why I mention it's an extreme long shot," Olimova said.

"Even then there would likely to be some evidence," Eongen replied. "The colony had the usual object trackers. If there were a black hole large enough to eat the entire colony, they would have noticed the gravitational warping long before it became a threat. If it was small but slow they could probably have found it too. If it was small and fast enough not to be noticed, then even a direct hit wouldn't be able to eat it all. At least some debris or energy from the collision would be in evidence."

"Can we look for that?" Fris asked.

"Sure," Eongen said. "We have the equipment. I'm just saying that we probably would already have some evidence of that."

"All right. Next?"

"What if the colony's hidden?" another Garvinn scientist said.

"How do you hide an asteroid large enough to house fifty thousand people?" Fris asked.

"Nanobot cloaking," Eongen said. "We've all used it to hide skip drones and ships."

"Not *all* of us," said Ong Vannak.

"The Conclave and the Colonial Union have used it," Eongen amended.

"That's a lot of cloaking," Fris said. "And it doesn't explain why it was done."

"Right now the why isn't important," the Garvinn scientist said. "Just that it was done. It could hide the entire asteroid, visually and all across the electromagnetic spectrum."

"But not gravitationally," Bethany Young said. "Unity's asteroid is large enough to have its own gravity well. It's shallow but it's trackable. And we know where it's supposed to be."

"Could you track it gravitationally?" Fris said.

"You wouldn't even have to," Ong Vannak said. "You could just shoot something at where it's supposed to be." Ong took a moment to register the surprised and shocked faces around it. "I'm not saying something *destructive*. A probe, not a missile. But if we know where it's supposed to be, then any nanobot shielding wouldn't stop it from hitting the asteroid's surface."

"We could do either," Young said. "Although checking for the gravity well is probably easier, and less a risk of damaging our equipment."

"Anything else that comes immediately to mind?" Fris asked the crowd.

I raised my hand. "The Consu," I said.

Fris considered me for a moment. "What about them?"

I hesitated, remembering that the information I had been given by Clock back on Phoenix was still at least nominally confidential. Threading this needle without suggesting that I knew more than I was supposed to was going to be the thing, here. "If there's any species who could make an entire asteroid disappear, it would be them."

"All right," Fris said. "But unless you have a Consu here with you to ask if they had done something with Unity Colony, I don't know what we can do with that at the moment."

"Even if you had a Consu here, you'd have to fight it for the right to ask," Bradley King said, then looked at me directly. "Or so I've *read*."

"We don't need a Consu," Olimova said. All eyes turned to her. "We don't need a Consu," she repeated. "At least, not yet. What we need is evidence the Consu have been here recently."

"How would you do that?" Fris said.

Olimova shrugged. "Every spaceship propels itself through real space. Look for propellant."

"That is, if Consu use the same sort of propulsion as we do," a Garvinn said. "They're so far advanced from us they might as well be using magic half the time."

"We're going to run scans for known propellants anyway," Olimova said. "If we find anything that doesn't look like it's from a spaceship or drone that we can already identify, that's going to be something we can work on further. Maybe that will be Consu, maybe it won't. Either way it will be evidence."

"Then we have our initial set of goals," Fris said. "Confirm the findings we've already been given from earlier drone searches. Look for gravitational wells and anomalies. Check for evidence of people and species who weren't supposed to be here."

"It's not much," Ong said.

"It doesn't have to be much," Fris said. "It has to be a start. So let's get started."

In short order this much became evident:

The initial scans from drones were correct. There was no substantive evidence of debris of any sort that suggested that Unity

Colony had been destroyed. Nothing that looked like fragments or dust from the asteroid itself, or anything that showed the composition of any of the metals, alloys or other building materials used by Obin in their initial construction, or by the colony in creating subsequent structures. What we were seeing, all along the path of the orbit of the colony, was the cosmic dust endemic to the Karna-Hlaven system.

There were no gravitational anomalies anywhere within fifty astronomical units of our ship. Every gravity well we could register or could find evidence of had been charted and described by the Obin years before, when they first surveyed the system with an eye toward colonizing it. Everything was where it was supposed to be, gravitationally speaking—except for the asteroid that housed Unity Colony. There was no gravity well there at all, so the idea that Unity Colony had been cloaked was right out the window. It wasn't cloaked. It just wasn't there.

Nor was there any evidence of propellant from unknown sources in the local area ("local" in this case being a tube of space ten thousand kilometers in diameter, charted along the expected orbit of Unity Colony's asteroid), either in heat signature or in a cloud of chemicals. If someone was visiting Karna-Hlaven, they hadn't come near Unity Station.

"Unless they skipped in," Keiward Eongen said. "Skipped in at a zero velocity and then didn't move."

"Until what?" Feruza Olimova asked. She looked up at him from her workstation, next to Bethany Young's. Eongen had come over to consult with Olimova and, possibly, to flirt with her. "Unless they disappeared alongside Unity, anything that skipped into this system would still have to get to minimum skip distance to leave."

Eongen shrugged. "Maybe they *did* disappear with Unity."

"Unlikely, and anyway skipping in at zero velocity makes no sense here. Unity Colony's asteroid wasn't massive enough to have its gravity well drag anything along with it, like a planet would. If something skipped in at zero velocity near the colony, the colony would see it zoom by and that would be that. If something skipped in, we would see it traveling to skip out."

"Unless there's some way they've changed how skipping works," Young suggested, from her workstation.

"Sure," Olimova said. "And while we're entertaining that idea, let's entertain the idea that we can make chickens spontaneously appear from the vacuum of space."

"Hypothetically—" Eongen began.

"If you say anything about the quantum field I will strangle you," Olimova warned him.

Eongen smiled at this.

"So between our three delegations and a dozen scientists we have nothing," I said.

"We have nothing, but we were expecting to have nothing at this point. It's early yet," Eongen said to me. "We went for the low-hanging fruit. We would have been surprised if we had come up with anything. Now we have to get creative."

"You don't strike me as the creative type," Olimova said to Eongen.

"A lot depends on what I'm asked to be creative about," Eongen replied.

Weirdly, it was Bethany Young who blushed at this.

"How long do we stay out here?" I asked Merrin, three days after our skip. We stood in front of the massive display in the cargo hold, looking at literally nothing. All the scientists were still cranking away on their work; we nonscientists had very little to do at this point. The Colonial Union security detail, who had even less to do than we did, were at a table, teaching their Garvinn counterparts how to play poker.

"We were told we have two weeks to find something," Merrin said. "If we don't come up with any information about the whereabouts of Unity after that, then we're called back and they start working on the next phase of the problem."

"What's that going to be?"

Merrin grimaced and looked at me. "Coming up with a reasonable excuse about how fifty thousand sentient creatures suddenly disappeared without a trace."

"We're going to lie about the deaths of all these people?"

"Probably, yes."

I stared at him for a moment. "There's no possible way that's going to fly," I said.

"It all depends on how it's done," Merrin said. "Fifty thousand people is a huge number. But you can hide those fifty thousand in the millions of people who die every day across the dozens of sentient species represented at Unity. You don't do it all at once. You drop a name here and a name there over several months. I'm pretty sure we can figure out plausible demises for our three thousand colonists over the course of a year."

I flushed with anger, thinking about Magdy. "These are actual people, you know."

"Yes, I know," Merrin said. "And if you recall I know more of them than you do. Maybe I don't know them as well as you know who you know. But you can be assured they're not just *statistics* to me, Gretchen."

I took a breath and let it out. "I'm sorry," I said. "I didn't mean to blow up at you."

"You can blow up at me," Merrin said. "I'd rather you blow up at me than at someone else."

"I apologize for implying you didn't care."

"It's fine. I do care. Rather a lot. But whether I care or not doesn't mean much for how our governments are going to handle this."

"They could just be open about it."

Merrin shook his head. "There's no universe where that doesn't blow up the tripartite treaty. If all the nonaligned alien species find out the Conclave was off colonizing while forbidding them from doing the same thing, they're going to raise hell. Then the Conclave might withdraw from the treaty, purely as a defensive response, and start colonizing again. Then the Colonial Union will do the same. We'll be fighting for the same planets all over again. A decade's peace, shattered. None of us can afford that right now."

"So we paper over fifty thousand lives," I said.

"For now," Merrin said. "The truth will come out sooner or later. But the later it is, the better it is for all of our governments. That's the plan, if we don't find Unity Colony. Find a way to outrun the consequences. If it all comes out now? It's war. But fifty years from now?" He shrugged. "It might not matter at all at that point."

"I didn't know you were this cynical," I told Merrin.

"It's not cynicism. It's experience."

Before I could respond to this there was a whoop from the direction of the Earth delegation's work area. Merrin and I both turned to see Bethany Young raising her arms in victory. She saw us looking at her and quickly put her arms down. "Sorry," she said.

"Don't be sorry," I said. "Just tell us why you're whooping."

"I found something," she said.

"Something related to Unity?" Merrin asked.

"Uh . . . maybe?"

"Maybe? What does that 'maybe' mean?" Merrin pressed.

"It means that I don't actually know what it is or what it's related to," Young said. "It's something that probably shouldn't be here at all. All I know is that I've found it."

"If you don't know what it is, why are you so excited?" I asked.

"Because it's not what it is that I'm excited about. It's *where* it is. *That's* the exciting part."

EIGHT

"A couple of days ago Feruza and Dr. Eongen were talking about things skipping into the space around Unity Colony," Bethany Young was saying to, basically, the entire assembled delegations in the common room. She was standing in front of the large display screen, which was showing nothing, but a deeply significant nothing. "Dr. Eongen mentioned things skipping in with zero velocity, and Feruza said that the colony's gravity was so weak that it wouldn't drag anything along with it, they would just see the colony zoom by in its orbit."

Young nodded to Olimova, who pressed a key at Young's workstation. The large screen brought up a representation of Unity Colony's orbit, with two points on the arc highlighted, one in yellow, one in green. She pointed at the yellow one. "This represents where we inserted after we skipped in," she said, "and this"—she pointed to the green dot—"is our best guess as to where Unity Colony would have been when it disappeared."

"We've already looked there," one of the Garvinn scientists said. "There was nothing there."

"That's right," Young said. "Nothing that we *looked for*. We looked for debris and we looked for evidence of ships having gone through that space. We were looking for very specific things, and we didn't find them. But then I started thinking about one of the early ideas we threw out, the one about the colony being cloaked with nanobots. I combined it with the idea of something skipping in at zero velocity."

Young looked at Olimova again; the image returned to the blank space. "So then I surveyed the area again, scanning for two things: anything barely above the ambient temperature of space, and anything with a mass more than a metric ton, which is close to the minimum mass that will show up on the gravity scanners we have with us. This is what I found."

Olimova clicked, and suddenly on the screen was a small dot, only barely lighter than the surrounding darkness.

"What is that?" asked Fris.

"I haven't the slightest idea, but it is something," Young said. "Something that shouldn't be where it is, and cloaked, so we weren't meant to see it. Well," she amended. "It's not meant to be seen. We don't know who this thing is hiding from, or if it's trying to hide at all."

"So this thing, whatever it is, is just hanging out there in space," Ong Vannak said.

Young shook her head. "It's moving. It's slowly falling in toward the Karna-Hlaven star, which tells us two things. First, that it really did skip into the system with zero velocity relative to Unity Colony, and two, working backward given its mass and current rate of movement we can very precisely estimate when it arrived in-system, which was within an hour of when we estimate the colony disappeared."

"So whatever this is had something to do with the colony's disappearance," Caspar Merrin said.

"We won't know for sure until we find out more about it," Young said. "It seems too coincidental for it not to have some relationship to the disappearance, but until we examine whatever it is, we can't say for sure."

I remembered Olimova saying that despite her age, Young was a good scientist, and I took this precise bit of hedging as an example of that. "What *do* we know about it at this point?" I asked.

Young pointed up at the image of the featureless sphere. "The diameter of the sphere is just under fourteen meters, and its mass is roughly ten metric tons. Whatever it is, it's not especially large."

"We could fit it in this cargo hold," Fris observed.

"Not this one, please, we're using it," Ong said. This got chuckles and clicks.

"*Could* we put it into one of the cargo holds?" Merrin asked Fris. "I'm not asking whether it's physically possible. I'm asking if we can retrieve it and bring it on board."

Fris considered this. "We'd have to find out what it is first. I'm sure the captain of this vessel would rather not put anything on its ship that represents an active danger to it."

"So if it's safe we can grab it."

"This ship has four cargo holds. We're using two of them, one for this common area and one for equipment and probes. I don't think the other two are being used for anything. If the captain is willing, we could easily fit it in one of those holds."

"What are you thinking?" I asked Merrin.

"I'm thinking that whatever it is, if we take it back with us, we're in better shape than if we come back with nothing."

"*Or,* we could send a skip drone, let our superiors know what we've found, and let them dispatch a different ship and crew to pick it up," Ong said. "Maybe one that's staffed with military, and not scientists and diplomats."

"Obviously we let them know we've found it," Merrin said. "And if they tell us to back off and let them deal with it, fine. We have a couple drones at skip distance, so we can get a quick answer. But I'd be surprised if they send anyone else. If any of our governments wanted their militaries involved, they'd have sent them already."

"Then the question would be which military," Fris added. "It's not realistic to expect *them* all to share a ship like we are."

Merrin nodded at this. "Regardless, we don't have to wait on our superiors to find out more about this thing, whether we bring it onto the ship or not."

"What do you suggest?" Ong said.

"Well, we do have *probes*," Fris answered.

"Congratulations, it's a featureless black globe," Keiward Eongen said. He was navigating the probe that was now hovering next to Young's mysterious sphere, pacing it as it moved slowly but with incrementally increasing speed toward the Karna-Hlaven star. The visual feed from the probe was now filling the common room monitor screen and appeared to show nothing. "A whole lot of nothing" was a common theme on the monitor in the last few days.

I, Caspar Merrin, Fris and Ong Vannak were crowded around Eongen's workstation; everyone else, including Ran, had been excused from the room. Bethany Young in particular was unhappy with this. It had been her discovery, after all.

"Can you put a light on it?" Fris asked.

"I already have a light on it," Eongen answered. "This material is swallowing it up. Almost nothing is bouncing off of it."

"Is it nanobotic technology?" Merrin asked.

"Maybe? It's hard to say what it is without taking a sample of it."

"So take a sample of it," Ong Vannak said.

Eongen looked back at the Earth diplomat. "Maybe things are different back on Earth, but in the Colonial Union, these probes cost a boatload of money, sir. Who knows what this thing will do to this probe if there's physical contact. Maybe nothing. Maybe it will fry it into particles and go after us next."

"We brought the probe out to learn more about this thing," Ong replied. "Right now all you're telling us is what we already know: that it's an unknown sphere of black. If we have a probe, we should use it to probe."

Eongen looked over to me and Merrin. I looked to Merrin, who shrugged. "It's a probe," he said.

"None of you heard me say the part about maybe it being blasted to bits and us along with it," Eongen said.

"I heard you," Merrin said. "We're five thousand klicks away. We should be fine."

"You understand the speed of light, right? Like if this thing has laser or particle defenses, five thousand klicks means nothing."

"Dr. Eongen," I said.

Eongen held up his hands. "Fine, I did my due diligence as a scientist and a person who doesn't want to die. What do you want me to do now?"

"How far is the probe from it?" Fris asked.

"About fifty meters."

"What tools does it have on board?"

"It has an extendable sampling arm."

"Get close enough and extend it, please."

Eongen looked again at Merrin, who nodded. "All right," he said. "Just remember not to bill me for this." He navigated the probe forward, and extended the probe's telescoping sampler.

"Contact in three, two, one," Eongen said.

On the screen, nothing happened.

"Whoa," Eongen said.

"I don't know this word," Fris said.

"Whoa?" I said. "What do you mean, whoa?"

"You didn't see that?"

"See what?"

Eongen motioned to the screen. "The sphere of cloaking material collapsed!"

I looked. "The screen is still black."

"It's a *different* black," Eongen said. "Hold on . . ." He did something at his workstation.

A featureless gray rectangular prism suddenly appeared in the viewscreen.

"Whoa," I said. I saw Fris look at me.

"I widened the light field," Eongen said. "I focused it directly on the sample arm before."

"What is that?" Ong asked, pointing to the prism.

"You got me," Eongen said.

"It looks like a shipping container," I said.

"What is a shipping container doing floating in space with a cloaking field around it?" Fris asked.

"Once again, I say, you got me," Eongen answered.

"It's probably not a shipping container," I suggested. "It's just a very simple form holding whatever's inside."

"So, a *container*," Ong said to me.

"This ship's a container, if you're going to define it like that."

"This ship has other things going on. Like propulsion, and life support and artificial gravity."

I pointed to the prism. "And that was able to project a cloaking field of some form."

"Did you get a sample of that field?" Merrin asked Eongen.

Eongen shook his head. "It collapsed the moment contact happened. There was nothing to collect. The probe's sensor registered a tiny electrical flash from the field collapsing, and a significant increase in local temperature as the residual heat from inside the field was exposed to space."

"Residual heat from what?" asked Fris.

Eongen pointed to the prism. "From that. Whatever's going on with that thing, it's warm."

"Could there be something alive in there?" I asked.

"Maybe," Eongen said, looking at his workstation. "The temperature radiating out of that thing is about zero centigrade. That's about the freezing temperature of water," he said, to Fris.

"The translation makes conversion units," Fris assured him.

"Okay," Eongen confirmed. "That's not warm enough to keep anyone currently on this ship very happy, but it's enough to keep something alive if its insulated or in some form of stasis."

"That's not actually warm," Ong said.

"It's warm relative to the ambient temperature of space," Eongen replied. "Which is actually something I think we need to be aware of. That cloaking bubble wasn't just keeping us from seeing whatever this thing is. It was acting as an insulator, shielding this thing from the cold of space and from the radiation of the local star. We've just made it a lot harder for whatever this is to regulate its own temperature, and we don't know how it's going to handle that."

"It was already falling in toward the star," Merrin said. "After a while it wouldn't have mattered. Shielding or not, it would have fried."

Eongen pointed at me. "We're making the assumption it's just a shipping container again."

"If it's not just a shipping container, then it can regenerate its cloak," Ong said.

"Maybe," Eongen said. "But right now, it's not doing that, and in fairly short order the temperature differential is going to start affecting it one way or another. We can observe what happens, but if you want to examine this thing in its pristine state, the clock is ticking."

"I'm open to suggestions," Fris said to us all.

"If we bring it into the ship we can control the ambient temperature," Merrin said. "I'm sure the cargo holds can be set to zero degrees."

"We're still waiting to hear back from our overlords about that," Fris said. A skip drone had been sent back to Phoenix Station with updates and queries; the return skip drone has yet to arrive.

"Also, that solves one problem by introducing another," Eongen said. "This ship's artificial gravity is set to one g, which is tolerable to all of us, but who knows what it will do to whatever's in there, alive or machine."

"That's a good point," Merrin said.

"Plus, once more as a person who would not like to die needlessly, we don't know what's in that thing and what would happen if we try to get into it."

"We could sequester the cargo hold and ask the Obin to turn off its artificial gravity," Ong said. Eongen groaned. Ong shot him a look. "What?"

"Artificial gravity doesn't really work that way," Eongen said. "Not usually. Not without a lot of energy expenditure. If you were going to keep one cargo bay in the current state of microgravity that this thing is experiencing, we're probably going to have to set the whole ship to that."

"I don't see the problem."

"See if you're saying that after half our people are vomiting uncontrollably, including me," Eongen said.

"How did you ever get into space at all?" Ong asked him.

"Honestly, it's a really good question."

"Before we do anything else we should find out more about the thing," I said, and pointed to the prism on the screen.

"Let me get the probe around it and get a scan of the entire surface," Eongen said. "Then we can pull it up on the monitor and see if there's anything that can give us a clue about its origin."

The scan took five minutes, and when it was done we were looking at a three-dimensional representation of a featureless gray rectangular prism.

"Well, that didn't help much," Ong said.

"We know one thing," Eongen said. "It's *not* a shipping container. At least not one from Earth or the Colonial Union. They're all standardized in sizes going back centuries on Earth, and the Colonial Union adopted those sizes as well. These dimensions are off from those." He turned to Fris. "I have no idea if the Conclave has standardized their shipping containers yet."

"We have not," Fris said. "It's a real mess for trade."

"Interesting," Eongen said. "Besides this, there are no other things like labels or connectors that shipping containers would have to be functional. It's just a prism. I don't think any of us are actually surprised by this, but I wanted to say it out loud."

"What is it made of?" I asked.

"I don't know."

"But we can find out," Merrin pressed. "We have the sampler arm."

"You want me to go up and scratch it?" Eongen asked.

"You already popped its bubble," Ong said.

Five minutes later Eongen's sampler had scratched off a

microscopically small amount of the prism's surface and sent it back into the heart of the probe for analysis.

"Whoa," he said, after a moment.

"There is that word again," said Fris.

"So, it's not exactly metal," Eongen said.

"What does that mean, not exactly metal?"

"It means there are some . . . *unusual* metal oxides here in a composite with bioceramics, and it's making a material that we don't have in our databases here on this ship. And since the databases we brought with us on the ship were updated to the day we skipped, that means this is a mystery material."

"Who uses bioceramics to make spaceships?" Ong asked.

"Good question, and the answer is no one," Eongen said. "They're not generally suited for that task. You want to build new bones, bioceramics are great. You want to build a spaceship, you use other materials."

"And yet there is this thing, made of bioceramic, floating in space," Fris said.

"I'm not here to explain it; I'm here to tell you what it is."

"You said the composite isn't in our database," I said. "Is it close to something that is?"

Eongen raised his eyebrows at this and typed something into his workstation.

"Whoa," he said, two seconds later.

"And there it is again!" Fris exclaimed.

"What is it?" Merrin asked.

"Come look at this and tell me I'm not imagining it," Eongen said to him.

Merrin went over to the screen, looked at it and then looked at me.

"What?" I asked.

"The closest compound we have in the database for this is the one that makes up the Consu carapace," Merrin said to me.

Fris and Ong and Eongen swiveled their heads to look at me.

"Oh," I said, weakly. "That sure is interesting."

There were three pings at that moment, from the PDAs

attached to Fris and Merrin and Ong. They pulled them out and looked at them, and then looked at each other.

"What is it?" I asked.

"We got word back from Phoenix Station," Ong said, still looking at the PDA.

"What did they say?"

Ong looked back up at me. "'Deal with it,'" he said. He looked at Merrin and then to Fris.

"What do you want to do?" Merrin asked Fris.

"I want to get that thing on the ship," Fris said.

NINE

Caspar Merrin crooked his finger at me. "I need to talk to you," he said.

"All right," I said, and turned to excuse Ran, who was once again shadowing me, as usual.

"No," Merrin said. "Ran too." He started walking toward his quarters, which as it happened were right next to my quarters. Ran and I followed.

Merrin's quarters were no less cramped and unadorned than mine were, which is to say they were a square only a shade over two meters to a side. The quarters had been a somewhat hasty bolt-on on the part of the Obin, who, lacking most measures of modesty or interest in the perks of hierarchy, tended to sleep in dormitories, pretty much stacked one on top of the others. On this trip the diplomatic leaders were allowed their own quarters; the scientists and security staff had cots and roommates. They were not quite as stacked together as the Obin were.

The three of us stuffed in, Merrin closed the door and turned to me. "What aren't you telling me?"

"This is about the Consu thing, isn't it?" I asked.

"I think that's obvious," Ran replied.

"Thank you, Ran, but I was actually directing that at Caspar."

"Oh." Ran fell silent.

"Ran took the words out of my mouth," Merrin said.

"I had a meeting at the Obin embassy the night before I came to Phoenix Station," I said. "A colleague there told me that the

Obin had noticed the Consu regularly spying on the Obin, including here at Karna-Hlaven. That's how I knew to ask about the Consu."

"Technically I was the one who was told and Gretchen was in the room," Ran said.

"Yes, this is the polite fig leaf covering telling me something I wasn't cleared to know," I concurred.

"And you chose not to tell me this, why?"

"Clock—my counterpart at the Obin embassy—told me that the Obin had informed the State Department of all of this," I said. "I thought you knew."

"If I had known, I would have told you," Merrin said.

I shook my head. "If you had known, it would have been information over my clearance level. You would have been told not to tell me. At least that was my assumption."

"Yes, of course," Merrin said. "And I would have told you *anyway*, because I would want you to have full operational knowledge of the mission. As you should have believed *I* should have, Gretchen."

I nodded. "Yes, all right. You're right. I'm sorry. I wasn't trying to hide it from you, but that's not an excuse."

Merrin nodded and looked at Ran. "And what about you?"

"I hid it, and it caused me substantial distress," Ran said. "Obin don't like lying by omission."

"Well, that's good to know," Merrin said, amused. He returned his attention to me. "What else did your Obin diplomat say that would be useful?"

"It gave me a basic history lesson of how the colony landed here, and it told me that the Consu started being interested in the Obin again after the events of Roanoke. Possibly because the Obin had contacted the Consu at the behest of Zoë Boutin-Perry, and the resulting events caused a significant change in the events in this part of space."

"Why would the Consu care, though? They don't regularly follow what we lesser beings do."

"That's not true," Ran said.

We both looked at the Obin. "Go on," Merrin said.

"The Consu think of us like we might think of lesser animals. Livestock for Obin. Pets for other species. It is a tenet of their belief system that it is their role to guide other species toward perfection."

"Yes, that's their excuse to show up and pick a fight with other species," Merrin said, with a smirk. "Kill a couple thousand sentient creatures in rigged battles and call it progress for them. We've known about that for a while."

"It would be a mistake to minimize what they do," Ran warned. "Combat is a rite for the Consu, and just because it is the only one the rest of us see does not mean it is the only one, or that it is not significant, both in itself and in the larger context of their other rites and rituals."

"And you know this how?" Merrin asked Ran.

Ran straightened itself up, as much as possible in a room where it had to crouch. "The Obin more than any other are the Consu's special pets," it said. "They created us, for their own purposes. They neglected us when we disappointed them. When we questioned them they took from us a cost higher than any other species ever had to pay to them. They are our specialty. You might say they are our obsession. Any Obin could tell you what I have told you."

Merrin turned to me. "You work with this all the time."

"The Obin can be intense," I said. "In their defense, they are literally at the dawn of individual consciousness. Everything for them is intense."

"I try to be personable," Ran said. "Sometimes it is difficult."

I put a hand on Ran's shoulder. "You're doing great, Ran."

There was a ping on Merrin's PDA. "Speaking of the Obin, our hosts have brought your prism into the ship, into one of the empty cargo holds. They're not going to be able to cut the artificial gravity, but they are holding the space at zero degrees. Remember to bring a jacket."

"Me?" I said. "This is a security detail thing."

Merrin shook his head. "You're the one who told us the Consu might be involved. The closest thing out there to what this thing is, is a Consu shell. We all agreed this means you win the 'first contact' prize." He looked over to Ran. "You can go along too, if you want. You appear to know more about the Consu than anyone else on this ship."

"Aside from every other Obin," Ran corrected him.

"Yes, but they are already busy."

"I'm not prepared to examine an alien artifact," I said. "I don't have protective gear. I don't even have gloves."

"None of us were expecting to bring something onto the ship," Merrin said. "Eongen probed it when it was in space. It seems fine."

I narrowed my eyes at Merrin. "Says the man who is not volunteering to be in the room when it opens up and I'm exposed to who knows what is inside."

Merrin looked at Ran. "Any records of other species catching viruses from the Consu?"

"No," Ran said. "They are usually more direct when they want to kill others."

"There you go," Merrin said, to me.

I looked to Ran. "You're not helping," I said.

"In retrospect I see how I did not support your position," Ran agreed.

"And we still don't know if that is a Consu artifact in there," I said, turning back to Merrin. "All we have to go on is the fact its composition vaguely resembles a Consu shell."

"We go with what we have," Merrin said.

"And how am I going to get into it anyway?" I said. "There are no visible openings or seams. Do you expect me to *knock*?"

Merrin held up a hand. "Don't get ahead of yourself, Gretchen. When you get into the room, you'll see what you're working with and you'll go from there. If you don't find a way into it, we'll figure out something else."

"I'm not happy with this," I said. "It feels sloppy."

"It is *extremely* sloppy," Merrin said. "But if it helps us understand what happened to Unity, then sloppy will have to do."

I looked at Merrin glumly. "If I get infected by an alien virus I will go out of my way to make sure you're the first person I pass it on to."

"That seems fair."

"I'm serious. If my skin melts off, yours is melting right after mine."

"I won't run, I promise," Merrin said. He glanced back down at his PDA. "The captain says it's in and the cargo hold's secured. They're ready when you are."

"Don't worry, ma'am," Bradley King said to me. He and his security detail were standing directly outside the entrance to the cargo hold, weapons at ready. "We have cameras on you and will be inside the perimeter the second anything goes wrong."

"Thank you," I said. I knew King was trying to be reassuring, and I appreciated the attempt. I also knew that if that prism opened up and something inside of it decided that I would be a tasty snack, I would be dead faster than he and his pals could pile through the door.

I looked over at Ran, who was standing next to me impassively. It had turned its consciousness off, the better to be more efficient in my defense if it came to that.

"Are you ready?" I asked Ran.

"Yes," Ran said, in the flat affect it always had when its consciousness was off. If you weren't conscious, you weren't emotional. This was useful for the moment, but I had a second to reflect that this meant conversation with Ran in this mode was a series of monosyllables and short declarations. It turns out you need at least some emotion to carry on a discussion of any weight.

On the other hand, that flat yes was more reassuring than I had anticipated. There wasn't any question that Ran would defend me, to the death if necessary. That yes was flat, but it was also eternal.

I smiled at Ran, and then at the Colonial Union security detail, and then entered the cargo hold, Ran following behind.

The cargo hold was cold as promised, and entirely empty save for the space prism, which was positioned about two-thirds down the length of the space from where I entered. I made my way to it in short order and got my first good look at the surface of the thing. It wasn't entirely smooth; the surface looked like finely pebbled porcelain, each of those tiny pebbles in turn roughly textured. There was no pattern to the pebbles or texture as far as I could see. This prism could have been manufactured, but it could have equally likely been grown, or possibly accreted. I resisted the temptation to run my fingers across it, for now.

I walked around the object and looked for anything that would appear to be a door or even a seam. There was nothing. The object was too tall for me to look at the top plane, and the lower plane was on the floor of the cargo hold, but if there had been any obvious variation on those, they would have been seen during the load-in and I would have been told about it.

"I'm not seeing a way in," I said to Ran. "Are you?"

"No," Ran said.

As I had prepped for the examination Merrin had told me that the Obin did an initial scan of the object with equipment they usually used to check cargo. The scan passed through the outer material but was blocked by something inside. This reminded me of something we did on Roanoke; when the Conclave were hunting us and even the smallest bit of radioactivity might give us away, we manufactured just enough nanobotic cloaking material to coat the inside of an actual storage container, and put what very few bits of electronic equipment we could use into it. No radiation escaped, and none got in. Walking into that storage container's anteroom was like walking into a pitch-black room.

That storage container at least had an obvious entrance. This thing had nothing. No obvious way in and, equally, no obvious way out.

I completed my circuit of the prism and stood in front of one of its shorter sides, staring at the gray, roughly and seemingly randomly pebbled surface.

"Well, hell," I said. I looked at Ran. "Any ideas?"

"No."

I grunted at this and looked back at the prism side. "Fuck it," I said, and then reached out and knocked.

Nothing.

I looked back at Ran. "Didn't hurt to try," I said.

Ran pointed past me. "Look," it said.

I looked back. There was a vertical seam in the prism surface where there hadn't been one before.

"Whoa," I said, and then briefly, randomly thought of Fris.

"Stand back," Ran said to me. I took a step back.

The previously vertical seam sprouted branches, and the petals of surface created by the branches suddenly unfolded and then expanded outward. Inside the prism was a void, and a tunnel, at the end of which was something I couldn't immediately identify.

And then, a voice from out of the void.

"A human! Unexpected."

There was a pause.

"And an Obin. Less unexpected. Well, I've already set my translator, and I'm not going to bother to do it again. The Obin can keep up or not."

"I understand you," Ran said, to the voice at the end of the void.

"How nice for you." A pause. "I see you have one of those abominable collars on you. Is your so-called consciousness switched on?"

"No."

"For the best. They're the worst thing that has happened to your species, not the least because it's tied all of you to *them*." Even through the darkness I could sense being pointed at. "You were meant for more, Obin."

"I'm Gretchen Trujillo," I said, to the voice. "I'm a diplomat from the Colonial Union."

"I don't recall asking for your name or your occupation, but very well," the voice said.

"What may I call you?" I asked.

"I also don't recall giving you permission to learn my name, human."

"Well," I said to the voice. "If I had any doubt that you were a Consu, that's over now."

"This isn't a human ship," the voice-who-was-probably-a-Consu said. "I can tell by the hum of it. By the vibration through the floor, now that I've opened up my sanctum. What are you doing here, human?"

"I'm looking—*we're* looking—for Unity Colony. It was housed on an asteroid. It's disappeared."

There was silence at this.

"Why are you here?" I asked.

"I was dying," the voice said. "On a journey toward my end, in which all restrictions and obligations have been relieved, which is why I may speak to you at all without interminable procedure. It was to be a sacred death. Which you have now interfered with."

"I'm sorry."

"I don't think you are, yet." There was the sound of movement, and then from within the prism lights turned on and I could see to whom I was speaking. It was indeed a Consu, and now I understood why I wasn't able to identify it earlier: It, like I presume everything else inside the prism, was upside down.

Despite everything, I giggled. "We can get you out of there, if you like," I said.

"I'll be staying. But there is something you can do for me."

"What is it?"

"You're going to be getting visitors very soon now. They will want me, and they will want me alive. You will need to keep them away from me until I have time to prepare."

"You just said you wanted to die," I said.

"It's not that simple. There are forms to observe, which have been interrupted. I would have to start over. That would take even more time."

"I will kill you," Ran offered.

"I'm sure you would, Obin. I said I want to die. I did not say I wanted to be killed. The distinction might escape you, but it is vitally important to me."

"Why?" I asked.

"You might call it a political statement," the Consu said. "Right now, none of that is relevant. What is relevant is that pulling me out of my shell means that my whereabouts are now known. If they are known, they are coming for me. I am, for the moment, doomed to stay alive. Whether it is with you or with those coming for me is your decision."

"Why would it matter to us?" I asked.

There was a momentary silence. Then, "Are you trying to bargain, human?"

"I'm trying to understand why where you stay alive is important to me or anyone else on this ship."

"That's a yes, and I note you don't have the courage to say it," the Consu said. "So here is the deal I propose. You keep me alive and on this ship, and I will share with you the fate of this colony you're looking for. If I'm captured, you get nothing. If I am killed, you get nothing."

"You know what happened to Unity Colony."

"Intimately."

"Is it safe?"

"If I am safe, then you will find out. Not before."

"It's not all up to me," I said.

"It will have to be. You don't have time for a committee."

"Who is coming for us?"

"Does it matter?"

"We have to know who we're defending you from."

"Heretics."

"Consu heretics?"

"I wouldn't be concerned with any other kind," the Consu said.

"We need to know more," I pressed.

"Another bargain," the Consu observed.

Before I could answer, a siren went off, loud and insistent, across the ship.

"You're out of time, human," the Consu said to me. "Protect me or don't."

I nodded. "We'll protect you," I said, and turned to go.

"There is one other thing," the Consu said.

I turned back. "What is it?"

"The ones who are coming for me will not bargain with you to get me, or leave you alive if they take me. They will kill each of you on this ship, individually until they have me, all at once when they do. Don't expect them to follow the typical Consu rules of engagement. They're heretics. The moment they have me, you will, all of you, die."

I stared at the Consu. "You could have told me that earlier," I said.

"You could have said yes earlier," the Consu, still upside down, said. "Now leave. I have things to do which will take time. You are wasting both of ours."

I ran toward the exit of the cargo hold, Ran racing behind me.

TEN

"It is a Consu ship," said Mouse, the captain of the Obin ship, pointing to the control monitor on the Obin ship's bridge. "But it is not one of the ships they usually use for their military missions."

"Our guest says that these are heretics," I said to Mouse. I was there with Caspar Merrin, Ong Vannak and Fris; Ran was still shadowing me, since it had also spoken to our guest, but it stood away from us, taking care not to include itself in decision-making. "If they're heretics it's possible they don't have access to what would be Consu capital ships."

"Is that an advantage for us?" Ong asked.

"No," Mouse said. "Even the most modest of Consu vessels is more capable than our ship is. We can't outrun it. If the ship attacks ours, we will likely be destroyed."

"Our guest says that the heretics want it alive," I said. "That precludes them blasting us out of the sky."

"You think they will board the ship," Merrin said to me.

"I don't know," I admitted. "I'm just telling you what I was told."

"The Consu also usually fight on the level of their adversaries," Fris said. "That's part of their code for interacting with us. So if they board, we might be able to fight them."

I shook my head. "Our guest said not to expect them to follow their usual rules. The heretics want it alive, and that's the only thing we know is a priority. Everything else we don't know."

"We know they will kill us if we get in their way," Ong said.

Merrin turned to Mouse. "Have they tried to contact you? To negotiate or to threaten?"

"No," Mouse said.

"So no idea how they will attack, if they do board no idea how many there will be, and no idea what weapons they will have," Merrin said.

"All our security people are armed," Fris said, to Merrin and Ong. "We have combat rifles, and I know you have the same." He turned to Mouse. "I assume you have offensive weapons as well."

"Yes."

"They're not going to do much good against the Consu," Ong said.

"The Consu can die like any creature," Fris reminded him.

"I understand that," Ong replied. "But if they're not condescending to stoop to our level, then we don't know what they will use to kill us. But I'm betting whatever it is will kill us a lot faster than we can kill them."

"If they can reach us at all," I said.

"What does that mean?" Fris asked.

"Consu are the size of small trucks," I said. "This ship is designed on Obin lines. They're larger than our two species"—I motioned to Fris and Ong—"but they're still physically smaller than the Consu. "They're not going to come marching through the ship. They can't fit in the corridors."

"Which means at least we can keep our scientists safe," Merrin said.

"Unless Trujillo's new friend is wrong and they just blast us out of the sky," Ong replied.

Fris motioned to the Consu ship on the screen. "If they were going to do that they would have done it already. I think we can assume they mean to board us."

"When?" Ong asked.

We all turned to Mouse. "Soon," it said.

Merrin turned back to me. "You said our guest needed time. For what and how much time?"

"I don't know in either case," I said. "I don't get the sense it thinks we are worth giving details to. But the implication was that with enough time, it could neutralize the heretics."

Merin nodded. "So we have to buy it the time."

"If you were a Consu, where would you board the ship?" I asked Mouse.

Mouse said something to one of its bridge crew, and a blueprint of the ship appeared on the control monitor. "There." It pointed to an area aft of the cargo holds. "Our ship plan is a common one for Obin ships. The Consu would know it. They would know we would be holding our Consu in one of our cargo holds but not which one. They would not want to damage the cargo holds and kill their intended captive. This area is storage for our cargo handling equipment and other things. It is large enough for the Consu to enter, and easy for them to access the cargo holds and to take their captive out from. This is the obvious entry point."

"Unless they try to surprise us," Ong said.

"No," Mouse said. "They are Consu. They will not consider us to be a serious threat. They will use the most efficient route."

One of the bridge crew said something to Mouse. The image on the control monitor switched back to the Consu ship. From the ship, a transport boat was departing and headed toward us.

"How long until they get here?" Fris asked Mouse.

"Fifteen minutes to arrive. Another ten minutes to attach to and access our ship," Mouse said.

"What do you want to do?" Merrin asked Fris.

"Hide our scientists," Fris said. "Get our security people in place. Fight like hell until we're dead, the Consu are dead, or a miracle happens."

I had a thought, and turned to Mouse. "You said you were confident the Consu wouldn't think we were a threat."

"Yes," Mouse said.

"Do they think we're weak, or do they think we're not very smart?"

"Both."

"I think we can work with that," I said.

Our first problem was when our rifles exploded.

Actually, that was the second problem. The first problem was the Consu transport attaching to our ship from underneath the storage area and then tearing a hole into the hull from which a dozen Consu swarmed out.

The Garvinn security team, our first line of defense, opened fire on the Consu with their rifles and were shocked when their rifles blew up in their claws, shearing themselves into pieces.

"What the fuck just happened?" Fris said. He, Caspar Merrin, Ong Vannak, Ran and I were watching events on the common room large monitor. I was briefly and irrelevantly impressed that his translation medallion had that word in its vocabulary and understood the nuance that made it the best word to use in this context. Fris clicked into his PDA, telling his team to hold back.

A light went on in my head. "Oh, shit," I said, and looked at Fris. "I know what this is."

"Tell me."

"It's a sapper field," I said. "I've seen this before, at Roanoke. Zoë went and won one from the Consu through combat. It's what we used to defeat the second Conclave attack on the colony. It takes the energy from weapons and makes them unworkable."

"So our firearms won't work," Merrin said.

I shook my head. "It can be tuned to work at different energy levels. Jane Sagan tuned ours to let our defenders use crossbow bolts and flamethrowers. I wouldn't count on these Consu allowing even that."

"So how do we fight with them?" Ong asked.

"Hand-to-hand," I said.

Ong looked at the monitor, and at the part of it that showed video of the massive Consu using whatever it was to tear through the bulkheads. "We have to fight *those* with our hands."

"If they're using a sapper field, then yeah," I said.

"Can *they* use firearms?" Fris asked.

"No," I said. Fris got back on the channels to his people.

Ong looked at Merrin and me as Fris did this. "How is this the first time I'm hearing about this thing? About Consu tech the Colonial Union clearly knew about?"

"I've never heard of this before," Merrin said.

"As far as I know we weren't allowed to keep it," I told Ong. "It was a 'single-use' sort of thing."

"It wasn't in the movie," Ong said.

"Oh my God," I said. "Stop with the movie."

On the monitor the Consu and the Garvinn were sizing each other up.

"There are twelve of them and four of my people," Fris said. "I'm not going to tell them to go after the Consu hand-to-hand with those numbers."

"What are you going to do?" Merrin asked.

"Move on to the next part," Fris said, and clicked into his PDA.

On the monitor, the Garvinn moved from their protected firing position to directly in front of the entrance of one of the cargo bays, pulled out their combat knives, and started clicking their defiance at the Consu.

From the host of Consu, six detached and closed the distance between them and the Garvinn, not bothering to take a defensive posture.

"How far does this field extend?" Fris asked me as we watched the Consu advance.

"The one we used covered the entire colony."

"So this one could cover the entire ship."

"Yes." I remembered something else. "But it didn't last very long."

"How long? Be specific."

"Something like five to ten minutes. The colony was bigger than this ship, though. This one might last longer."

"Was the field generator portable? Something the defenders could carry around?"

"No," I said. "It's got to be in their transport."

On the screen, one of the Garvinn—I think it was Bertk—turned his head to look at his fellows, clicked something at them, and then launched himself at the nearest Consu. The Consu unfolded itself, revealing its massive slashing arms, and posed itself almost as if it was welcoming the Garvinn into an embrace. The other Consu paused to consider the fight.

Their battle was brief. Then the Consu closed ranks and kept heading toward the remaining Garvinn, leaving Bertk's remains on the floor.

"Why did he do that?" Ong asked. "That was suicide."

"Quiet," Fris said, watching the screen.

The three remaining Garvinn, looking uncertain now, stepped back from their line and retreated behind the entrance to the cargo hold. The Consu, unrushed, followed, entering through the cargo hold's wide entrance.

Fris pressed a button and the monitor split its screen, one half showing the former view and the other half showing the interior of the cargo hold. In it the remaining Garvinn were racing through it while the six Consu were proceeding at a measured pace, looking around their environment. They were clearly looking for something that they were not finding.

Fris's PDA clicked to life just as the Consu paused in their movement.

"They're secure," Fris said to us, then switched a communication channel to speak to Mouse.

On-screen the Consu looked back as a shield on the entrance through which they came slammed down with explosive force. Then they disappeared, as the exterior doors to the cargo bay were blown open by emergency detonations. Those explosive packs on the cargo doors were meant to be used when the doors were damaged or otherwise unable to be moved by conventional means. But they worked marvelously to remove interlopers as well. The Consu were sucked out into space, along with anything else unsecured and not massive enough to withstand sudden hurricane-force winds.

"*That's* why he did it," Fris said, looking at Ong. "He sold the idea we were defending that hold. He cut the invading force in half. It was a good trade."

Ong didn't say anything to that.

"They won't fall for it a second time," Merrin said.

"No," Fris agreed.

"We have eleven security staff remaining," Ong said. "Not counting the Obin. There's six Consu remaining. We could take them."

"You saw what that Consu did to Bertk," Fris said. "And no offense, Ong, but my security staff is far more capable than yours or Merrin's. If you put any of them up against the Consu without weapons, they will die even more quickly than mine did."

"What do you suggest we do?" Merrin said, to Fris.

Fris looked at me.

"What?" I said.

"This sapper field generator," Fris said. "You've seen what one of these things looks like?"

"Briefly. A long time ago."

"Could you disable the thing if you saw it?"

"I have no idea."

"Well, that'll have to do." Fris lifted his PDA. "I'm getting you a security detail. You're going to that transport."

"No," Ran said.

Fris looked up at this. "What?"

"Keep your security where they are," it said. "We can get to the transport."

"You're diplomats," Fris said.

"You missed the display the other day where she took down one of your security detail," Ong said, to Fris.

Fris looked to me. "Well?"

I turned to Ran. "I need a weapon."

Ran produced a knife and gave it to me. "I have another," it assured me.

"I should come with you," Merrin said.

"No you shouldn't," I said, bluntly.

"I don't have a knife for you," Ran pointed out, rather more diplomatically.

"What's your plan?" Fris asked.

"First, I'm going to pay a quick visit to our friend in the cargo hold," I said. "To see how much more time it needs."

"And then?"

"And then I'm going to need to keep a line open to Captain Mouse. I'm going to need it to do something for me."

"I was wondering when I would see you again," our visiting Consu said to me as I and Ran entered its prism. It was engaged with some apparatus and did not look directly at me. "The humans you have guarding me at the moment are not sufficient for the task, I should tell you."

"How much more time are you going to need?" I asked, ignoring the provocation.

"I heard a terrible noise a few moments ago. What was that?"

"We blew some of your heretics into space."

"They should have been smarter than that," the Consu said.

"I asked you a question."

"I need as much time as I need and that is all you need to know."

I shook my head. "We're already dying defending you, and your friends aren't going to fall for the same trick again. They've been thinking about how to proceed, but that's not going to last. Soon they're going to figure out where you are."

"Your humans have firearms with them," the Consu said. "Surely you've told them how useless they are at the moment."

"You know about the sapper field?" I asked.

"It interfered with my work the minute it was switched on. I've made adjustments, but it's slowed my work down."

"So if we get it turned off you'll be done faster," I said.

"You won't be doing that, so it's immaterial."

"Answer my question. If it's turned off, can you get what you're doing done faster?"

"Yes."

"And what are you doing?"

"You'll see."

"Will it do anything about your heretics?" I asked.

"No, of course not," the Consu said. "You're still going to have to kill them all. Also, I would do it quickly. If you truly did blow some heretics out into space, they'll be sending more. And they won't play as nicely as these ones you already have do."

"You let me worry about that."

"That was always my intention, human."

"If I get the sapper field down, how much more time will you need?"

"*If* you get the sapper field down, then a few of your minutes will be all I need. If you don't, then more heretics will be upon us and it won't matter."

"This better be worth it," I said to the Consu.

"Whether it's worth it to you doesn't concern me at all," it replied.

I stomped out of the prism and went to talk to Bradley King, who was stationed directly outside of the prism with his team.

"Secure yourself," I said. "It's going to get weird."

"We were told," King said. He looked over at Ran and then back at me. "Permission to speak freely?"

"Sure."

"You two are insane," he said. "We saw what that Consu did to the Garvinn. I don't care how many tricks you have up your sleeve. It's not going to be enough."

"I appreciate the vote of confidence."

"I just don't see the point of dying unnecessarily."

"I'll try not to die, then," I said. "But if you're really concerned you can come out with me."

"If you asked me to, I would," King said. "I'm here to protect you."

"Thank you," I said. "But you're going to be needed here."

"You're the boss."

"I'm glad you know it," I said. I looked at Ran. "Are you ready?"

Ran made a motion and turned off its consciousness, to be more efficient and effective for what came next, and I can't say I didn't envy it. "I am ready," it said, flatly.

We walked toward the entrance that led us to the storage area.

There were six Consu waiting there for us.

"If you leave now, Ran and I will spare your lives," I said to them, and it would have been a badass line if my voice hadn't cracked three times as I said it.

I didn't know if the Consu could understand me because they had no response at first. Then they all separated from each other slightly, and unfolded their slicing arms.

"Okay then," I said, presented my knife, and ran screaming at the lot of them, Ran following silently behind. The six started advancing on the two of us.

Just before we made contact with the Consu, both Ran and I dropped and slid, coming in full contact with the floor of the storage area. It hurt. A lot.

The Consu nearest us moved to slash us to pieces—

—and then tumbled away weightless, rotating wildly as they did so, because our sliding to the floor was the signal for Captain Mouse to kill the artificial gravity on the ship.

The Consu shrieked like metal scraping against more metal, but I was trying not to pay attention to that, focusing instead on the hole on the storage area floor that the Consu had boiled out of, underneath which was their troop transport. The slide was meant to keep me on a vector closely parallel to the floor, but I had misjudged slightly and was slowly rising up. As I came to the first lip of the hole I reached down to grab at it and missed, and caught the far lip with the tips of my fingers. My whole mass yanked against my arm, which wasn't fun, but my momentum was halted and I pushed my way into the Consu transport—Ran, who had performed *its* slide perfectly, following directly behind me.

Inside the transport was a Consu.

Ran and I weren't expecting to find one in the troop carrier. But then, it wasn't expecting to see us show up, either. The three of us literally stared at each other across the transport's threshold, a small human and a large Obin, and a creature the size of a personal vehicle, if the vehicle had massive cutting arms bolted to the hood. Then the Consu started to unfold those terrifying slashing arms, screeching like a busted metal door as it did so.

Which was a stupid thing to do. One, it was literally floating inside the transport with nothing to anchor it. Two, Ran had switched off its consciousness when we had left the common area to run to the transport. It wasn't scared of the Consu no matter how loud it screamed.

Ran anchored itself against a transport bulkhead and then leapt at the creature before it could fully extend its arms, pushing the Consu into the transport and sliding between those slashing arms to get close to the Consu's more vulnerable parts. The scream stopped with a slightly surprised *urk* as Ran grabbed the Consu's neck for leverage and then drove its combat knife into the Consu's skull.

I stared for a moment. This was not the first dead body I had ever seen, human or alien; that had happened back at Roanoke. It *was* the first time I had seen a dead Consu. And it was the first time I had seen Ran kill. It did the killing so fast I barely had time to process it happening.

"You really *were* holding back when you were sparring with me," I said, which was not the smartest thing I could say in the moment, but I think I might have been a little bit in shock.

"Yes," Ran said, flatly.

Ran's flat, emotionless response dragged me back to reality and the reason why we were at the transport at all.

The transport was almost Obin-like in its minimalism. Beyond the floating heap of the Consu corpse were what I assumed were navigational controls for the transport; Ran had most likely slaughtered the pilot. Even if the Consu grabbed our visitor, they might not be able to take it off the ship after all. And that was an encouraging thought.

I had other things to focus on, however.

"I think this is it," I said, pointing to a cube of machinery that seemed slightly at odds with the rest of the transport. Its aesthetic was different, and more detailed, than everything else.

"Are you sure?" Ran asked, still unplugged from its consciousness.

"Not at all," I confessed. I looked for anything that might resemble a control panel or a switch. "I can't find anything to turn it off," I said.

Ran stared for a moment, went to the Consu corpse, shoved it up against a bulkhead, and with its knife hacked off one of the Consu's immense cutting arms. It hauled the raggedly severed limb over to the cube.

"Move," it said to me.

I moved. Ran bolstered itself and then swung the slashing arm directly into the cube, puncturing it and driving the point of the bladelike arm far into the machine. With some effort, it pried the arm back out, and then drove it back in again.

Ran did this three more times, and then turned to me. "That's enough," it said.

I got on my PDA and contacted Merrin. "We think it's disabled," I said to him.

"Get out of that transport," Merrin said.

I didn't need to be told a second time. Ran and I floated our way out of the Consu ship and then hung on to the lip a second time, hugging the floor as closely as possible. I looked down the storage area and saw the six Consu near the far end of the room, three of them floating awkwardly in the air, presumably after having bounced off the far wall, and the other three on the far wall itself, cautiously making their way toward the entrance of the cargo hold where our guest was staying.

"Any time now," I muttered to myself, and then let out a little *oof* as the artificial gravity kicked back on and I fell the several centimeters to the floor.

It was worse for the Consu, who all fell from a height of several meters. Their size meant their mass was substantial, and they all took damage of one sort or another. One fell awkwardly on one of its slashing arms, wrenching it into a shocking angle, the snap of the breaking limb like a gunshot. A second fell on its back, the dome of its shell cracking as it did so.

The metal-on-metal screams of the falling Consu were so loud that at first I didn't hear the sound of gunfire as King and his crew entered the storage area and started firing at the Consu.

"Oh, crap," I said, and Ran and I ducked for cover.

The Consu also scrambled away, except for the one with the cracked carapace. It absorbed a whole lot of gunfire and then didn't move after that. The other Consu fled across the room while the four humans knelt and fired and then proceeded to sweep the room carefully. The Consu were flushed out and dispatched until three remained and one, waiting until one of its compatriots was being attacked, bolted toward the cargo hold door.

King, seeing the movement, turned to train his weapon on the runner; the Consu slashed at him and his head rolled from his body. The remaining Consu, emboldened, ran at what was left of the security detail. One of the Consu fell, but the other closed the gap and flung itself at the three.

I bolted from my cover and ran for the cargo hold, Ran racing behind.

The heretic Consu was closing on the prism and there was no way I would cover the gap in time. I yanked out my PDA, opened a circuit, yelled "cut the gravity!" into it, and tossed it away.

From my vantage point I could see into the prism, to the

Consu inside, who was looking at the heretic almost on its threshold. The heretic stopped, unfolded its slashing arms, and with its smaller, almost human arms grabbed something cylindrical it was carrying, possibly a stun grenade of some sort. It reared back to throw the weapon, and I launched myself at the heretic, and then the gravity switched off and I slammed into its carapace at full speed.

I am small. The heretic Consu was not. My mass slamming into its mass did not send it tumbling. But I did wreck its aim; the grenade or whatever it was plinked off the bioceramic edge of the prism and floated away. The Consu, unmoored, teetered sideways across the floor, scrambling for purchase. I grabbed onto its carapace and held on.

The heretic, realizing I had grabbed on, tried to dislodge me, pushing off from the floor of the cargo hold as it did so and causing us to rotate lazily. I was at a spot on its carapace that it couldn't easily get at, so all its slashing and grabbing did was jerk us around even more. Below us I saw Ran; its momentum had carried it across the cargo hold and it was looking for a way to secure itself.

By now the heretic and I were heading toward the ceiling of the cargo bay. If we got there, there was a possibility the Consu could use it to reposition itself, shake me loose and run me through. I could push off away from the Consu, but if I did that there was a good chance it could slash off some vital part of my body before I got a safe distance away.

I looked to Ran, who by this time had secured itself against some machinery. "Tell them to turn on the gravity!" I yelled to it.

"It's not safe for you," Ran said back.

"I know! Do it anyway!"

Ran used its consciousness harness to speak to Merrin, and then looked back up to me. "Three seconds," it said.

I counted to two and then pushed off from the Consu, up toward the ceiling, turning it slightly as I did so. It took the opportunity to slash at me.

It could have been worse. It could have sliced me right in half. As it was, it only slashed me from belly button to sternum.

And then it fell, easily ten meters, directly on its back, cracking its carapace like a rotten egg and splashing its insides all over the cargo bay floor.

Then I fell, easily more meters than that, not landing on the cargo bay floor but on the shattered Consu, which broke my fall after a fashion, which is to say not a lot, but enough that I didn't die. And my insides, at least, stayed inside.

The momentum tumbled me off the corpse of the heretic, and then I landed on the cargo bay floor, staring up at the ceiling and wondering why everything was so goddamned painful.

I figured that *now* I was going to die, and lost consciousness.

BOOK TWO

ELEVEN

I opened my eyes and saw a ceiling.

"Ah, you're awake," a voice said, from somewhere else in the room. It was not unfamiliar, but at the moment I couldn't place it.

"Where am I?" I asked.

"Well, you're not dead," the voice said.

"I know *that*," I murmured.

"How are you so sure?"

"The afterlife wouldn't have such harsh lighting." I closed my eyes.

The voice laughed. "There's the Gretchen I knew."

I opened my eyes again and looked toward the voice.

It was attached to Magdy. Older than the last time I saw him, but still very much him.

"Hey." Magdy reached out to settle me as I tried to sit up. "Don't do that. You have tubes in you. Lie back. Relax."

"Are you kidding me?" I said, still trying to prop myself up.

"I'm not," Magdy insisted. "Lie back down, Gretchen. I spent a lot of time putting you back together again. I don't want you ruining all my work."

I flattened myself back down on the bed, unhappy. "What do you mean, you put me back together again?" I asked.

"Let's see," Magdy said. "When I got to you, you had a serious concussion, a couple of broken ribs, lots of internal bleeding, and a really impressive slash that ran the entire length of your abdomen right up into your chest."

"I got into a fight."

"Yes, I heard."

"With a Consu."

"This was also communicated to me."

"And then I fell ten meters onto its corpse."

"You were always an overachiever, Gretchen."

I laughed at this and immediately regretted it.

"Yeah, maybe don't laugh for a bit," Magdy said, noticing my discomfort.

"Don't laugh, don't sit up," I groused. "Is there anything I'm allowed to do?"

"Work on breathing for a while," Magdy said.

"I'm allowed to talk, though?"

"In moderation."

"It's amazing," I said. "Two minutes with you again, I already want to punch you."

Magdy smiled at this. "I missed you too, Gretchen."

"All right," I said, after a moment of breathing. "For real this time. Where am I?"

"You're in the human wing of the hospital on Unity Station," Magdy said.

I nodded and immediately regretted *that*, too. "Second question. How did we get here?"

"Your ship skipped into Unity's space."

"Where is Unity?"

"In the Karna-Hlaven system."

"That's not possible."

"We've been told that by your fellow shipmates," Magdy said. "And yet, if you could look out a window you would see Karna-Hlaven's sun, and all the other stars in the galaxy exactly where they're supposed to be."

"You *disappeared*," I said. "We went to the Karna-Hlaven system and looked exactly where you were supposed to be. Your colony wasn't there. Your entire asteroid was gone. Not hidden or cloaked or blown up. Just gone."

"You're at Unity Colony now," Magdy assured me. "We're not hidden or cloaked or blown up. We're here."

"Not possible," I said again.

"Very possible," Magdy said. "That said, for the last two weeks we haven't received a single skip drone from either the Conclave or the Colonial Union, or from Earth. That's worrying. We also haven't received shipments of supplies or food, either. That's much more worrying. Every skip drone we sent out to Phoenix or Earth or the Conclave's capital went unanswered."

"It's because you *disappeared*," I said.

"*We're* not the ones who disappeared," Magdy said. "Not from our point of view, anyway."

I lay there and stewed for a few minutes. "Has anyone figured this out yet?"

"There are theories," Magdy said. "Actually more like hypotheses. Actually, more like guesses. That's what I hear, anyway. I'm just a doctor. No one's in a rush to tell me about state secrets. Most involve a Consu that apparently you know."

"I wouldn't say I know it. I just talked to it."

"That counts."

"It really doesn't."

"It counts if that Consu has decided it won't talk to anyone else but you."

"What?" I tried sitting up again at this.

Magdy put out a hand again. "Relax."

"You tell me to relax again and I really will punch you."

"It's going to be a really weak punch," Magdy said.

"You'd be surprised."

"I won't be surprised. I remember all your days out practicing murder with Zoë. But seriously, right now you're weaker than you think you are and you're still recovering. I've patched up your wounds and administered sealant and growth compounds for your ribs. But that concussion is still going to mess with you if you try to get up. Trust me, I'm a doctor."

"No deal," I said. "I remember you when you *weren't* a doctor."

"Fair enough," Magdy said. "Then at least trust me when I say I want you to get well enough that you *can* land that punch."

"I don't know that I like this new, vaguely responsible Magdy Metwalli," I said.

"Also fair. But listen to me anyway."

"At the very least, tell me when I can get out of here," I said. "I need to go slap around a Consu."

"Your boss—Caspar Merrin?"

I nodded, very shallowly.

"—was asking me the very same question while you were out."

"Which, yeah, how long have I been out?"

"A couple of days."

"I've been unconscious for *two days*?"

"Two days and about six hours, to be more exact."

"Why was I out so long?"

"Because I was soft-pedaling your injuries to you," Magdy said, and pointed to my abdomen. "If that slash had been a fraction of a millimeter deeper, you probably would have ruptured your intestines out on that cargo hold floor. Not to mention that whatever microbes the Consu have on them, they really like human flesh. The ones that got on you when you got slashed started necrotizing your body almost immediately, and got into your bloodstream. I had to medically induce you into a coma to deal with that, and even then it was touch and go for too long, in my opinion. You almost died, Gretchen. A couple of times."

"So what you're saying is that I'm going to have an *amazing* scar," I said, after a minute of considering this information.

Magdy smiled. "Probably not," he said. "Modern medicine is better than that."

"Maybe I wanted a scar," I protested.

"If you want to add one on after you heal, that's your business," Magdy said.

"You still haven't said when I'm getting out of here," I pressed.

"I want you here at least one more day," Magdy said. "Like I said, I fixed most of the big things, but that concussion you got was no joke. I want to be sure that brain of yours is going to be all right."

"I need to talk to that stupid Consu," I said.

"Again, I have been told this by your boss and, I think, his boss? An alien named Freeze?"

"Fris," I said. "Not his boss. Just acting like it."

"It's a pretty convincing act. My point is, the Consu doesn't appear to be going anywhere. Neither do your bosses, and neither are we, speaking collectively. One more day, two at most, isn't likely to make much of a difference to them. It will make a difference for you. As long as you listen to your doctor and rest, and refrain from taking a swing at him."

"I promise nothing."

"Of course." Magdy came to the bed, leaned over, and gently kissed the top of my head.

"Not the most professional bedside manner," I said, smiling.

"Maybe not," Magdy admitted. "But I am really happy to see you, Gretchen. Happy to see you and very glad you didn't die."

"You're not going to get rid of me that easy," I said.

"Let's hope not." He stepped back. "Now, believe it or not, I have other patients, including a couple from your ship. I'll come check on you again before my shift ends."

"I'll be here," I promised. "Not moving."

Magdy smiled and left my room.

I experienced a mad jumble of emotions that I was too fatigued to process effectively, and decided to deal with them by falling back to sleep almost instantly.

"You're alive," the Consu said to me, two days later. It, and its prism, had been hauled off the Obin ship and deposited into a new and different cargo hold on Unity Colony. This cargo hold was much larger than the one on the Obin ship; if I fell from near its ceiling, I would die no matter how many Consu I fell on first.

"It was a close thing," I told the Consu. I nodded to the cane I was leaning on. "I'm still healing. I got slashed by one of your heretic friends."

"Then you were lucky indeed."

"It wasn't the cut that was the problem," I said. "It was the microbes the heretic carried. Apparently Consu are filthy."

"As with everything, the Consu consider their weapons. Our heretics knew they would not be using projectile weapons, so they chose the weapons they could use. One of those weapons were microbes."

"So not filthy, just evil."

"Not evil, effective. You did almost die, human."

"Almost. But I'm not dead yet."

"Fortunate for your compatriots," the Consu said.

I knew why it said that. "Why wouldn't you speak to any of them?"

"For my own reasons. I spoke to your Obin pet"—and here I bristled at Ran being labeled a *pet*—"just enough to let them know nothing more would be forthcoming for any of them until you came to speak to me."

"Why will you speak to me?"

"Because you amuse me and because you held up your end of our agreement," the Consu said. "You threw yourself at the heretic who was attacking me and contributed to my avoiding harm. That was stupid of you, human."

"In retrospect, I agree," I said. "Also, you're welcome."

"As recognition of that, at least for now, I will answer your questions, and only your questions. More accurately, I will answer some of your questions and ignore the ones I think are not worth my time. If they are not worth my time, they will not be worth yours either, although that fact is not a primary concern of mine."

"Let me start with an easy one," I said. "What should I call you?"

"You already asked me that once."

"That was before I kept you from being captured," I pointed out.

"I don't care what you call me."

"Fine. I'll call you 'Kitty.'"

"As you wish," Kitty said.

"We're at Unity Colony."

"Yes."

"Which, the last time I was awake, had disappeared."

"So you believed."

"How is it we're here now?"

"I brought us here."

"How?"

"The same way all of our species get anywhere," Kitty said. "I caused your ship to skip here."

"To the Karna-Hlaven system."

"To a Karna-Hlaven system."

I pointed. "That," I said. "Explain it."

"It should be obvious."

"Assume I'm a stupid human."

"I had already assumed that," Kitty said. "Do you understand at all how skip drives work?"

"Not really," I admitted.

"Then I will let someone else explain them to you, because I would be bored doing so. For now, all you need to know is that this"—Kitty touched the side of its prism—"is a skip drive. It is of a different design than what has come before and offers certain advantages. The consequences of those advantages are far-reaching. One small consequence is that it has taken us here, to your missing Unity Colony."

"This new skip drive," I said. "Was this why the heretics wanted you?"

"Again, this should be obvious."

"Why you?" I asked. "What makes you so important?"

"Because I am the judge of consequences," Kitty said.

"That's not helpful," I said.

"That's not a concern of mine," Kitty replied.

"We escaped the heretics," I said.

"Yes."

"Can they follow us here?"

"They do not know the way," Kitty said.

"So we're safe."

"One of the problems with species like yours is that you believe 'safe' is a beneficial condition."

"I didn't hear you complain when I kept you safe from these heretics attacking you," I said.

"If you had not, things would have been different," Kitty said. "That's all."

I was beginning to get a headache speaking to Kitty. "Are you being cared for?" I asked. "Is there anything you need?"

"Your colleagues have made the decision that it is advantageous to keep me alive. I am offered this space and they have presented me with food that is sufficient for my needs. I have things I need to do. I am content."

"What things do you need to do?"

"What I was doing before you interrupted me, human. I need to die."

I nodded. "How long will that take?" I asked.

"As a courtesy, I will let you know when I am prepared."

"But not today."

"It would be unlikely," Kitty said, and then waved at me, dismissively. I understood what that meant. I hobbled away with my cane.

Ran was waiting for me at the other side of the cargo hold entrance. "I do not like you being with that Consu alone," it said to me.

"I can handle myself," I said.

"No you can't," Ran said. "You can barely walk."

"Thank you for that assessment, Ran."

"I apologize for being blunt; however, I am not wrong."

"No, you're not," I said, and then sighed. This was the first time in my life I had ever felt particularly weak—actually, "weak" wasn't the right word. *Vulnerable.* Recovering. I didn't like any of it.

"What did you learn from the Consu?" Ran asked.

"I learned that before we do anything else, I need to speak to a skip drive physicist," I said.

"There should be some on this colony," Ran said.

"Good. Let's get them."

"How many do you need?"

"Let's get all of them, and go from there," I said.

TWELVE

The meeting with the skip drive physicists did not go as planned.

"This is a joke, right?" said Arturo Lavagna, the human skip drive physicist, after I gave a precis of what Kitty had said to me. He was one of two on the colony—or more accurately, the colony had several physicists, none of whose job, on a daily basis, dealt with skip drives, but these two at least had training in the field. The other skip drive physicist was from a species called the Orga, which was a new species to me, and also, looked distractingly like a weasel. "This has to be a joke. You're joking with us."

The three of us were in the chambers of Unity Colony's governing council, which had been given over to us for this hasty meeting ahead of a larger debrief between our mission's diplomatic leaders and the colony's heads of government. For this meeting, Caspar Merrin was present, along with Haimi Bava, one of the councilpeople representing the colonists from Earth. Ran was present, too, because Ran was always present; it was its job now, being present.

"It's not a joke," I said. "I'm telling you what the Consu said. A whole new sort of skip drive, which brought us here."

"Your Consu friend is lying to you," said Ghen Horvni, the Orga. "The physics of skipping simply don't work how it described them to you. Or at least, how you've just now described them to *us*."

"I told it to you exactly as it was told to me."

"Perhaps you've misremembered."

"It wasn't that long of a message."

"There might have been a translation error, then. Because this is not how skip physics work."

I looked at Horvni like the smug little weasel he was and tried not to audibly sigh in exasperation. "I understand that what it described doesn't conform to skip drive physics as we know them," I said. "Again, that's *why* I'm telling you this. Because if it's accurate then we have something new on our hands."

"We don't," Horvni assured me. "The physics of skipping are well understood, and have been for decades."

"I believe you believe that," I said.

Horvni moved to speak again, no doubt snidely, and then a hand went up. It belonged to Haimi Bava. "Excuse me," she said, "but for those of us who are not engineers or physicists, what *are* the physics of skip drives, as we understand them?"

"That covers a lot of ground," said Lavagna.

"Well, then, you can cover that ground, and quickly," said Bava, sharply. "And do it with far less condescension than both you and your colleague here have been showing so far."

Lavagna had the grace to look briefly ashamed at this dressing-down. "Apologies, Councilor Bava, Ms. Trujillo. We're all aware of the gravity of the situation."

"How excellent to hear," Bava said. "Prove it, please."

I looked over at Bava, who was now my new personal hero. She caught my glance and gave me the smallest of smiles.

"Most people think of skip drives like propulsion drives, sending us across physical space," Lavagna said. "But that's not accurate. What skip drives basically do is create a hole in the multiversal fabric."

"Also not accurate, but close enough for nonscientists," Horvni clarified.

"Yes," Lavagna said. "Not accurate but accurate enough for this conversation. We make a hole in space-time, we leave one universe at one position, and arrive in another universe in a different position."

"Meanwhile, in the universe we just left, another version of us arrives, from an entirely different universe," Horvni said. "And so on, and so on."

Lavagna pointed to Horvni. "That's right. And in all these cases that's possible because the universes are so similar—literally just an electron position of difference between them—that we never notice anything is different."

"They have to be that similar, otherwise the skip couldn't happen," Horvni said.

"Why is that?" asked Bava.

"It's a lot of math to explain that," Lavagna said, and immediately held up his hand when he saw Bava stiffen. "This is not to imply that you couldn't understand it, just that you want us to cover this ground quickly. Just know that as a matter of physics, it gets exponentially more difficult to go to universes with higher levels of dissimilarity."

"The other thing that is exponentially more difficult is initiating a skip inside of a significant gravity well," Horvni said. "That's why our ships—*all* our ships"—and here the weasel looked at me significantly—"have to travel to a place where space-time is flat enough to make the skip."

"There are some exceptions for very low-mass objects at things like Lagrange points," Lavagna said.

"Yes, yes," Horvni said, dismissively. "But that wouldn't apply in *this* circumstance."

"Do we ever go back to our original universe?" Bava asked.

"No," Lavagna said. "There's no way to go back to the universe we started from. Once you've skipped, you've left it forever."

"That's unsettling," Bava said.

"Only in the most literal sense," Horvni assured her, not particularly well. "Each universe is so similar to the others that functionally there's no difference. They have to be for the skip drive technology to work at all." Horvni turned his head to me. "Which is why what Ms. Trujillo is telling us makes literally no sense. She's saying this 'new' skip drive skipped an entire ship from *inside* a significant gravity well into a universe so far away from her own that our asteroid didn't exist in it until we arrived."

"Don't forget the assertion that our entire asteroid was somehow skipped without any of *us* knowing," Lavagna said.

"Which in itself is impossible!" Horvni exclaimed. "Nothing remotely as massive as the Unity asteroid has ever been skipped. It's so large that its *own* gravity well would prevent it from being skipped."

"So you're calling us liars," I said, motioning to Caspar Merrin. "Us and the Consu."

"I'm not going to fall into a trap of calling anyone a liar," Horvni said. "I am merely pointing out the extreme unlikelihood that what you are saying is accurate in any way that relates to physics at all."

"That sounds a lot like calling me a liar," I said.

"Not at all," Lavagna said. "You might just be ignorant, or misinformed. Those are two entirely separate conditions."

"Or it's something else entirely," Horvni said.

"Explain that," I said.

"Ms. Trujillo, please look at this from our point of view," Horvni said.

"You've told me your Consu friend informed you it has a new sort of skip drive that allows it to do things no other skip drive *in the history of the universe* has ever done, and that as a result, we are in a new universe so different from our own that this asteroid didn't exist in it. That means *this* asteroid skipping into *that* sort of universe is so improbable that under the laws of physics we know and have *repeatedly* confirmed, it would take an amount of time exponentially longer than the age of this universe to happen."

"Significantly longer," Lavagna said. "As in, the age of this universe hundreds of thousands of times at least."

"I do know what 'exponentially' means," I said, to Lavagna.

"So, did an apparently miraculous skip event actually happen?" Horvni continued. "Or is it something much more plausible? Like, as just one example, our various governments choosing to stress test our colony by cutting it off for a certain amount of time, and then sending a ship full of diplomats to observe how we've handled the isolation?"

"A ship with battle damage and a bunch of Consu corpses," I pointed out.

"I don't know anything about *that*," Horvni said. "But even if that's true, that's still almost infinitely more probable than what you're suggesting."

Bava, who had been absorbing all this, turned to Lavagna. "And you agree?"

"I don't know what to think," Lavagna admitted. "But I do know Occam's razor suggests we're still in the same universe as we've always been, and that their ship"—Lavagna pointed at Merrin—"skipped in the normal way, regardless of any Consu that came with them, dead or alive."

"That's a conspiratorial view of galactic politics you have," I said, to Lavagna and Horvni.

"It's not conspiracy, it's probability," Horvni countered.

I was about to punch a weasel, but Merrin held up his hand. "Councilor Bava, do you think we're lying to you?" he asked. "Or at the very least, misrepresenting the circumstances of our arrival?"

Bava thought for a moment, then pointed at the physicists. "They're just saying what others on the colony are saying," she said. "Not about the skip drives, but all the rest of it. People here know you've said the colony disappeared, but there was nothing on this end that would suggest that happened. If there was a skip, we didn't notice it. What we noticed was supply ships and data drones no longer arriving, and our own drones disappearing unanswered. That doesn't feel like physics. That feels like neglect."

"We didn't abandon you," Merrin said to Bava. "We came looking for you."

"And fought Consu to get here," I added.

Bava glanced at my cane. "There's no doubt about that last part, at least. But honestly I would prefer that you're lying. If you're lying, it means that we can expect supplies again. This colony isn't yet self-sustaining. Very soon now, we're going to run out of things to eat."

Merrin returned his attention to the physicist. "What can we do to convince you, as scientists, that we're not lying or being lied to?"

"You could let us talk to this Consu ourselves," Horvni said.

"Kitty only talks to me," I said.

"Excuse me, what?" Lavagna said, eyes widening. "Did you just call the Consu 'Kitty'?"

"I asked it for its name and it wouldn't tell me," I said. "I decided to call it Kitty."

"Unbelievable," Lavagna said.

"What's a kitty?" Horvni murmured to Lavagna. Lavagna picked up his PDA, opened it, and navigated, I presume, to a picture of a kitten. "That looks nothing like a Consu," Horvni said, after a moment.

"It doesn't really matter what we call the Consu," Merrin said. "It's made it clear that it won't speak to anyone but Gretchen. You could give her technical questions, perhaps."

"Kitty doesn't want to bother answering those," I said. "That's why it told me to go speak to skip drive physicists in the first place."

"If we can't speak to the Consu," Lavagna said, emphatically not calling it Kitty, "then at least let us look at its equipment."

"Yes," Horvni said. "If nothing else it would solve another mystery, which is how your Consu was able to power a skip drive at all, without taking energy from your ship to do it."

"I can ask," I said. "I wouldn't expect a yes. If Kitty won't talk to anyone else"—I noticed Lavagna wincing at the name—"then I don't expect it will want us in its space either."

"You could force the issue," Horvni said.

"With all due respect, if any of us want to find a way back to the rest of civilization, we need to keep Kitty happy," I said. "Or whatever passes for happy."

"Interesting," Lavagna said.

"What?" I asked.

"You said 'if any of us want to find a way back.'"

"So?"

"So either you're very good at keeping your story straight, or you really do think you're trapped in this particular universe with us."

"What does that mean?" Bava asked.

"It means that if our ship tried to skip away from here, we would just skip to a universe similar to this one," I said. "Where our civilizations might not even exist, just like they don't exist here. There's a reason your data drones aren't getting replied to."

"Which would mean the universe is even more removed from the ones we're used to," Lavagna said. "It's one thing for a star system not to have a particular asteroid in it. It's another thing for entire civilizations not to have existed."

"Which makes your story even more unlikely," Horvni pointed out.

I held up a hand. "I get it," I said. "But it still means that we're not going anywhere until this is figured out."

"Ms. Trujillo, I would love to believe you," Lavagna said. "But if we don't have access to either the Consu or its equipment, you're not giving us much to go on. If you want us to believe you, you have to help us."

I nodded at this, because there wasn't much else to say.

Bava was having none of this, however. "Don't put it all on her," she said, to the physicist. "While she's working on that, you two have work to do as well."

"What do you want us to do?" Lavagna said.

"Assume she's correct," Bava said. "And find a way to make the physics work."

"They *don't* work," Horvni began.

"Prove that," Bava said, cutting him off.

Horvni looked over at Lavagna. "That's . . . what we've *been* doing."

"No, you've been expressing an opinion," Bava said. "An

informed opinion, but an opinion nonetheless. Now I need you to show me your *opinion* has some basis in fact."

"We can't do that," Lavagna said. "You don't have the math for it."

"There are fifty thousand people in this colony, all of them with specialized skills. I will find someone with the math. But you have to do the math first."

"It's a waste of time," Horvni said.

Bava narrowed her eyes. "I don't think the two of you understand," she said. "When it comes down to it, I don't care about the details of the science one way or another. What I care about is that in a matter of weeks, we run out of food and other necessary supplies." She pointed at me. "If she's correct, then we need to find a way back, and you two are the only ones *with the math* to tell us how. If you don't, and she's right, we die. All of us. Even you. So, if you please, waste a little time on this."

"There's only two of us," Lavagna said. "And this will take us away from our actual jobs as it is."

"We brought some scientists with us," Merrin said. "They're not doing anything at the moment. Most of them have had math."

Bava nodded and returned her gaze to the physicists. "Find some space. Let me know when you're ready. We'll send over the help. Then get to work."

Horvni and Lavagna stared at her for a moment. Then they nodded, looked at each other, and left.

"I want to be you when I grow up," I said to Bava.

"That was the easy part," she said, looking over to where the two physicists had departed. "In less than an hour, we get to try to explain all of this all over again, to all the other councilors, who have even less math than we do. They're not going to believe you, either, and they won't even have an informed opinion about it."

"But you believe us," Merrin said. "You believe we're telling the truth."

"I believe that we need to prepare the colony like you're

telling the truth," Bava said. "Because if we don't, things are going to get grim, fast. But I will tell you this, Mr. Merrin, Ms. Trujillo. If it turns out you have been stringing us all along, and that we are where we're supposed to be, and this is just some stress test of this colony, you and every other member of your mission's diplomatic corps will have a few solid minutes to think about the stupidity of such an action before I have you cycled out of an airlock."

"Reasonable," I said. "Bad for us, but reasonable."

"I'm glad you think so," Bava said. "Now, let's go through all of this again before my colleagues arrive. I have a suspicion I'll be doing a lot of explaining."

Magdy was waiting for me outside of the colony council chamber after the meeting. It had taken the better part of four hours, and when it was done I understood why revolutions happened.

"You don't look great," Magdy said, as I came out of the chamber and used my cane to hobble over to him through the crowd of people outside the chamber. Ran started following behind me, but I waved it off. It stood a reasonable distance away, ready to knife Magdy, or anyone else, if need be.

"That's because I have a shit doctor," I replied, coming up to him fully.

"I walked into that," Magdy admitted. "Which is still better than you can do right now."

"I can still murder you," I promised him.

"That's not saying a whole lot."

"True. You were always soft."

"Ouch."

"How did you know where I was?" I asked. I had left my PDA in my temporary quarters, which were sparse yet also depressingly cramped. As far as I knew, Magdy had no idea where I would be or how to reach me.

"As your former partner, I have a special, almost psychic bond that allows me to know, almost innately, where you are anywhere in the universe, and also the council meeting was broadcast across the entire colony," he said.

"Oh, well, *that's* great."

"I was going to invite you to dinner tonight, but considering how we are now instituting strict rationing, we'll have to figure out something else."

"Well, I'm already ahead of the rest of you," I said. "I haven't eaten all day. I haven't eaten, I'm tired, and I crave the sweet release of unconsciousness."

"Here," Magdy said, and fished something out of his coat pocket. It was a protein bar. "In lieu of actual dinner."

"Do you always walk around with a protein bar, or are you just happy to see me?"

"I never said I was happy to see you."

"Not only can I murder you, I can have Ran do it too," I reminded him. "You can be murdered twice."

"Also, yes, I usually do have a protein bar on me. Three doctors and five nurses for five thousand humans on this colony. They keep me pretty busy."

I took the protein bar, unwrapped it, and made a very fine effort not inhaling the whole thing at once. Being yelled at by physicists and politicians was apparently hungry work.

Magdy noticed. "Chewing is recommended."

"You're not the boss of me," I said.

"This was a constant theme in our relationship, yes," Magdy observed.

Protein bar inhaled, I started walking toward the colony's transport system, which would take me closer to my terrible quarters, where I planned to collapse onto my substandard bed. Magdy walked with me, Ran ten steps behind. Magdy noticed.

"How is it having your own Obin bodyguard?" he asked.

"Strangely familiar," I said. "Zoë had hers, and after a while you just forgot they were there. It's kind of the same here."

"No one else forgets you're being trailed by an Obin," Magdy pointed out.

"No, I suppose not," I allowed. "So, did you watch the actual council meeting?"

"Not all of it," Magdy said. "I caught bits of it. I mostly followed the responses on the community forums."

"And how were they?"

"Pissed. Pissed at having been cut off for weeks, pissed at the new limitations on food and supplies, pissed at the council, pissed at our various governments, and pissed at you."

"Me?"

"Not you specifically, the 'you' of your mission. Not the least because you're another few dozen people sharing our food and resources."

"I'll try to breathe less," I promised.

"That's the spirit."

"We're not happy about any of this either, you know. We're stranded here now, too. We have to find our way back, and the only thing we have to go on is whatever Kitty decides to tell us."

"Kitty?"

"That's my name for the Consu."

"You named a Consu 'Kitty'?"

"Do you have a better name?"

"Several."

"Shut up. My point is, that's all I have to go on to help us. And it is up to me, since the stupid Consu won't speak to anyone else, and who knows how long it'll keep that up before it gets bored and stops responding at all. If that happens we're all screwed."

"So talk to the other Consu," Magdy said. "Maybe that will help."

I smiled ruefully at this. "Sadly, I can't magically conjure Consu out of the air," I said. "My powers at the moment are limited to hobbling and inhaling protein bars."

Magdy stopped and looked at me. "You don't know."

I stopped too. "Know what?"

"There's another Consu on the colony. One from your ship."

I gaped at Magdy. "We killed all the rest of them," I said.

Magdy shook his head. "You killed most of them. One of

them survived. Your people put a lot of slugs into it, but none of them penetrated particularly deeply. One of my colleagues volunteered to operate on the Consu. The Consu nearly took her head off. We gave it a tray of surgical tools and antiseptics. It took care of its own wounds."

I turned to Ran. "You didn't tell me another Consu survived."

"To be fair to your bodyguard," Magdy said before Ran could say anything, "Ran was mostly stationed in front of the door of your hospital room most of the time you were out. It was not on top of current events otherwise."

I nodded at this and turned back to Ran. "I apologize, Ran."

"Thank you," Ran said. "The human wing of the hospital is isolated away from the rest of it. It would have been difficult to gather information."

"Why is the human wing away from everything else?" I asked Magdy.

"Part of it was because we had to utilize the infrastructure the Obin already had in the asteroid, and so it was luck of the draw where the human wing would go," Magdy said. "The other part of it is the Conclave citizens have some latent bigotries to work out."

"They don't like humans?"

"No one likes humans," Ran said. "This is well-known."

"Thank you, Ran," I said.

"Your bodyguard is not wrong," Magdy said.

"Unity is not so unified?"

"It's complicated."

I nodded. "Where is this other Consu?"

"Still in the Conclave part of the hospital, I believe. It's pretty big. There's almost nowhere else to put it."

"All right. Let's go."

"Now?"

"Yes, now."

"I thought you said you were tired," Magdy said.

"I was tired," I said. "But then I had a protein bar."

THIRTEEN

"You know what I've noticed," I said to Magdy as the colony transport system took us toward the hospital complex three stops away.

"I can't possibly imagine," Magdy said.

"As a colony, you haven't done a whole lot of decorating here," I said. I gestured out of the transport car at the colony as it rolled by, or more accurately as *we* rolled by. The colony common spaces, at least along the transport line, were unremarkable, gray and utilitarian.

Magdy gestured to Ran. "Your bodyguard knows why."

"This is where I am supposed to inform you that Obin don't do ornamentation," Ran said to me. "Your ex-boyfriend and current doctor is trying to hide his being intimidated by me by including me in the conversation in a friendly way." Ran looked at Magdy. "I am correct about this?"

"I would have put it differently," Magdy said.

"Of course you would," Ran informed him.

"Also, how does it know we used to date?" Magdy asked me.

"You did more than date," Ran said. "You also had sex."

This announcement got the attention of some of the other people in the transport car, at least some of whom remembered to have the tact to keep their reactions mostly to themselves.

"You're not wrong," Magdy admitted, looking around at the other passengers. "But maybe this was not the best place to make that statement."

"Are you ashamed of having sex with Gretchen?" Ran exclaimed.

"Okay, you explain this one," Magdy said, to me.

"He's *probably* not ashamed of having sex with me," I told Ran. "But humans generally don't discuss their sex lives on public transportation."

"It's just sex," Ran said.

"That's very liberated of you, Ran," I said. "I'll explain it to you later. For now, take my word for it."

"I will," Ran said. "From now on, no more reminding Dr. Metwalli that the two of you had sex while you are on public transportation."

There were several variations of giggling at this from several species of person.

"Or pretty much anywhere else," I suggested. "And that applies to nearly all humans."

"This widens the restriction considerably," Ran said, doubtfully.

"Yes it does," I said.

"Perhaps you humans are overly neurotic about sex."

"It's entirely possible," I admitted.

Ran nodded and looked at Magdy again. "I will no longer speak of you having sex with Gretchen, or with anyone else."

"Well, thank you," Magdy said.

"Publicly."

"That will suffice."

"This naturally precludes me speaking of you having sex with him," Ran said, to me.

"By commutative property, yes, it does, thank you, Ran." I turned to Magdy. "To get back to your original question—"

"Thank *Christ*," Magdy muttered.

"—Ran knows because I told it. One of the reasons I'm on this mission at all is because you're here. When Unity disappeared Dad felt guilty that he asked you to be part of the colony. I explained all this to Ran, with the additional context that you and I were an item."

"So you told your bodyguard we had sex," Magdy said, quietly.

"No, I asked," Ran answered, loudly.

"*Ran*," I said.

"Oh. I am sorry," it replied, and went silent.

"Ran wanted to have a complete understanding of our former relationship, including why we broke up," I said to Magdy.

"That's because you left Roanoke," Magdy replied, with a hint of jokey reproach that I knew wasn't entirely jokey at all.

"So did you, *Dr.* Metwalli," I pointed out.

"You left first."

"You could have gone to medical school on Erie."

"No I couldn't have," Magdy said. "This was in the before times, remember, before the Tripartite Agreement. My residency choices, in both senses of the word, were Zhong Guo or Roanoke. Roanoke wasn't far enough along to have a university, much less a medical school. So Zhong Guo it was. What?" Magdy caught me looking at him thoughtfully.

"I'm just thinking about the fact that when we were an item, you were kind of a meathead," I said. "And now you're a doctor."

"I wasn't a meathead," Magdy protested. "I was just young."

"Is *that* what we're calling it."

"You weren't always such a great prize yourself, you know," Magdy said. "Little Miss I'm Going To Stab You With My Wit."

"And also with a knife, don't forget that," I reminded him, and then stopped and considered him at length.

"What?" Magdy said.

"I just realized I haven't asked you if you're involved with anyone."

"Like a girlfriend?"

"Unless you've had some personal growth in a direction I don't know about, yes."

"I have indeed had personal growth, just not that way. I am currently between relationships," Magdy said.

"Who was the last one?"

"Nneamaka. She's a gastroenterologist."

"And what happened?"

"She couldn't stomach me anymore."

"He made a pun!" Ran said to me. "It was very clever."

"Actually, not really," I said to Ran, then looked back at Magdy. "You're a child."

"Sorry. It was right there. To be fair, by the time it was over she really couldn't stand me."

"Not *you*," I exclaimed.

"And what about you?" Magdy asked. "What is your primary relationship now?"

"Gretchen has a cat," Ran volunteered. "Its name is Lucifer."

"That cat name is very on brand for you," Magdy said to me. "Any nonfeline significant others?"

"I was engaged once," I said.

Magdy almost looked hurt by this, which, *good*, but then he recovered. "So that's a lot."

"It was a lot," I agreed.

"So what happened?"

"I became too much."

"You have also made a pun!" Ran said, to me. "Not as good, however."

"Thank you, Ran," I said. "It wasn't meant to be a contest."

Magdy looked at me for a moment. "I'm sorry about your engagement," he said to me, quietly.

"It's fine," I said. "And it was for the best."

"How so?"

"You're not the only one who has had time for personal growth," I said. "Look, I think this is our stop."

Magdy took the hint. He wasn't lying about the personal growth.

The three of us got off the transport into a small square in front of the hospital complex. Calling it a "square" was making it seem more grand than it was. The ceilings of this area were—accounting for Obin height—as low as they were anywhere else, and the square itself was unadorned. It was more a widening in the traffic way than anything else.

"To go all the way back to our first topic of conversation, before we got sidetracked into sex and recrimination," Magdy said as we walked to the hospital, "yes, Ran was right. The Obin were the ones to build out this whole asteroid, and everything they do is about strict utility."

"You've been here for two years," I said. "You could have added some ornamental plants. Strung up some lights."

"If you ever manage to get to the areas where the colonists actually live, you will see some of that," Magdy said. "So far, you've been to the hospital, nearly unused guest quarters, and the council chambers."

"She has also been to a cargo hold," Ran said, helpfully.

"I'm sure that was very festive," Magdy said, to Ran, and then turned back to me. "At some point, if you like, you could visit me. At my apartment. In the part of the colony that has, you know, decoration."

"Uh-huh," I said. "Calm yourself, Doctor. I'm still convalescing."

"I just want to show you my houseplants," Magdy assured me.

I laughed at that, and we went into the hospital.

There were a clutch of Obin guards in front of the (large) room that held the convalescing Consu, and none of them seemed particularly interested in letting me speak to their captive. I tried being calm and logical with them, and when that didn't work I tried being charming and manipulative with them. That didn't work either, probably because as far as I could tell none of them had their consciousness harnesses turned on.

"I'm not getting anywhere with this bunch," I said to Magdy and Ran.

"You could go over their heads," Magdy suggested.

"That would take time and I'm already here."

"Patience was never one of your strong points."

"You of all people don't get to lecture me about patience," I shot back.

"May I try?" Ran asked, interposing itself before Magdy and I could lose our tempers. "Talking with the guards."

"Be my guest," I said, filing away the plan to get into it with Magdy later.

"What are you going to do?" Magdy asked Ran.

"I have an idea," it said, and then walked past us to the guards, speaking to them in Obin. As it did so, it would occasionally gesture in our direction. Heads would bobble in our direction, then bobble back to Ran. One of them, I expect the head of the guards, spoke back to Ran, flatly. It didn't look good for us.

Ran was silent for a moment and then said something else. The guards all touched their harnesses. Ran turned to me and Magdy.

"I just asked them to turn on their consciousnesses," Ran said. "Whatever happens next, don't panic."

Then Ran turned back to the guards and screamed at them in Obin. I don't speak the language, but I know a real verbal reaming when I hear it. The guards, utterly unprepared to be chewed out, much less by another Obin, began to tremble uncontrollably.

Ran did this for another minute or so, then stopped and barked a command. The guards parted. Ran turned to me.

"You may enter," it said.

"Come on," I said to Magdy.

Magdy seemed surprised. "Me?"

"You don't want to be hanging around when these guards turn off their consciousnesses."

Magdy was about to say something else, probably along the lines of how he would rather take his chances with the Obin than a Consu, then stopped and nodded. So he could be taught, which was indeed a change. The two of us walked past the guard, Ran following after.

"I am turning off my consciousness now," Ran said. "Screaming angrily is very stressful."

"Yes it is," I agreed. "I didn't know you had it in you, Ran."

"I always wanted to do it," Ran said. "And now I never want to do it again." It reached up and flipped its switch and went entirely blank.

And with that I turned and faced the Consu in the room.

It was on a platform, in lieu, I supposed, of a hospital bed, which, being the size of a small vehicle, it would not have fit on anyway. Its carapace showed evidence of both projectile impacts and surgical saws; both cuts and punctures seemed to be spackled with some sort of surgical mortar, which I assumed would be its equivalent of stitches. The creature was shackled and its mobility compromised. It was both patient and prisoner.

"Hello," I said, to it.

It regarded me and then let out a screech that sounded like it was trying to scour the inside of my skull. Beside me, Magdy winced at the sound, and I remembered this was actually his first time in the presence of this particular, highly advanced species. No doubt we were being insulted, but neither of us spoke metal screeches.

"Oh, right," I said, stupidly. I borrowed Magdy's PDA, set up a translation circuit and then placed it on the ground between me and the Consu.

"That should help," I said, and the PDA made a tinny scraping noise. "Would you repeat what you just said?"

"You are unclean," is what the Consu said.

"That's just rude," I replied.

"You cannot speak to me," the Consu continued. "You are unsanctified, and not fit to be in my presence. Speaking even this to you demeans me in a manner that threatens my soul. I will require purification."

"Here's the thing about that," I said. "You and your heretic friends invaded my ship, killed my friends and tried to kidnap someone who was under our protection." I lifted my cane. "I was injured and almost died. I think that deserves an explanation. Unclean or not, you owe me."

"If I were unshackled you would be dead," the Consu said.

"But you're not, and so here we are," I replied.

The Consu stared at me, silent. I hobbled over with my cane.

"You know, the longer you don't speak to me, the more you're going to have to purify yourself," I said.

"You called me 'heretic,'" the Consu finally said, after another minute of a staring contest.

"That's what Kitty called you," I said. "The Consu you were trying to kidnap."

"It is still alive."

"Yes," I said. "One of you almost grabbed it. I prevented that."

"Foolish."

"That's what Kitty said."

"Their name is not that."

"It wouldn't give me its name, so I gave it one," I said. "You could tell me your name, if you like."

"I will not."

"Then I'll call you 'Bacon,'" I said.

"I don't care what you call me," Bacon replied.

"Funny, Kitty said that, too. So, are you?"

"Am I what?"

"A heretic?"

"That's not a concern for you."

"If it's the reason you killed my people, it is."

"If the traitor had done its task, your people would not be dead."

"Traitor? Kitty's a traitor? Traitor to whom?"

Bacon paused. "You know nothing," it said.

"No, I don't," I said. "That's why we're talking. There are things I need to know, and I want you to tell them to me."

"There is no reason to speak to you."

"If you want to get home there is," I said.

"Human," Bacon said. "Don't think you can motivate or bargain with me. There is nothing you can offer that I want or need. Not even my life. I was sanctified and death is not a thing I fear."

"Shame the doctors spent all that time patching you up."

"It did not ask for that and would not have wanted it.

Because of it I have missed my"—and here was some untranslatable scraping—"and I will have to begin again."

"Help me and I will do what I can to help you begin that journey," I said.

"Human," Bacon said again, and I noted that the word sounded even more condescending coming from it than from Kitty. "There is nothing you can do, and if you knew what you were saying you would not say it."

"Why not?"

"It is not something you deserve to know."

"Tell me why Kitty is a traitor. Tell me what it was doing. What you were doing. Tell me about this new skip drive. Tell me how we got here. Tell me why."

"You should ask your Kitty," Bacon said.

"I did."

"What did it say?"

"It was as maddeningly obtuse as you're being."

"The traitor and I may not agree on many things," Bacon said. "But we agree that you are not worthy of knowing what we know."

"Tell me what I want to know," I said.

"No," Bacon replied, and then said nothing else, no matter how much I asked, pleaded or provoked it.

"That was not as successful as I think you hoped it would be," Magdy said to me, once we were on the other side of the door, and then immediately raised his hands when he caught my look. "Sorry, that came out snarkier than I meant it. I just meant it wasn't very forthcoming."

"Kitty made me forget the utter contempt the Consu have for us lesser beings," I said. "I lost my temper."

"Maybe a little," Magdy said. "But you were provoked. By the sound of it, the only thing on this colony it hates more than you is that other Consu."

Bing. "Yes," I said. "*Yes.*" I secured my cane in the crook of my arm, reached over to Magdy, put my hands on either side of his face, pulled him in and kissed him on the lips. Quickly. No heat.

"Okay," Magdy said when I was done, smiling. "I'm not complaining, but I am confused."

"You used to like that."

"I still like it. But I thought you were convalescing."

"That's for giving me an idea." I turned to Ran. "Do you think the guards will still talk to us?" I asked it.

"Yes," Ran said. "They seem to have recovered from my shouting at them."

"Then ask the leader if the Consu in there is stable enough to move."

"All right," Ran said, then paused. "Where will we be moving the Consu to?"

FOURTEEN

Kitty watched as we brought in Bacon and set it up with its own space in the cargo area and said nothing until that was done.

"They are confined," Kitty said to me after Bacon's holding pen was constructed and a sedated Bacon hauled in and set into it. All the workers and handlers had left, and it was just me remaining, with Ran by the door, silent and ready.

"It killed some of us and threatened to kill me," I said. "So unlike you, it's a prisoner."

"If we were where we came from, you and everyone on this asteroid would be killed for imprisoning one of us," Kitty said. "It is not to be borne."

"I acknowledge your extreme chauvinism," I said, "and also, we're *not* where we came from, and as far as I know you are the only two Consu in this entire universe, so any advantages you might have had there don't carry over."

Kitty changed the subject. "Why did you put this one with me?"

"The hospital needed the room, and this one was well enough to move. Also, we've already fitted this cargo hold to deal with your personal comfort and needs. It doesn't make sense to do it all over again. So now you have a roommate."

"I would not choose this," Kitty said.

"I will pass along your complaint to management," I promised.

"Nor would this one choose to be near me."

"It invaded our ship to retrieve you."

"Not out of fellowship."

I nodded. "It did call you a traitor when I spoke to it," I said. "I don't suppose you would care to explain that."

"It is not your concern."

"I thought that's what you would say." I pointed to Bacon, who was still out of it. "This one was even less helpful than you are, and at this point I'm tired of trying to be patient with your species. If you would like to be useful to me, then that would be fine. Let me know. Until then, well, once Bacon here wakes up, you will have each other to speak to." I nodded to Kitty and then walked out of the cargo hold, Ran close behind.

"Do you think they know you have recording devices in the cargo bay?" Ran asked me, once we were outside of the bay.

"I think the more accurate question is whether they *care* if there are recording devices or not," I said. "I don't think they do. It's like a human caring if a dog is listening in to a conversation. The dog can't understand what's being said."

"You are not a dog," Ran pointed out.

"You and I know that, and maybe even Kitty knows that," I said. "But I don't think Kitty believes it, and I'm pretty sure Bacon doesn't. When Bacon wakes up, they're going to start talking. And what they are saying to each other is going to be very different than what they would ever say to me."

Ran considered this. "What do you think they will talk about?" it asked.

"For one thing, we think they were lovers," said Feruza Olimova, of the two Consu, whom we could see and hear in our monitor, screaming and gesticulating.

I blinked in surprise at this. "The hell you say."

"That's just speculation," said Keiward Eongen. He, Olimova and Bethany Young had volunteered for Consu spying duty, since all the other scientists we brought with us were busy helping Horvni and Lavagna rethink skip drive physics. They had set up shop in a spare conference room of Unity Colony's government complex, which was now littered with monitors, water bottles and protein bar wrappers. Scientists, at least the human ones, were untidy.

"It's not really speculation," Olimova said.

"They could just be friends," Eongen countered.

Olimova and Young looked at each other, shared a significant glance, and then Olimova looked back to Eongen. "You have never had a lover's spat?"

"Not . . . recently," Eongen said.

"Perhaps you would like a refresher," Olimova replied, and this is how I learned their flirtation stage had moved on to actual banging.

"I'd rather not."

"Then you can trust me, there is a certain level of rage that can only be leveled against someone you've been fucking," Olimova said. She pointed at the screen. "This is that level."

"I have to admit I've never thought about Consu fucking before," I said.

"I imagine it's complicated," Olimova said. "So much carapace. But however it is done, I am certain these two have done it. A lot of their conversation is about betrayal."

"Well, Bacon did call Kitty a traitor."

"I still can't believe that's what you call the Consu," Eongen said.

"What's wrong with it?" I asked.

"It's so *undignified*."

I shrugged. "They're just people."

"They're just people with about a twenty millennium technological head start on us," Eongen pointed out.

I pointed to the monitor. "Who still have relationship issues. Probably about Kitty being a traitor."

"That's it," Young said. "Apparently . . . *Kitty* was pretending to be part of whatever faction that Bacon is part of. Kitty was supposed to use the new skip drive technology to send the colony somewhere else. Instead it sent the colony here and faked its own disappearance. Or something."

"It's a little muddled," Olimova said, and pointed to their computer. "The translation isn't very good. The two of them are using some version of their language that is significantly grammatically different than what they usually use with us."

"The Consu use a very specific dialect to talk to lesser species," Ran said. "They would not stoop to use their own language to speak to us."

"You could have told us this earlier," Eongen said.

"I assumed you knew."

"Not every species has as singular a focus on the Consu as yours does."

"I'm sorry you don't," Ran said.

"Does that mean our plan to spy on them isn't working?" I asked the scientists.

"No, it's working," Olimova said. "It's not entirely incomprehensible, but we're missing some stuff and have to piece it together through context. Machine translation is already going to miss subtleties. We have to go through the transcriptions and try to make it make sense."

"Which is why I'm saying they might just be friends," Eongen said.

"Some things you don't need a translator for, Kei," Olimova replied.

"What else have we pieced together?" I asked.

"There was some discussion of the thing Kitty was in when we found it," Young said. "The prism, I think you call it."

"What about it?"

"Bacon was saying something about how Kitty took a risk by engaging its skip drive, that it was barely powerful enough to move itself, much less the ship that it was in."

"What did Kitty say about that?"

"It said something along the line of it intentionally fed the other Consu misinformation about the command center's capabilities. I assume 'command center' here is this prism of yours."

"Then Bacon said they knew more than they let on, and then Kitty said it doubted that, and then the translation gets wonky again," Olimova added.

I nodded at this, but it was an earlier part of this discussion I was interested in. "You said 'command center,'" I said to Young. "How sure are we about that translation?"

"Pretty sure?" Young said, and pulled up the translation transcription, scrolling back to that part of the Consu's argument and highlighting that phrase. "The translation program gives it a sixty-eight percent confidence. It might also be 'command pod' or 'operations center.'"

"But no matter what, the prism is where Kitty ran things from."

"Seems like."

"Okay," I said. "What was it operating or commanding?"

"It was operating the skip drive that moved the colony," Eongen said.

"Right, but Bacon just said it was barely powerful enough to get the ship here."

"And Kitty said otherwise."

"Sure, but there is a huge mass difference between our ship and Unity Colony's asteroid," I pointed out. "Besides, the colony skipped, but Kitty's command pod stayed behind."

"Meaning that whatever it was that skipped the asteroid came along with it," Olimova said.

"Something big enough to skip this asteroid would have been spotted," Eongen pointed out. "The people here say they didn't know they had swapped universes until we told them. A lot of them still don't believe it."

"They wouldn't see it if it were cloaked," Young said. "Just like the command center was."

"You were the one to find the command center," I said, to Young. "You think you could find whatever it was that skipped this asteroid?"

Young nodded. "The program I ran to find the command center should work just as well for this," she said. "We're looking at temperatures and microgravity wells. The only problem is the equipment I need to run the scans is still on the Obin ship. I'd have to connect remotely."

I looked over to Ran, who caught the look. "I will get in contact with Captain Mouse," it said, and stepped back to run the call through its consciousness harness.

I looked back to the monitor, where Bacon and Kitty were still clearly yelling at each other. Eongen caught me looking. "Be glad you're not in that room," he said. "That probably sounds like two ships crashing into each other for an entire hour. It's instant migraine, at least until you lose your hearing."

"Yes," I said. "But I find it comforting."

"Comforting? You're going to have to explain that one."

"You said it yourself," I said. "Here is this species that is so vastly ahead of us that we can barely comprehend it most of the time." I waved at the screen. "And here they are, fighting with each other. Exactly like we would do. Exactly like most species we know would do, in their own way. They're supposed to be gods, and they're acting like this."

"The gods always were poorly behaved," Olimova said.

"Right, but that's because our gods were always just a version of us." I pointed to the screen again. "The Consu aren't a version of us, and never have been. But here they are, fighting like jilted lovers."

"So they're not that different from us," Young said. "They just have better tech."

"I'm not comforted by them being not that different from us," Eongen said. "We have a hard enough time getting along with our same species, much less any other." He motioned to the Consu on the screen. "Give us the same tools as they have, we probably would have wiped out every other species in the galactic neighborhood, and then started working on ourselves."

"I bet you're fun at parties," I said to him.

"Tell me I'm wrong," Eongen replied.

"Captain Mouse says that it's had the ship open a connection for you, Dr. Young," Ran said.

Young nodded, grabbed a keyboard and started typing. A few minutes later she smiled to herself and wiped the monitor of the squabbling Consu, replacing it with a generated map of the local space, with Unity Colony asteroid at the center and the Obin ship, currently under repair, floating off to the side.

"Let's see what we can see," she said, and pressed a key to execute her search.

"Holy shit," Eongen said, a few seconds later, looking at the monitor.

"You got that right," I said.

On the monitor, a constellation of objects floated around the asteroid, encircling it.

"It's not one skip drive we were looking for," Young said. "It's dozens."

"One hundred twenty-eight of them, if you're being precise," Olimova said, looking at the tally in the monitor.

"Well, at least now we have something to show the people who don't think we were skipped into another universe," I said. "Hard to argue with one hundred twenty-eight rebuttals."

"You underestimate human stubbornness," Olimova said.

I smiled. "Don't remind me."

"So, what now?" Eongen asked me.

I looked back to the monitor. "Kitty won't tell us how its command center works," I said. "And I'm pretty sure it would sabotage the thing if we tried to get in there without its permission. So we grab one of these instead."

FIFTEEN

"There's news," Arturo Lavagna said to me. "Whether it's good news or bad news is up to you."

"Believe me, at this point, any news is good news," I said.

We were in a colony cargo hold, one separate from the one holding our two Consu. This one held one of the one hundred twenty-eight skip drive satellites, which was currently being crawled over by every scientist on the colony with a physics background. Wrangling it into the bay had taken a couple of days, first to get permission, which took more persuading than I thought absolutely necessary, and then to get a tug to drag one into the cargo bay without destroying it.

While Lavagna was talking to me, Ghen Horvni was in the background conferring with physicists of varying species over some specific issue. He was gesticulating wildly, which, inasmuch as he looked like a weasel to begin with, gave him the appearance of a stuffed animal being shaken by an excitable child. I decided to keep that observation to myself.

"Well, then, the good news is that this thing almost certainly houses a skip drive," Lavagna said, pointing backward to the satellite. "Its basic design looks enough like what we know to be a skip drive that we're able to see the family resemblance. This isn't too much of a surprise because nearly all modern skip drives derive from technology we got from the Consu one way or another. But it's a confirmation that some version of a skip drive is what we're dealing with here."

"Which means you're no longer skeptical of the idea that we're not in our universe anymore," I said. This was a question in the form of a statement.

Lavagna took it as such. "Let's just say my and Horvni's skepticism is a lot less pointed at this juncture," he said. "I wouldn't consider *that* good news, considering what it means for us. There's also the fact this skip drive we have raises more questions than it answers for us."

"Tell me about those new questions," I said. "Because after I'm done talking to you I have to go talk to the colony council about it. Which means I have to be able to explain it to them, so use words as small as possible, please." I did not tell Lavagna that I, also, would need the "small words" explanation.

"All right, let me put it this way. The skip drive as we know it today? It's the equivalent of an airplane in, say, the early twentieth century back on Earth. Canvas wings, single propeller, extremely basic." He waved in the direction of the satellite. "This is like a spaceship. A *skip-drive-capable* spaceship. It's *that* much farther ahead than any skip drive any of the rest of us have."

"It's not a surprise that the Consu keep the best of their technology to themselves."

"No, it's not, but this feels like having my face rubbed into that fact." Lavagna smiled ruefully. "There I was a couple of days ago being condescending to you about what was possible with skip drive physics, and now here this is, reminding me that I'm a Neanderthal banging rocks together."

"Your apology is accepted," I said.

"I appreciate that, Ms. Trujillo."

"And what has the Neanderthal learned that I am going to be able to tell the council?"

"Honestly, not much," Lavagna said. "We can see just from the design of this skip drive how much more advanced it is, and we know—or, apologies, still must hypothesize—that it is capable of operating within a gravity well and can go to far different universes than our drives can. But we don't know enough right now to connect those two things together. It's a lot of math."

I smiled at this. "I'm confident you all can figure it out. They had to have built these new drives that way for a reason."

"Well, maybe not."

"What does that mean?"

"The drives themselves are not the only way these things are advanced," Lavagna said. "The fact that they—hypothetically—work in connection with other skip drives is mind-blowing."

"Why is that mind-blowing?"

"You don't have the math for it," Lavagna assured me. "But even getting one skip drive to work is like herding cats on a quantum level. Getting two in tandem would require exponentially more computing power and energy to work, and is more than *we* can do right now. Getting one hundred twenty-eight of them to work together is staggering. But if you want to move something as massive as this asteroid, that's what you would need to generate a field wide and strong enough to drop it into a completely different universe."

Lavagna waved back toward the satellite a third time, this time catching the attention of Ghen Horvni, who started to walk over. "And this is why I think the ability to drop things into unlikely universes isn't intentional. The energy and computing power is required *just* to create a field large enough to move the asteroid. The part about having the ability to travel to vastly different universes is a side effect of this massive power and computational draw, if you will. An emergent property."

"A bonus feature at no extra cost," I suggested.

Lavagna pointed. "Yes! That."

I looked over at the satellite. "It's not that big," I said. "Where is all the power coming from?"

"That's what Ghen's been working on," Lavagna said, pointing to his alien counterpart, who had come up to us during the last part of the conversation.

"We just have guesses at this point," Horvni said.

"I'll take guesses," I said.

"Antimatter," Horvni proclaimed.

I blinked at this. "We brought *antimatter* onto the colony?" Antimatter and matter annihilate each other almost perfectly, releasing appalling amounts of energy. Even a tiny amount would be enough to blow up a fair chunk of the colony.

"It's weirder than that," Horvni said. "There's a tiny modified skip drive in there that we think opens up to a stream of antimatter particles by way of vacuum energy."

"That's a lot of words," I said. "But the part that sticks out for me is 'stream of antimatter particles.' I promised Haimi Bava that bringing that thing onto the colony would pose no danger. Now I'm worried I was a liar."

"There's no danger unless we try to turn it on," Lavagna said.

"Which we would like to!" Horvni said, excitedly.

"Oh my God," I said.

"Not on the colony," Lavagna rushed to explain. "We would put it back where it came from first."

"There is a problem, however," Horvni added.

"*Besides* the antimatter?" I asked.

"No, it's the *other* type of power. The computing power. There's not enough of it on the satellite for what it would have to do. Not only to make a successful skip on its own, but to coordinate with other satellites to create a larger field like we think these must do."

"Then how does it work?"

"We don't know," Horvni admitted. "We would *like* to know, because if these were a part of us getting here—regardless of universe—then they will have to be part of getting back."

"Did your Consu say anything about how the computing was done?" asked Lavagna.

I shook my head. "All they said was that preparing would take it some time."

"Can you ask it more specifically?"

"I don't know that it will talk to me anymore," I said. "It spends most of its time screaming at its ex now."

"I don't know what that means," Lavagna said, after a moment.

"I'll give it another shot," I promised. "Just don't expect miracles."

"A miracle is what we're needing," Horvni said. "So try for one anyway."

"I wish you would have your PDA on you," Magdy said to me. He was waiting for me outside the cargo hold. He pointed to Ran, who was waiting with him. "I have to contact your bodyguard to know where you are."

"Back on Phoenix Ran is actually my assistant," I told him. "So even if I had my PDA on me, you would still have to go through it to make an appointment."

"You're her assistant?" Magdy asked Ran.

"I am," Ran said.

"How is she as a boss?"

"I think this is an attempt to incriminate either her or me with regard to our employment-related behavior," Ran said.

"Maybe a little," Magdy confessed.

"She's mostly acceptable as a boss," Ran said. "And I am a model assistant."

"Mostly acceptable?" I said to Ran.

"You're sometimes idiosyncratic," Ran said. "For example, your refusal to carry your PDA on a regular basis, which is inconvenient and irritating to others."

"It's not wrong," Magdy said to me.

"This is why I am a model assistant," Ran said. "I understand my superior's quirks and failings."

"And are happy to talk about them to anyone who asks," I said.

"I understand how you may not find that a positive," Ran acknowledged.

"I like your assistant," Magdy said.

"You would," I replied. "Not that it's not nice to see you, but why are you here?"

"It's lunchtime and since we're now rationing calories, after I ate a protein bar I had free time. Since I've hardly seen you for over a decade, I thought I would come to see how you're doing. Seems a better idea than counting the seconds until I can have another protein bar."

"You can eat things other than protein bars, you know."

"I actually like the protein bars. Well"—Magdy quirked his mouth here, which made him suddenly a lot cuter, which annoyed me because I didn't want the distraction—"it's more like I've gotten habituated to them. Jam one in, I'm good for three or so hours."

"So you're saying that even if we had gotten to have dinner, it just would have been more protein bars," I said.

In response to that, Magdy reached into his pocket, pulled out a protein bar, and offered it to me.

I laughed. "No thank you."

Magdy turned and offered the protein bar to Ran, who took it, gravely. "Thank you," it said, to Magdy.

"Have you ever had one of those?" I asked Ran.

"I have not," Ran said. "But I would like to try it. Obin food is extremely functional but not interesting."

I pointed to the protein bar. "That, too, is functional but not interesting."

"I understand why you say that," Ran replied. "But there is a difference between Obin 'functional' and human 'functional.'" It placed the protein bar in its utility belt.

"So many differences between species," I said, sarcastically.

"It's not the only difference," Ran said.

"This is where it is going to go into detail about being a hermaphrodite," I told Magdy.

"I am," Ran confirmed.

"Hold that thought, please," I said to Ran, who promptly paused its dissertation. I turned back to Magdy. "I have to go make a report to the council about the progress here. You could come with me if you want."

"You have the entire council waiting on you," Magdy said. "Impressive."

"Not the whole council," I confessed. "Just Haimi Bava. She's been appointed my handler. I think the rest of the council finds me enervating." I started walking toward the colony transport line. Magdy kept pace, Ran behind.

"No cane today," he said.

"I decided I didn't need it."

"What she said was 'fuck this thing,' and then threw it back in her room," Ran said.

"That's accurate," I confirmed. I looked over at Magdy. "Is that all right, Dr. Metwalli?"

"As your physician I probably would have suggested you keep it around for a couple more days in case you got fatigued," Magdy said. "Also I am aware that just saying that would have made you even more determined not to use it."

"She does have oppositional behavior," Ran added.

"Oh, I am *aware* of that," Magdy said.

"And you don't?" I asked him.

Magdy shrugged. "Less now than when we were younger. Less of a call for stubborn doctors than you might think. Now I'm the one who has to be the responsible adult."

I smiled at this. "How is that working out for you?"

"It could be better," Magdy admitted. "Trying to be a responsible adult is what got me here. Your dad played that particular string pretty hard."

"I'm sorry Dad pressed you to take the gig," I said.

"I can't blame it all on him," Magdy said. "I thought coming here would eventually get me to other places. It seemed like a good career move at the time."

"And now?"

"Well, if nothing else, I get to see you again," Magdy said.

"Wonderful," I said. "We'll get to starve together."

"I mean, I have a lot of protein bars."

We got onto the transport car. I looked around at our fellow passengers, who were looking at the three of us with something more than polite stares.

"Did something happen?" I asked Magdy, quietly.

"What?" Magdy looked around. "Oh. No, nothing happened. Actually, that's not true. Word about the satellite swarm is out. People know that we're actually really lost, and what that means. They've had a couple of days to have it sink in. The denial stage is mostly over. Anger is setting in. On top of the anger everyone already had."

"That's not great," I said.

"Also they know you now," Magdy added.

"What?"

"You're famous. They know you from the broadcasts and they know you have a relationship with the Consu, whom they distrust. Some of them now distrust you by association."

"That's also not great," I muttered.

"You have a bodyguard," Magdy noted, nodding at Ran. "And have your own particular set of skills."

"Employing either will make me even less popular," I said.

"I would also prefer not to stab anyone," Ran said, not quite quietly enough to have the comment go unnoticed.

"Let's change the topic, please," I said.

"What are you going to tell Councilwoman Bava?"

"That we've made a whole lot of progress that doesn't do us any good," I said. "We know the satellites zapped us into another universe, but we don't know the math to describe how they did it. We know they used an enormous amount of energy to do it, but the best hypothesis we have for that power is something like vacuum magic. And none of the satellites have the processing power required to coordinate all of their skip drives at once. So: Zip. Zilch. Nada. Nothing. But! Our scientists are very excited about all the nothing we know. So that's something."

"The satellites are most likely using internal processing," Ran said.

"What?" I said to Ran.

"The satellites are most likely using internal processing," Ran repeated.

"What does that even mean?"

"We believe Consu have prostheses in their bodies, not unlike your Colonial Defense Force soldiers do," Ran said. "These prostheses are designed to allow the Consu to use their brains to process enormous amounts of information, and to use it in their technology."

"So the Consu have supercomputers in their brains," I said.

"It's the most sensible explanation for observed behavior," Ran said.

"Lavagna and Horvni said the amount of processing power required is orders of magnitude more complex than anything we have available," I said. "You're saying that a single Consu has that amount of processing power available in *one* body."

"Yes, of course." Ran looked at my and Magdy's shocked faces. "They are more advanced than all the rest of us," it said. "This is not just something we tell ourselves because otherwise we would feel inadequate. They are in fact almost beyond our comprehension."

"And *you* know this how?" Magdy asked.

"It's common knowledge among the Obin," Ran said. "The Consu are a special concern to us."

"And you're telling me all of this *now*," I said to Ran.

"I was not in the cargo bay with you when all of this came up," Ran reasoned.

I pinched the bridge of my nose. The transport slowed and opened its doors. I pushed Ran out of the transport, following after it. Magdy, curious, followed me.

"This is not our stop," Ran said.

"Shut up," I said. Another transport going the other direction rolled up. I shoved Ran onto it.

Presently the three of us were back at the cargo bay. I whistled to Lavagna, who came up, wondering why he was being whistled at.

"This is Ran," I said, pushing my assistant and bodyguard at the scientist. "It is a veritable trove of information about the Consu, which apparently you will only ever find out if you ask it very specific questions. So please start asking it *very* specific questions about the Consu and how they might be operating these satellites. Start with—" I turned to Ran. "What is it?"

"Internal processing," Ran said to me.

I pointed to Ran. "That," I said to Lavagna. "I'll be back for Ran in a few hours. Please wring it utterly dry of all the information it has. And if there are any actual Obin scientists in the crew of the ship that brought us, draft them into helping you with this."

"All right," Lavagna said, somewhat confused.

I looked up at Ran. "Be helpful," I commanded.

"Yes," Ran promised. I walked out, Magdy following.

"You're beginning to limp," he said to me.

"That's because I'm tired and furious," I said. "Is there a morgue on this colony?"

"A morgue?"

"Yes," I said. "You know, a place where you keep dead bodies."

"I know what a morgue is," Magdy said, slightly irritated. "I want to know why you want to see ours."

"Because I want to see some dead bodies," I said. "Specifically, I want to see the Consu we killed."

"I don't know if they're there," Magdy said. "Consu are pretty big."

"Let's go and find out," I said.

"What are you going to do with the Consu bodies?"

"I'm going to cut into them," I said.

Magdy looked at me. "Are you, now."

"Actually, *you're* going to do it," I said, to him. "I'm going to watch."

Magdy glanced down at his PDA. "Well, leaving aside I know nothing about Consu physiology, my lunch hour is over."

"Tell them you're busy."

"You're going to get me in trouble," Magdy said.

"You got me in trouble a whole lot when we dated," I said. "You owe me some trouble back."

SIXTEEN

"Hello," I said, to the person I assumed was the chief medical examiner, whom we had summoned out of the morgue at the hospital and who was meeting Magdy and me in the hallway immediately in front of it. "I am here to see a dead body."

The I-assumed-the-chief-medical-examiner stared blankly at me, and then swiveled their eyestalks at Magdy. "*You*, I know," they said, and made dismissive hand waves at me. "This one, I do not."

"Dr. Gurrrrv, Gretchen Trujillo," Magdy said, by way of introduction. "Gretchen, Dr. Gurrrrv."

"Lovely to meet you," I said.

"How do you know this one?" Gurrrrv asked Magdy.

"It's complicated," Magdy said.

"When a human says that about another human I assume it means they're having sex," Gurrrrv said, to Magdy. "Humans will do many inadvisable things for the people they're having sex with. It's a scandal across the other species."

"It's not a sex thing," I assured Dr. Gurrrrv. "It's a diplomatic thing."

This brought the eyestalks swiveling back to me. "You're a diplomat."

"That's right."

"You came over in the ship, yes?"

"I did."

"And you are telling me that something about you being a diplomat requires you to gawk at corpses."

"I wouldn't put it that way, but yes."

Dr. Gurrrrv's eyestalks went back to Magdy. "I preferred the 'I want more sex' rationale."

"We need to see one of the Consu," I said. "We have to examine its brain."

"For what purpose?" Gurrrrv asked.

"There's something in it I want to take out and look at."

"So in addition to seeing the corpse, you want to cut into it."

"Well, not me, obviously," I said, and jerked a thumb back at Magdy. "This is why I brought him."

"I told her this was not a good idea," Magdy said to Gurrrrv.

"You should have tried harder," Gurrrrv told him, and then brought their attention back to me. "Ms. Trujillo, did you know that the Consu bodies we have here are the first ones that any of our species have ever reclaimed?"

"I did not," I admitted.

"This was told to me by a Garvinn named Fris, who delivered these bodies with another of his kind named Tav."

"I know both of them."

"*They* were lovely to deal with," Gurrrrv said, and even through a translation speaker I did not miss the implication. "When they brought the bodies around they mentioned that in every other encounter any of us have ever had with the Consu, the species policed the bodies of their dead after the conflict was over, and that even if we had wanted to examine the bodies, we had no choice in the matter."

"That makes sense," I said.

"The one named Tav mentioned that there were once a people called the Xtackcha who decided to try to capture a Consu in order to understand more about their physiology. Ms. Trujillo, have you ever heard of the Xtackcha?"

"No," I admitted.

"Neither have I, and it is my literal job to know about all the species in the Conclave and outside of it, so I can understand their general cultural taboos about their dead bodies. Now, Ms. Trujillo, perhaps you are not concerned about what might happen if you, or Dr. Metwalli here, merrily cut into the corpse of a species that apparently has the means and will to perpetrate a genocide against a people who had the temerity to attempt to kidnap a single one of them. I confess, however, it concerns me just a little."

"Well, they're all in another universe entirely," I pointed out.

Gurrrrv narrowed their eyes at me, which was not a thing I would have imagined someone with eyestalks could do. "Tell me, does this particular negotiating strategy of yours work in other places?"

"You'd be surprised," I said.

"I regret to say I would not. Nevertheless, Ms. Trujillo, the answer is no to you, and no to Dr. Metwalli, who at least seems to understand the extreme inappropriateness of your request. In fact"—and here eyestalks swiveled in the direction of Magdy—"I'm not sure why you consented to be part of this misadventure."

"Honestly I wanted to see what would happen," Magdy confessed.

"This lowers my opinion of you, I'm sorry to say."

"That's entirely fair."

"Let me try this again," I said. "What do *you* need from me in order for me to be able to examine a Consu?"

"Nothing comes to mind," Gurrrrv said. "I'm not operating a tourist attraction here, Ms. Trujillo. This office acts as morgue and mortuary. We are required to treat each body that arrives here with respect in accordance with their established rituals and personal wishes. We do medical examinations when required by the colony or medical personnel. *Qualified* medical personnel," she stressed, "which does not include Dr. Metwalli. Nothing cultural, institutional or scientific justifies your request—and regardless of your assurance the Consu are in another universe, I won't risk potential annihilation of this colony.

Now, unless there is something else, less obtuse than this, that I can help you with, I am going back to work."

Neither Magdy nor I had anything to say to that, so Dr. Gurrrrv went back to their work, the doors swiping back and forth behind them.

"Give me your PDA," I said to Magdy.

"'Please' would be nice," Magdy said, "and also, what for?"

"Dr. Gurrrrv said that medical examinations happen when required by the colony," I said. "I'm going to call the colony."

"You're going to go over her head."

"I am, and also, thank you, I was unclear on gender, if any. Now, *please*, give me your PDA."

Magdy shook his head. "She had a point about consequences."

I shrugged. "We can always space the body afterward." This got a hard stare from Magdy. "I'm joking," I said to him.

"I'm not sure about that."

"I'm *mostly* joking about that."

"Why does it matter if *you* see inside the Consu?" Magdy asked. "You're not a doctor. You wouldn't even know what you're looking at."

"*Somebody* needs to look at them," I said, spitting out the words, because I was tired and I hurt and also I was fed up with everything. "We're slow-walking our way to starvation; the living Consu we have speak to us in cryptic puzzles that *I'm* supposed to figure out because I'm the only one that either of them will talk to, plus apparently they are both trying to die in some ridiculous ritual way, so being *helpful* isn't on either of their list of things to do. The only really useful information I get is from an Obin who is just as likely to mumble on about sex as it is to tell us something *useful*. I don't know what questions to ask it to get anything out of it that might save us. So maybe I want to look at a Consu brain because no one else will do it, and even if *I* don't know what I'm looking at it, maybe something in there will make me think of something I can ask a question about, to Ran or to one of the Consu or *someone*. Because I would rather do that than try to manage our path to oblivion."

"Are you okay?" Magdy asked, after a minute.

"Obviously *not*," I said. I leaned up against a wall, closed my eyes, and allowed myself a nice relaxing thirty-second mental breakdown.

When I was done, Magdy was still staring at me. "Stop that," I said.

"Sorry."

"Actually, scratch that. Go ahead and keep looking at me. I just remembered that I like it when you do that."

Magdy smiled at this. "All right."

"You know what else I like?"

"When I give you my PDA so you can make a call so you can get permission to do an autopsy on a Consu."

"I was going to say 'kissing you,' but actually your suggestion sounds better," I said, and held out my hand.

Magdy got out his PDA, but held it away from me for a second, looking at it thoughtfully.

"I'm emotionally and physically fragile right at this moment, but I could still absolutely take that away from you," I pointed out.

"No, I know that," Magdy said. "I just had a thought, though. One that might get you what you want without exposing us to, you know, the outside risk of genocide."

"I'm willing to be persuaded," I said.

"Let me make a call first. Then I will give this to you and you can make a call. And after this, start bringing your PDA to places."

"Pushy," I said.

"I didn't even say please," Magdy said, and made his call.

"I want it on record how inconvenient and annoying this was," Dr. Gurrrrv said. "And also that, just because we consider this to be a 'noninvasive scan,' doesn't mean that the Consu might not treat it the same as if we took a bonesaw to one of their number."

"Your objection is noted," said Haimi Bava, who was present

in the room, as was Caspar Merrin, Fris and Captain Mouse, Ran still being questioned by the physicists and their crew. Magdy, who was no longer strictly needed, was still around. He had gone up to his department and rescheduled his appointments for the day. I wanted him there, and no one thought to object to my request.

The room we were in held a medical scanner large enough to examine an elephant, not because there was an elephant on the colony but because sentient creatures came in a wide range of sizes, and it was considered both prudent and economical for the hospital to have a single medical scanner that could accommodate them all.

Inside the medical scanner at the moment was a dead Consu. I had arrived as hospital staff were wrangling the corpse onto the scanner floor; it took some doing and there was considerable leakage as a result. The corpse, despite having been kept in a storage room held to just barely above freezing, had clearly begun to putrefy from the inside. It smelled absolutely *delightful*.

I wasn't the only one to notice this. "Can we get started, please," said Fris. "If this takes too long I may vomit, and it takes a lot for a Garvinn to do that."

Bava nodded. "Begin your scan, Dr. Gurrrrv," she said. Gurrrrv made a sound that I'm sure signaled exasperation, and pressed a button on her command console. The scanner came to life with a distinct clank and a pop, and then hummed for roughly five minutes before switching with another hard clank. A few seconds later, and we were all looking at a three-dimensional model of the internal structure of a Consu.

"What are those?" Bava asked, pointing out some notable striations.

"Those are where the creature was shot," Merrin said.

"You didn't skimp," Bava observed.

"We didn't have time to be precise."

I ignored the striations and focused on the thorax, where the Consu's brain was. Most species had the brain in the head, and the Consu *did* have a supplementary brain there—one important enough that stabbing it would usually kill the Consu in question. But practical experience (which is to say, killing lots of them) had suggested the species' primary brain was in its thorax. Unusual but not entirely unheard of, especially in a species like the Consu, whose head was fairly small in comparison to the rest of its body.

This Consu's brain was where it was supposed to be, as was its secondary brain, each connected to the other with a thick nerve stem clearly designed to keep the communication channels between the two wide open. As a percentage of its body mass, these two brains seemed within line with most species, although the didn't necessarily mean anything in terms of general intelligence; large brains could have relatively few neural connections, and small ones could have many. There was one intelligent species that was only a few centimeters tall and whose intelligence was squarely in the middle of the galactic bell curve. Don't ask me how their brains worked. I just know they did.

Since I was neither a scientist nor a doctor, the Consu's brains didn't look like anything particularly special to me. It was, as far as I could tell, a perfectly standard-issue set-up for the Consu, from what we'd already pieced together.

The brain material in all the rest of its body, however. *That* was interesting.

"Is that cancer?" Merrin asked, pointing to the brain matter distributed throughout the body.

"I don't think so," Magdy said. He turned to me. "Was this what you were expecting?"

"I had no idea what to expect," I said. "Except that Ran said they suspected the Consu had BrainPal-like prostheses in their brains. The computers the CDF have in their heads."

"I think these *are* the prostheses," Magdy said.

"That's organic material," Gurrrrv said.

"Doesn't mean it's not a prosthesis," Magdy said, still staring at the distributed brain matter. "There's a rumor that the latest versions of the BrainPal are either partially or completely organic. If we have that technology, it wouldn't be a problem for the Consu to have it." He frowned suddenly.

"What is it?" Fris asked.

Magdy turned to Gurrrrv. "Can you bring the nervous system into higher relief?" he asked.

"Give me a second," Gurrrrv said, and fiddled with her console. A moment later a network of filaments glowed brighter than they had previously.

"Do you see it?" Magdy asked me.

I looked at the nervous system of the Consu for several seconds, not seeing anything, and then suddenly realized what it was that I wasn't seeing. "The other brains," I said. "They're not connected."

"You got it," Magdy said.

"What does that mean?" Bava asked.

"The extra brains don't have neural connections," Magdy said. "They're connected to the Consu's circulatory system and its equivalent to the lymphatic system, so they're being fed and maintained. But they're not connected to the Consu's nervous system at all."

"So they *are* cancer," Merrin said.

"No, they're *wireless*," I said, and waved at the image in front of us. "The Consu didn't want to have to wait for neural signals to go from one part of their body to another. They wanted to have a speed-of-light connection directly to their actual brains."

"That or they want to run their brains in parallel, and that's easier to do when there's no lag," Magdy added.

"There's nothing in their brains that looks like a wireless implementation," Gurrrrv said. "At least, not that I can see here."

See, that's why we should have cut into the thing, I thought, but did not say. Instead I said, "They are a few millennia ahead of us. Their implementation might be something we haven't thought of yet."

"All right," Bava said. "So now we know that the Consu have

extra brains in their bodies. That's great. How does this help us at all?"

I turned to Captain Mouse, who had been quiet through all of this, very much unlike Ran would have been. "The Obin know more about the Consu than any of us," I said. "I would welcome your thoughts here."

"All of this is as new to us as it is to you," Mouse said. "Most of the information we have has been through observation of behavior. This new knowledge does not surprise me. It fits our observational model. I am surprised about the multiple brains and that they do not have a hard connection."

"What's surprising about that?" I asked.

"It's poor security."

The words hung in the air for a moment. "Are you suggesting Consu brains can be *hacked*?" asked Fris.

"I do not suggest anything," Mouse said. "I am saying it is poor security."

"This is an incredibly advanced civilization," Merrin pointed out. "I would guess the internal security of their brains is significant and constantly updated."

"Maybe for the live ones," I said.

We all looked over at the Consu corpse.

"I would like to remind you all that the Consu erase entire civilizations when people get invasive," Gurrrrv said.

"And this one is beginning to rot anyway," Fris added.

"There are more," Captain Mouse said.

"How is this one's brain matter?" Magdy asked Gurrrrv.

"It's in better shape than the rest of it," Gurrrrv answered. "There's some degradation, because it's been dead for a while now. But it's still largely intact."

Bava looked at me. "How do you want to do this?"

"Me?" I asked.

"You're the one who brought us here. You're the one who demanded this. I authorized this, but it's being done at your behest. Make a call here."

"Do you have technicians you can spare?" I asked Mouse.

"Our ship's systems are now repaired, and my crew have little to do," Mouse said. "We can see if we can retrieve information from these brains."

"How are you going to do that?" Merrin asked.

"I do not know," Mouse said. "I do request that we be allowed to take the Consu bodies back to our ship."

"For what purpose?" Bava asked.

"So that when we cut into them none of the rest of you can be blamed," Mouse said. "Dr. Gurrrrv's apprehension is not misplaced. If the Consu discover what we are doing, they will not be sparing in their retribution. You fear them and that is reasonable. We are Obin. We fear nothing, unless we choose to."

"There's the problem of the bodies when you are done with them," Merrin said.

"Space has already claimed several Consu. It can claim these as well."

I looked over at Magdy when Mouse said this and raised my eyebrows as if to say, *See*. He shrugged and looked a little annoyed.

"If we discover anything of use I will report it to Ms. Trujillo," Mouse concluded.

"If you could speed it along, that would be great," Bava said to Mouse.

"It will take the time it will take," Mouse informed her.

Bava opened her mouth to reply, remembered that Obin are extremely literal, closed it, and nodded. "Anything else?" she said to me.

"I think I'm going to visit Kitty and Bacon again," I said.

"What's that going to do?" Fris asked.

"They're currently both planning their ritual deaths."

"Yes, you've told us that."

"Well, all this talk of tossing bodies into space has given me some ideas."

"You're going to go threaten two Consu," Magdy said.

"I might," I admitted.

"Well, no one would ever say you're boring."

"Does this threatening need to be done right now?" Bava asked me.

"I'm on a roll," I said to her.

"You are," Bava agreed. "But it's going to take time for Captain Mouse and its crew to gather their information, and we have two other teams of scientists gathering data as well. From what I've learned about the Consu there's no advantage in trying to coerce them without as much information as you can get first."

"Time isn't on our side," I pointed out.

"No, it's not. All the more reason to use it wisely and not rashly." She turned to Merrin here. "Would you agree?"

"I do," Merrin said, looking at me. "Beyond that, I know you're still recuperating. It's late and you need your rest."

"It's not that late," I said.

"Dr. Metwalli?" Merrin asked.

"Oh, I don't want to get anywhere near this," Magdy said.

"Thank you," I said to him.

"That said, I did see Ms. Trujillo limping earlier and showing other signs of stress and fatigue."

"It's settled, then," Bava said. "We'll give our teams more time to gather information, and then Ms. Trujillo can meet up with the Consu. In the meantime, we could all use some rest before we regroup. I'll have my assistant schedule a meeting. He'll be in touch." She nodded at everyone and left before I could offer a complaint. Everyone else wandered off as well, leaving me with Magdy and a large alien corpse.

I turned on Magdy. "'Oh, I don't want to get anywhere *near* this,'" I said to him accusingly.

"You *are* limping, you *are* stressed, and you *are* fatigued," he said. He motioned to the dead Consu in the scanner. "Present company excepted, I've never met a Consu, but I think if you rolled up on a live one right now, you might get chopped up into bits. And I don't want that."

"I've dealt with them before," I said.

"I know," Magdy said. "I patched you up from the last time,

remember. That was when you weren't stressed and tired and limping."

I looked at him grumpily. "You're still a traitor."

"I am history's worst monster," Magdy agreed. "Let me make it up to you."

"I don't want another protein bar," I said.

"I have another idea," he said.

SEVENTEEN

"All right," I said. "This was not what I was expecting when you said you wanted to make it up to me."

We were standing at the entrance to what seemed to be a vast park, the first thing I had seen on Unity Colony that had any amount of extensive green space to it. The park rolled off into the distance, and as it did so I noticed that save for a few places here and there, the acreage was taken up by crops. Not just the acreage at ground level; towers dotted the landscape, going all the way up to the top of the space, from which foodstuffs hung. Some of the crops I recognized as being for human consumption, but most of them were not. The result was a green space that felt both familiar and alien.

"What were you expecting?" Magdy asked.

"Honestly? Sex."

"You're still convalescing."

"I've convalesced enough for that."

Magdy smiled. "Maybe after you've had a nap."

"*Definitely* not the Magdy I remember."

"I remember you complaining about the fact that everything on the colony is gray and boring," Magdy said, ignoring my taunt, "because this used to be an Obin station, and the Obin don't decorate. You weren't the only one who noticed this. When they designed this part of the colony, they made it to feed us. But they also made it a place where we could walk around and decompress and get as close to 'nature' as you can get in a place like this."

I looked around as we walked. "There's not many other people here," I said.

"It's late in the day," Magdy said. "I don't know if you noticed, but Unity keeps a day that's about twenty-six hours long, which is a compromise number. Most people are on the same work schedule, and when they're done they want to go to the pub, or home." He opened his arms wide. "Which means that when I come here, I usually have the place to myself."

"Your own personal park."

"Yes. Which is meant to feed us, too, so there's that."

"If it feeds you, why are there food restrictions?" I asked.

"I said 'meant to,'" Magdy said. "This colony is only a couple of years old. This park was a priority, but it still took time to build and longer to start generating crops." He pointed to one of the towers. "Those are actually doing most of the heavy lifting for us right now. They're for fast-growing crops that don't need a lot of setup. Nutritious weeds, basically, for the various people on this colony. Everything else is taking more time. And even when they are fully ready they won't address all our nutritional needs. Some of us need or want proteins from other sources than plants."

"You didn't import cattle?" I asked, feigning shock.

"You will not be surprised that some of our human colonists asked that," Magdy said, and then pointed down to the ground. "No cattle. Not even rabbits. We do most of our protein gathering a level down from here. Aquaculture and various versions of insects—whatever can be grown in large numbers without having to invest too much of our crops in their feeding. Also algae vats and other such things."

"But it's still not enough?"

"It might be enough if there were just two or three types of people on the colony," Magdy said. "But there are a couple dozen species among the colonists. There's overlap—every colonist species has roughly the same physical requirements, breathes the same type of air, tolerates similar levels of gravity, and most have the same basic nutritional requirements. But even with that, there are things we can eat that others can't, and vice versa." He pointed out a tower of greenery we were passing by. "You see that?"

"I do," I said. "It looks lovely."

"It is lovely. To look at, anyway. It's called dylainaes, and it's a staple crop for the Oca, like rice or maize for us. They eat it with almost every meal. If you ate it, you probably wouldn't die; you would just wish you had."

"Personal experience?" I asked.

"For once, no," Magdy said. "But some of the stupider humans will occasionally eat some as a dare. If you eat a little bit, you'll be on the toilet all night. If you eat a little more, you come see me, and I throw you in a hospital shower stall until your bowels finally give up."

"Your bedside manner is deeply sympathetic."

"I didn't hear you complaining when you woke up."

"I *did* complain. I distinctly remember telling you I wanted to punch you."

"That was the drugs talking."

"Was it?"

"Anyway, my point *was*, because there's so many species with so many variances in their diet, this park doesn't produce enough for any one of our colony's species to subsist on. Not yet, anyway. Farther on in the colony there's a larger space that was meant to be a second farm, but it's not built out yet."

I looked around. "So we're going to starve despite all this greenery."

"All the greenery here will add another week to our general food supply. More or less. More for some species, less for others. For humans it will be a couple of days. The protein farm will add a few more days to that, and after that we're on to the algae."

"Everybody loves an algae smoothie," I said. I meant it to come off humorously, but in light of the actual possibility of starvation it turned out not to be funny at all.

Magdy gave me a look that suggested he understood what I was trying for, even if he didn't laugh. "They're going to start harvesting what we have here soon," he said. "If we come back here in a couple of days it's going to be mostly fallow ground and bare towers."

"That's why you wanted to come here," I said. "Isn't it?"

"Yeah. I wanted you to see it while it was still the nicest thing about the colony. And I wanted to see it for myself, too. Hopefully not for the last time. But if it is, then at least I saw it with you."

I gave Magdy an impulsive hug at this. Then a slightly less impulsive kiss.

I had plans for more than that, but then there was a pub fight.

Magdy and I had sat down at the Pub at the End of the Universe, which was a small bar near his apartment that had, somewhat unintentionally, become the possessor of the most accurate pub name in history. Despite restrictions, the pub was still selling drinks because, as the bartender put it, "Might as well get drunk now." It was hard to argue with that logic.

As we sat at a small table, beer in hand, Magdy's PDA buzzed. He picked it up, looked at it, and handed it to me. "Your assistant," he said.

I took the PDA. "Hello, Ran," I said.

"Congratulate me," Ran said. "I knew to call Dr. Metwalli before attempting to call your own PDA, which you refuse to carry with you."

"Yes, you are quite astute, Ran," I assured it.

"It's because you like him and wish to spend time with him."

"You're not wrong. Where are you?"

"I am leaving the cargo hold now," it said. "I was very helpful today, as you requested. I was planning to be more helpful, but everyone else went home."

"Well, come to us, then. We're at the Pub at the End of the Universe."

"There is no end to the universe," Ran said. "Any of them."

"You are correct," I said. "However, it's a name, not an address. Put it into your navigation tool and come find us."

"I have found it," Ran said. "I will be there very soon." It hung up.

"Thank you," I said to Magdy, returning his PDA. "You will be happy to know that Ran was smug about knowing I would be with you."

"It's more that *I'm* with *you*," Magdy said, taking the PDA and putting it away. "I'm the one who played hooky with you, after all."

I took a drink and looked around the pub, which was moderately crowded, in a specific way. "There are only humans in here," I said to Magdy.

"Ah," he said. "Well, there's a reason for that."

"It's not that alcohol is poisonous to every other species," I said. "I know lots of aliens who like a beer or five."

"Technically alcohol is poisonous to a lot of species, including our own."

"You sound like Ran when you nitpick like that."

"I'm just being precise."

"*Definitely* sound like Ran now."

"It's not because of the alcohol. It's because of the plumbing."

"The hell you say."

"You remember the park we were just at."

"Yes. I have good memories of it."

"I'm glad. It's fertilized and fed by the colony's waste."

"Gross but sensible."

"It's treated; it's fine. When they were planning the park they discovered that certain plants and plant-equivalents would only really flourish with fertilizer that heavily relied on their native biome."

"There's no poop like home," I said, raising my glass.

Magdy pointed, as if to say, *Exactly*. "To help facilitate with that, they put each species of the colony into its own neighborhood, each with its own sewer system, from which the relevant biological bits could be extracted before the rest of it was sent along into the common reclamation system."

"Seems complicated and overengineered."

"It is both," Magdy said. "Which we all know because the system fails in each neighborhood just randomly enough to drive everyone batty."

"I don't see what this has to do with only humans being in the pub, though," I noted.

"We were all sorted into separate neighborhoods because of our sewers," Magdy said. "It's not really the only reason, but it's a pretty big one. The population of the colony has remained static, so everyone's stayed in their neighborhoods. Which means that by and large, we associate with our own species." He motioned around the pub. "This is a neighborhood pub, and the neighborhood is human."

"You work with other species, though," I said.

"*I* do," Magdy agreed, "but not everyone does. And also, while I work with other people in the hospital, I am working in the wing set up for humans, away from the rest of the hospital, dealing almost entirely with human patients. So even then I spend most of my time with humans."

"It sounds like you think this is a problem."

"Isn't it? The whole point of this secret colony was to see if we humans could actually live with Conclave members in a way that doesn't have us all falling back to fighting for real estate. In all the time I've been here, what I've noticed is us keeping to ourselves, and other groups keeping to themselves. Now we're having a crisis that threatens all of us. Do you see us coming together as a colony?" He motioned to encompass the pub. "It doesn't really feel like it to me. I can't help thinking we might have sacrificed the larger goal to solve an engineering problem."

"You say that, and yet here we are in the human pub," I said. "You could have taken me somewhere else."

"Well, I like the beer," Magdy said. "And who knows how long it'll last."

I raised my glass again. "Here's to getting drunk now," I said. Magdy and I clinked glasses to that.

There was an audible gasp of surprise from elsewhere in the pub, and I looked around to see what was the matter. What was the matter was Ran standing in the doorway, looking for me. I raised my hand to identify myself. Ran gave a quick acknowledging honk and strode over in a few steps, creating a small bow wave of humans stepping out of its way.

"Hello, Ran," I said. "How was your day?"

"I already told you," Ran said. "Did you forget?"

"No, I was just making polite sounds with my mouth."

"Thank you for the polite sounds, which I will accept in the spirit in which they were offered."

"Would you like a beer?" Magdy asked Ran.

"Are these also polite sounds from you?" Ran asked back.

"They are," Magdy replied. "And also, if you would like a beer I would be happy to get you one."

"Thank you," Ran said. "I would not like a beer. I do not like the way it tastes to me."

"What does it taste like to you?" I asked.

"Metaphor is difficult for me, so I apologize if I get this wrong," Ran said.

"All right."

"Beer tastes like ass."

"No, you got it right," I told Ran.

"Interesting comparison," Magdy said, and took a sip of his own beer.

"It is only a metaphor," Ran told him. "I have not literally eaten ass. Why did you just spit out your beer?"

"I was not expecting that response," Magdy said, after some significant coughing.

"Are you all right?" I asked Magdy. Magdy nodded, still coughing.

"Beer is not for your lungs," Ran said.

"I know that, thank you, Ran," Magdy said.

"Also I think not for your mouth."

"It's an acquired taste," I admitted.

"Why would you acquire it?"

"For fuck's sake, shut up about beer," someone said from a nearby table.

We all looked over at the table, where three men were sitting with their own beers. There were several empty glasses between them. They had apparently been here for a while.

"Excuse me?" I said.

"I was talking to your creepy pal," the man said. "If the thing doesn't want a beer, it should shut about it. In fact, if it's not going to buy anything, it should just leave."

"I just arrived," Ran said.

"I know, you haven't stopped talking since you arrived. You sound mentally challenged, if you ask me. *Are* you mentally challenged?"

"Technically yes," Ran said. "I have a consciousness prosthesis that means that my mental capabilities are augmented, but which also presents challenges. As an example—"

"For fuck's sake, I don't actually care," the man interrupted.

"Then why did you ask?" Ran wanted to know.

"He was trying to insult you," I suggested to Ran.

"Oh! I understand now. He believes my mental challenges are something to be ashamed of instead of a fact of life."

"That's the gist of it, yes."

Ran looked over at the man. "That would make you a terrible person."

The man jumped off his stool, which was a cue for his friends to do the same. "The fuck did you just say to me?"

"I said you were a terrible person," Ran said. "It's not meant as an insult. It's a statement of opinion based on your behavior."

The man took a step toward Ran, which showed he really was drunk, because Ran was larger than—and generally terrified most—humans. This was my cue to get up and interpose myself between the two of them.

"You're going to want to rethink this," I said to the man.

"Get out of my way," he said.

"No."

"I'm not asking."

"I get that you're a 'tell' guy and not an 'ask' guy," I said. "I also get that you're drunk, and that for some reason you want to punch something. But you're about to make a mistake. Go sit back down."

The man looked past me to Magdy. "You need to tell your woman to back off," he said.

"We're just friends," Magdy said.

"Although you have had sex," Ran added, apparently forgetting it had promised never to talk about that in public anymore.

"Yes," Magdy confirmed. "But not recently. And *you*"—he returned his attention to the man—"should listen to her."

The man looked back at his friends, smirking, and then reached out to shove me aside, which was what I was waiting for. Two seconds later he was on his knees, screaming as I bent his fingers in ways they were not meant to be bent.

The man's friends looked at each other uncertainly, and then back at me. I smiled at them. "I haven't broken any of your friend's fingers yet," I said. "Take a step closer and let's see what happens."

One of the men held up his hands, placatingly.

"Thank you," I said, acknowledging his surrender. "Take a seat." The two friends sat back down.

By this time the entire pub was looking at me and the angry man on his knees. "This will only take a minute," I assured everyone. They did not seem convinced.

"I'm going to fucking kill you," the man said to me, through gritted teeth.

I squeezed his hand, which didn't injure the man, but which did really hurt. He grunted in pain. "Like I said, I haven't broken any of your fingers yet. But I *can*." And here I squeezed just a little more for emphasis, which brought another intake of breath. "And if you don't settle down, I absolutely will. And I will break them faster than you can use that fist you're making with your other hand to hit me with, which won't do you much good because you're on your knees, it's not your dominant hand, and you're drunk. If you don't believe me, take your shot."

The man thought for a second and unclenched his fist.

"Good choice," I said. "What's your name?"

"What?"

"What's your name?"

"Paulo."

"Hi, Paulo, I'm Gretchen," I said. "And my oversharing alien friend over there is named Ran. Say hello, Ran."

"Hello," Ran said.

"Ran, what would have happened if Paulo here had attacked you?"

"Nothing to me," Ran said. "I would have incapacitated him and his friends."

"Why is that, Ran?"

"Because I have trained to incapacitate any number of species, including humans."

"And what would have happened to Paulo and his friends?"

"That would have depended on them," Ran said. "However, there is a doctor here, which would have been useful."

Magdy waved at Paulo here.

"Thank you, Ran," I said, and looked back to Paulo. "As much fun as it would have been to see Ran kick your ass, Paulo, at this moment in time it would complicate matters. Everything's a little tense right now, and a bar fight between two different species is the last thing we actually need. Don't you agree?" I squeezed.

"Yes!" Paulo said.

"That's right," I said. "So I stepped in. Now it's just a run-of-the-mill human-on-human bar scuffle. Nothing for anyone to get upset about. And look at us. We're solving this problem amicably, without *anyone* getting any broken bones, because we're both making the conscious choice to be *sensible* about this, aren't we?"

"Yes."

"I'm so glad. Now, Paulo. I'm going to let go of your hand and take a step back. When I do, you're going to get up, you're going to settle your bill, and then your friends are going to take you home and you can sleep everything off, and tomorrow you'll be just fine, and that will be the end of it. If you do anything else, then let me just remind you that you're drunk, and I'm not, and while you are angrier, I am meaner."

"It's true," Magdy said. "Very mean."

"He's an ex," I explained to Paulo. "He may be biased." I let go of Paulo and took a step back.

Paulo grabbed his hand with his other hand, massaged it, and then stood up unsteadily. He looked over at Ran. "Fucking aliens," he said, and then stomped out of the pub, leaving his friends to settle his bill.

"I did nothing," Ran said, as Paulo stormed off.

"This is what I was saying about us not exactly coming together," Magdy said to me.

"I think he's just more of a garden variety xenophobic shithead," I said, sat, and reached for my beer. "How does someone like him make it onto a colony like this anyway?"

"Not everybody came here for noble reasons," Magdy said. "And some jobs are specialized enough that you'll take whoever can fit the bill."

"So you can be as xenophobic as you want as long as you can fix the overly complicated sewers."

"Sure, or if you're a doctor, since there's no reason to be classist about it."

"*You're* not xenophobic."

"I'm not, but I know some doctors who are—not necessarily human ones, either."

"How nice to know it's not just us humans," I said, wryly.

"We have the most xenophobic of all species on the station," Magdy said. "The Consu, remember. They think we're all bugs."

"Don't remind me of them right now," I said. "I have to talk to them soon. I know they'll talk to me. I just have to figure out how to actually extract useful information from them."

"I thought you were going to use their death wish against them."

"That's the plan," I agreed. "I could use a little more information about that, too." I looked up at Ran. "You wouldn't know anything about that, would you?"

"I know quite a lot about it. I will tell you it all," Ran said.

I held up a hand. "Yes to that, but not right now."

"You're not doing anything else at the moment."

"That's not true." I hoisted my beer. "I'm having a drink."

Magdy and I finished our drinks and considered having another, but as we were considering it I realized that a long day had fully caught up to me. We paid for our drinks and headed for the door.

"I'm just around the corner here," Magdy began, and stopped, looking past me down the street. I followed his gaze and saw a group of men standing there, Paulo at the head of them. Paulo was carrying what looked like a bat, as were a couple of the other men.

"You have security on this colony?" I asked Magdy.

"Of course."

"Go back into the pub where it's safe and call them," I said.

"What are you going to do?"

"Ran and I are just going to talk to them," I promised.

"Talk."

"That's what I said."

"I don't believe you."

"I don't see why not."

"You're *convalescing*," Magdy reminded me.

"I know," I said. "Seriously, Magdy. Just talking. We'll keep them busy until security comes to shoo them away. It'll be fine."

"I did a lot of work on you, you know."

"It doesn't sound great when you put it that way."

"You know what I mean, Gretchen."

I nodded toward the pub. "I know. Go call."

Magdy went back into the pub, pulling out his PDA as he did so.

I looked at Ran. "You ready?"

"Yes," it said.

We walked toward the crowd of men.

"I promised my doctor we would just talk," I said to the men as we stopped, five paces in front of Paulo.

Paulo smirked at this. "Lady, we're not here to talk."

I shrugged. "Okay." I positioned myself, Ran taking my flank. "Let's get to it."

The smirk on Paulo's face faltered slightly when he figured out Ran and I weren't trying to bargain with him. "You're serious."

"You just said you're not here to talk."

Paulo looked back at his crew. "There's ten of us and two of you."

"We can count."

"You should be worried."

"I've turned off my emotions," Ran said to Paulo, flatly. "I'm not capable of being worried."

This got a low, unhappy rumble from the crowd. I guessed Paulo had not communicated to the rest of them what, precisely, they were to be dealing with.

Paulo didn't know what to do with this statement of Ran's, so he turned his attention back to me. "You two can't take on all of us at one time."

"Christ," I said, exasperated. *"Paulo.* Your friends aren't going to do shit here. If you all were going to gang rush me and Ran, you would have already done it. But instead *you* just keep trying to scare us, and *they* keep waiting for you to do something. And by now the smart ones have figured out two things here."

"What's that?"

"One, that you weren't actually planning to fight. You just wanted to scare us with numbers, and that's really not working. Two, that Ran and I don't care about any of them. Just you."

"What?" Paulo asked.

"I thought I made myself clear in the pub," I replied. "The deal was, I let you go, and you were supposed to go home, and if you did anything else, there would be consequences." I motioned to his posse. "Obviously, you did something else. So now you're going to have consequences. If any of your friends want to share in your consequences, then that's fine. But *they* don't have to have them, unless they get in the way. And the fact is none of *them* are going to get to me and Ran before we can get to *you*. Because, again, you're the only one we care about."

"Hold on a minute," Paulo began, but I stopped him.

"No," I said. "It's late, and I'm tired, and I tried being nice but you had to go and ruin it. So now I have to be mean, and I want to get this over with so I can go to sleep." I held out my hand. "Knife."

Ran dropped a combat knife into my hand, keeping another one for itself. We stood there, knives in hand.

"Right, then," I said, to the crowd of men. "I'm counting to ten. Anyone left after that gets what Paulo gets." I started counting out loud, slow enough to let them think.

Paulo's pals had all walked away by six. Paulo watched them go, then looked back at me.

"Go to *bed*," I said to him, and kept counting.

He was gone by the time I got to eight.

Magdy stepped out of the pub. "Security is on the way," he said, looking at the retreating men. "Although it doesn't look like they'll be needed now."

"Not here," I said. "Someone might want to see where they go after this."

"What did you do?"

"It's like I said," I told him. "We just talked."

"And threatened," Ran said.

"Threatening is talking," I reminded them both.

"You've had an exciting night," Magdy said, to me.

"That's not the word I'd use for it. I did have other thoughts on how to spend it."

"It's not too late," Magdy suggested.

"It really is," I said. "Sorry. Right now all I really want is sleep."

EIGHTEEN

And of course I didn't sleep one goddamned bit.

For one thing, it doesn't matter how badass you pretend to be in the moment, staring down ten drunk angry men is going to shoot you full of fear and adrenaline. I had a good sense about Paulo's stupidity, but it had been a gamble about whether the other nine (well, minus the two who had already been with him before) were going to fall in line. All you need for an avalanche of chaos is one inebriated snowball.

Could we have handled them? Ran could have handled several, and I could have handled a couple. But neither of us would have gotten out of it uninjured; the ten of them being drunk and belligerent was in many ways worse than them being sober and strategic. Besides, I was still recovering from my injuries in our battle with the Consu.

Which was the reason for the threatening, and before that, the immobilization with the fingers. When mass and stamina aren't on your side, be quick and scary. It worked this time. It doesn't always.

In the aftermath of our barely avoided riot I was dealing with an adrenaline dump that both exhausted me and made me too agitated to sleep. Which kept me up in my terrible guest quarters bed.

And that gave me plenty of time to think about our current

situation, stuck on an asteroid colony, in an unknown universe, cut off from supplies and civilization with no way to get back except, possibly, by the graces of a Consu who gives no indication that it cares what happens to us, and who can't be bargained with because we have nothing it wants, and who is busy planning its own ritual death anyway.

"Fuck," I said, annoyed, after about two hours of this fun little panic spiral. More in frustration than anything else, I grabbed my PDA, the one I don't take with me, and opened it to see if there was anything there that would distract me.

There was, if you count alien autopsies as distracting. Captain Mouse and its crew had wasted absolutely no time in cracking open the Consu we had run through the scanner and parting it out for observation. Their plan, or so Mouse told me in its extremely factually presented brief, was to do a full examination of all of the Consu's systems and anatomy, which made me happy that the crew now had a hobby to keep them occupied. That said, Mouse acknowledged that at the moment, a closer examination of the Consu's extra brains had top priority, so that's what they were focused on at the moment.

"Brain structure divided," Mouse wrote. "Primary brain differentiated into lobes and areas indicative of processing centers and division of tasks, similar to most brain structures. Auxiliary brains not as obviously differentiated appear to be structured for pure processing. Only significant differentiation are nodes that appear to coordinate communication and cooperation between brain structures. Nodes present in all brains including primary brain." Well, this was not too surprising; it made sense that the Consu needed their actual brain to run their outboard brains.

What was surprising was what Captain Mouse wrote after that: "Initial analysis shows Consu auxiliary brains notably dissimilar to Consu primary brain; structure more similar to Obin brain."

Unexpected, but it also made sense in a weird way. The Consu had uplifted the Obin into sapience millennia ago, mostly just to see if they could. It worked, but the Obin brains never achieved individual consciousness. That had to wait for the brain prostheses the Colonial Union offered them. It's possible the Consu took some of the things they learned from the Obin and used them on themselves.

The Obin had made no progress into hacking into the brains of the Consu, but given the short amount of time they'd had them, the fact the Consu are unfathomably more advanced than the rest of us, and the question of whether the decomposition that had already begun might have already ruined any data that could be extracted, this was not unexpected.

Most of the rest of Captain Mouse's report was given over to images of the autopsy which, thank you, next.

Next was a digest of the conversations between Kitty and Bacon, to the extent that our team could parse them out; Feruza Olimova, in the notes to the transcripts, explained that the machine translations got worse the more emphatically the two Consu screamed at each other. Part of it was the dialect they were using, and the other part was simply that at top volume the two Consu overwhelmed the recording devices.

Nevertheless, from what the team could parse out, there were three major topics of conversation:

First, Kitty's apparent betrayal of Bacon and their team, which had required Kitty to do a specific thing with the skip of Unity Colony asteroid, which Kitty not only did not do but did not appear to feel in the slightest bit regretful about, which made the Consu's mutual yelling even worse. Subsumed in this was further discussion of Kitty and Bacon's relationship, which even if they were not lovers, had by all indications been significant enough that the betrayal had substantial personal overtones.

Second, both Kitty and Bacon were attempting to work their way through the ritual processes required for their meaningful deaths, but it appeared that each of them were also sabotaging the other's process, which I found to be an absolutely delightful level of petty coming from a species that were effectively gods to the rest of us. The result of the sabotage was that each of the

Consu had to begin their process over again, which also generated more high-volume arguing.

The third major line of discussion was on a subject that the machine translation had difficulty pinning down. It variously translated the topic as "pivot" or "edge" or "cusp," but whatever it was it had to be important, since neither Kitty nor Bacon yelled at each other about it. It was as close as the two of them ever got to having a rational conversation—and also the subject that our machine translation was the most at sea about. Whatever the discussion was about was something the Consu had never bothered to talk about in front of the children, the children being every other sentient species.

Which was interesting in itself but didn't give me anything to go on.

Finally, there was an update from the scientists working on the satellite. Ran's explanation to them about how the Consu work was interesting, but yielded no new breakthroughs—the tech was incredibly exciting and also entirely beyond them. They were optimistic that given enough time they could figure out how to make the satellites work. They were not optimistic that the colony had that much time.

I set my PDA down and stewed there in the darkness for another twenty minutes.

"Fuck it," I said, and then got dressed, opened the door to my guest quarters, and made a little scream as Ran was there, standing.

"Jesus, Ran," I said, after my heart slowed down and I was reasonably sure I had not actually peed myself. "What are you doing lurking outside my door?"

"I was not lurking," Ran said. "I just arrived."

"How did you know I was leaving?"

"I did not know that."

"Then why did you arrive?"

"You were awake."

"How did you know *that*?"

"You were signed onto the document that Dr. Olimova had

sent regarding the Consu. I saw that and came to make sure you were all right. As is required of me."

I stared at Ran, only a little grumpily. "Thank you. I'm sorry I made it sound like you were stalking me."

"It's not stalking if it's my job."

"That's . . . not entirely true, but I'll let it go for now," I said.

"Are you all right?"

"I'm having anxiety and mild depression with a side of adrenaline comedown."

"I am sorry," Ran said. "I once again offer you a healing hug."

"Thank you for offering," I said, smiling. "Actually what you can do is come with me to visit the Consu. If I can't sleep I can at least try to extract information out of them."

"How will you do that?"

"I think I finally figured out how to make their death fetish work for me."

The sound of Consu arguing was audible well outside the cargo hold and sounded like farm machinery fighting. In front of the cargo hold doors were a contingent of Obin guards.

"How do they stand it?" I asked.

Ran spoke to one of the guards in their language. "It says they turn off their consciousness when they stand guard. The noise remains alarming and unpleasant but only abstractly so."

"That's a pretty neat trick, actually."

"I do not recommend it for you," Ran said. "Humans do not turn off their consciousness in the same way."

"It's all right," I said. "I think they will stop screeching at each other when we go in."

This was true. When Ran and I entered the cargo hold, Bacon stopped screeching at Kitty and began screeching at us. My PDA, which I did remember this time, began translating Bacon's invective toward me. It was quite rude.

Eventually Bacon ran out of horrible things to say to me and instead glowered at me, in a deeply alien fashion, which was off-putting but less so than the goosebump-inducing noises. I nodded to Bacon, acknowledging its dissatisfaction with me, sat down my PDA with the translation circuit still on, and then turned to Kitty.

"We've gotten some noise complaints," I said to the Consu.

"You've been absent," Kitty replied, ignoring my comment.

"I've been busy," I said. "As you know we are in an entirely different universe and we are hoping to return to one like our own. And soon, because we will die if we don't."

"Death is not something to be avoided," Kitty said.

"Easy for you to say. Some of us have other things on our agendas."

"This would include capturing one of the elements of our drive chain."

"A what now?"

"Come now," Kitty said, and motioned about the prism. "I connected the elements of the drive chain and operated them from here," it said. "I knew what you were doing the moment you brought it onto your colony."

"We've been calling it a satellite."

"It doesn't matter what you call it."

"You could have told us this drive chain of yours existed and saved us some time."

"Saved you time for what?" Kitty said. "You have brought the chain element in and you have examined it, but you are no closer to understanding how it functions, nor can you operate it yourself."

"This much we figured out," I said. "We know that you control it using your brain as its primary computer." I nodded toward Ran. "It told us about you having something like a BrainPal inside your head."

"The Obin are known to observe us closely," Kitty acknowledged.

"More closely in some cases than others."

"She means that we have done an autopsy on one of your corpses," Ran said, to the Consu.

Ran's comments went through my PDA and were translated into Consu. Two seconds later, Bacon screamed loud enough to peel paint, and began to hammer the inside of its clear cage. The sound of the screaming overwhelmed my PDA's internal microphone, but it was clear from context that the Consu was extremely displeased at the idea of lesser beings rooting through one of their compatriot's bodies.

Ran watched Bacon as it screamed; I watched Kitty, who stood and said nothing. "You don't seem upset," I said to Kitty, once Bacon had exhausted itself. "Your friend here seems quite distraught. Murderously so."

"It is no longer my friend," Kitty said. "Nor do I care what you do to the bodies of its compatriots. They lost the right to be outraged over what you might do to them when they became heretics."

"You were one of us!" Bacon shouted at Kitty, not loud enough to overwhelm the translation circuit.

"I was never one of you," Kitty replied, hardly shouting at all. "You chose to believe I was, and it suited my purposes to have you believe it."

Bacon started to reply and then stopped, glancing at me and Ran. Obviously there were things it didn't want to say in front of us.

Kitty noticed. "You might as well say what you want," it said to Bacon, in the simplified version of their language. "They have been listening in on us this entire time."

There was another round of indistinct yelling at this. It went on for some time.

"You have rage issues," I said to Bacon, once it finished.

"I look forward to removing your head," Bacon said to me.

"You're only making my point."

Bacon hit at its walls and then turned away.

I brought my attention back to Kitty. "You knew we were listening."

"Obviously."

"Just like you knew we had one of your satellites and knew we were letting the Obin cut into the dead Consu."

"Yes to the first. I did not know about the second for certain, but I would have been surprised if you had not. You are desperate and looking for anything to save yourselves. If you've looked inside our bodies, then you know what we have done to ourselves."

"The extra brains."

"They are not extra," Kitty said, and there was a curl of distaste to its voice. "They are integral to who we are. They were one of our most important cusps."

"*That*," I said, pointing. "You were talking about that with Bacon, and we couldn't understand it."

"Tell them nothing," Bacon said to Kitty.

"Shut up," I said to Bacon, firmly.

Bacon drew back, clearly shocked.

"Tell me what a 'cusp' is," I said to Kitty. "Please."

"They are the times of great decision for Consu," Kitty said. "When competing schools of thought vie for the sentiment of our nation on a subject that impacts all of us. The conclusion that is reached sets the course for all Consu."

I looked at Kitty doubtfully. "This sounds like it's a debate club."

"It is war," Kitty said. "Wild and pitiless. The cusp that resulted in the Consu engineering our bodies to increase our mental capabilities nearly destroyed us. It was many of your millennia ago, and the Consu carry its scars to this day."

"And your factions had to fight," I said. "You couldn't just agree to disagree."

"It is not done."

"Why not?"

"You would not understand," Kitty said. "This is not dismissive or meant as an insult. I mean you don't have the mental capacity to comprehend the logic or racial compulsion for it."

I laughed at this. "I'm sorry," I said. "This is like being told by our physicists that I don't have the math to understand skip drives."

"They are correct," Kitty said. "You don't. Neither do they."

"But you do," I pressed.

"Yes, I do," Kitty agreed. It motioned again to the prism. "I alone developed this new understanding of skip physics. It is my life's work. Others created the machinery and mechanisms to make it function. This control center. The drive chain that surrounds this asteroid. But the understanding to make it work belongs to me alone." Kitty pressed one of its lesser arms against the expanse of its chest. "Developed and residing in me." They looked over to Bacon. "It is knowledge that others have wanted to use for their own ends. To force a new cusp for our people. To shatter the peace we have had among us for longer than your people, *any* of your people, have traveled in the stars."

"You hypocrite," Bacon said, to Kitty. "You stand there painting yourself a victim, when it was you who came to us, you who demanded we make tools for you, you who agreed to what use we would make of the tools we created for your use."

"We disagree on the sequence of events," Kitty said, to Bacon. "Nor am I a victim. It is possible that in my hubris I became a pawn, but that is my concern, not anyone else's."

Bacon responded with a noise that the translator couldn't guess at, but which definitely did not sound polite.

"Yes," Kitty said, to the other Consu. "But it hardly matters now. We're here, not there."

"We could go back," I said.

"No," Kitty replied.

I shook my head. "You're alive," I said. "You're undamaged, thanks to me." I pointed to his prism. "Your command center is fully functional, also thanks to me. So are all the elements in your drive chain. We haven't figured out how you power them, but we know you can. There is nothing stopping you from taking all of us back."

"You weren't listening," Kitty said. "The Consu are being pushed toward a new cusp, and the knowledge I keep with me is the key to it. If I return, I will be found. If I am found, then it is not assured my knowledge will stay with me."

"If you don't, then all of us will die," I said.

"The Consu don't care if you live or die," Bacon said, to me.

"This is true," Kitty said, and directed a hand toward Bacon. "Now, ask it what was the intended fate of this asteroid."

I turned to Bacon. "What was the intended fate of this asteroid?" I asked.

"It was to be used to return your peoples to the glorious path," Bacon said.

"That's vague and troubling," I said.

"The Consu believe their role is to push other species toward perfection," Ran said.

"I know. That whole 'We'll fight you with our hand tied behind our back and call it a sacrament' thing."

"It's not only then," Ran said. "They believe all conflict is perfecting."

"Is that true?" I asked Kitty.

"All conflict is a cusp; every cusp is conflict," Kitty answered.

"That's a cute little murder koan, but that still doesn't explain what was going to happen to this colony."

"For some time now, all of your species have avoided conflict with each other," Kitty said.

"Yes," I said. "The tripartite treaty of ours."

"This does not suit us. Nor do we believe it's beneficial to your souls."

"We disagree about that," I said.

"Of course you disagree; you are ignorant," Kitty said. "Within the Consu, there have been two schools of thought on how to continue the perfection of other species. One is to do nothing. Your peoples cannot abide peace. It is not in your nature, nor should it be. You may play at it, but you cannot sustain it. In which case all we need do is wait."

I thought about the goal of Unity Colony and how it was not particularly succeeding. "What's the other school of thought?" I asked.

Kitty inclined its head toward the other Consu. "To speed up the process."

"How?"

"The colony would have been moved into the path of a thing that has cultural and strategic importance to both groups of humans, and is also of interest to the Conclave," Kitty said.

I walked over to Bacon's enclosure. "Tell me what that is," I said.

"Earth," they said.

NINETEEN

"It fucking said *what*?" Ong Vannak yelled, and then there was commotion among the diplomats and colony leaders.

I rubbed my temples. The abrupt chaos from revealing the intended fate of Unity Colony was not unexpected, but also it was early in the morning and I had been up all night, first talking to the Consu and then wrangling this meeting of Unity Colony and diplomatic mission brain trust, and I was now extremely tired and working on a migraine. I also wanted coffee, which we did not have because it was now rationed and we had to be the example for everyone else, which was noble and also was not helping my incipient migraine at all. I wondered if I could text Magdy to bring me pain relievers, then remembered those would be even more rationed than coffee.

Ran, standing next to where I sat, noticed my temple rubbing and leaned in, solicitous. I waved it back, for now.

"How would they have been able to do that?" Haimi Bava asked me, when the din subsided enough for her to ask.

"How were they able to get here?" I asked. "Getting us to a universe vastly different from our own was the hard part, the part that only Kitty understood was possible. Popping this asteroid into Earth's gravity well was the easy part."

"But the Consu didn't do it," Fris said. "Kitty made sure of that."

I nodded. "Right. *But*, and this is important, not because it gives a damn about any of us one way or another. Right now there are two factions within the Consu: the one that wants to 'accelerate' our perfection by making us turn on each other, and the one that is content to wait until we just start killing ourselves without their input. Bacon is part of the first faction. Kitty pretended to be part of the faction, to gather information and to get the faction to waste its time and energy building a working version of the chain drive"—and here I waved out toward space—"that collection of satellites that brought us here. Kitty's role was to disrupt their plans and rat them out, which it did by sending the asteroid here. That anyone was on the asteroid is neither here nor there to Kitty's plan."

"But not to Bacon's," Caspar Merrin said.

"No," I agreed. "Their whole point was to shove this secret colony down the throat of the Colonial Union and the Conclave, to disrupt our peace treaty and send us back into war."

"And to destroy Earth," Ong said.

I looked over at him. "You're gonna hate this part," I told him.

"What part?"

"The reason the Consu targeted Earth was because it knew both the Colonial Union and the Conclave had interests in it. They didn't care about it for itself, and didn't see it as an important player or a threat."

"So we would be destroyed—eleven billion people murdered—to start a fight between *you two*," Ong said, moving his finger between me and Fris.

"That's about the size of it," I confirmed.

"*Fuck* the Consu," Ong said. "And I'm *still* pissed that you fucking named them 'Kitty' and 'Bacon,' like they're stuffed animals or something."

"At the time I didn't think it mattered," I said. "In retrospect I would have chosen differently."

"What I am hearing is that the eleven billion people of Earth have been spared, purely because of internal Consu politics," Bava said.

"That's accurate," I said.

"And the fifty thousand of us are going to die because these same Consu internal politics don't require us anymore."

"Yes," I confirmed.

Before I could go any further Ong spoke up again. "This asshole of a Consu could take us back to our universe. We know its tech still works. We know it knows how."

"It won't," I said.

"Maybe it would change its mind if we threatened to throw it out an airlock."

"That's not how they work," I said.

"I'd be willing to test that," Ong replied.

"Then you'd kill us all," I shot back. "You can't bargain with a Consu. You have nothing it values, and its perspective on life and death is not ours. When we found Kitty it had already prepared for its death. It wanted to die. All we're doing at the moment is continually disrupting that plan. If you try to murder Kitty, you'll just be giving it what it wants. If it doesn't toy with you first."

"Then what do you suggest?" Fris asked me.

"Well, as I was going to say"—I shot Ong a look—"we may have a long-shot option. You can't bargain with a Consu. You certainly can't threaten one. But if you can serve a function for it, if it can *use* you, maybe you can find a way to get what you want out of it."

"How does the Consu want to use the colony?" Merrin asked.

"Not the colony," I said. "Me." I looked over toward Ran. "Us, actually."

"I have an errand for you," Kitty said to me, after the shock of Bacon's declaration of the intended destruction of Earth had settled somewhat. "A task which I need to have done. If you undertake it and successfully complete it, I may give you what you wish."

"What do you think I'm wishing for?" I asked.

"The ability to save the creatures of this colony."

I wasn't thrilled with everyone on the colony being called *creatures*, but this was not the moment to complain about it. "Tell me."

"I cannot return to a universe like the one we came from," Kitty said. "The risk of ruining my death is too great. Nevertheless, there is business I left unfinished. I had satisfied myself that its unfinished state would not be a problem, but you have, against my will, given me more time to realize that unless that business is attended to, the perfection of my death will be marred. You must attend to that business."

I thought about this. "You are going to send me back—just me—to tie off some loose ends for you."

"If that is meant to suggest you will finish my business for me, then yes."

"What business is it?"

"I need you to deliver a message for me."

"A message."

"Yes."

"What's the message?"

"It's not important for you to know at the moment."

"Who will I deliver it to?"

Kitty waved in the direction of Bacon. "As it happens, its parent."

I looked at Bacon, who was doing the Consu version of glowering.

"How will I find this Consu?"

Kitty motioned to Bacon. "You will take it back with you."

"Will I now."

"When you do, it will be only a short while before its parent will appear to retrieve it. When it does, you will deliver the message."

"It's possible it won't want to bother with me," I said. "You Consu don't usually *mix*."

"You will be delivering it with my authority," Kitty said. "They will be unable not to receive it."

"Why not?"

"It is not done."

"You're serious."

Kitty motioned again to Bacon. "Ask it."

"Well?" I said, to Bacon.

"If it is offering the"—and here was an untranslatable scraping sound—"then my parent will not be able to refuse it."

I looked back to Ran, who stood there motionless. I thought perhaps for the first time I had learned something about the Consu that Ran did not already know.

But there was another problem, as far as I could see. "Bacon here has promised to murder me at its earliest convenience," I pointed out to Kitty. "I won't be able to deliver a message if my head has been sliced off my shoulders."

I swear to God, Kitty shrugged at this. "I do not foresee this as an issue."

"Easy for you to say, it's not your head."

Kitty bellowed something at Bacon, who bellowed back. For two minutes they had a conversation I could feel in my bowels. Then Kitty turned to me. "It will not kill you until after you offer the message to its parent," Kitty said.

"This is not entirely reassuring," I said.

"This is your problem to resolve," Kitty said.

I didn't like this answer at all, but there was something else pressing on my brain. "There is one thing I don't understand," I said. "You've said you can't go back, and I have to go back for you. But only you have all the information on how to work this new skip drive, and you have it all in your hea . . . in your brain." I motioned to the prism. "None of this works without you. So I can't go back without you. And you won't go back. So I'm wondering how any of this is meant to work."

"I will provide you the information you will need to operate this command center so you may travel and then, if you successfully deliver the message, return."

"How? Are you going to put it into some sort of device I can use?"

"It is information best suited for a brain."

I blinked at this. "You're going to download this information into my brain?"

"Obviously not," Kitty said. "Your brain is far too primitive to contain this information, much less process it. The transfer itself would kill you. If it did not, securing the information within your brain structure would. If you were dead, you could not deliver the message."

I glanced over at Bacon, who was still glowering. "So you're going to give the information about this new skip physics and how to operate the chain drive to . . . the person who hates you the most in this and probably every other universe."

"I would not."

"And now we're back where we started," I said.

"There is another option," Kitty said, and looked over at Ran.

"Excuse me, what?" said Bava. "Kitty wants to use Ran's brain to operate the new skip drive?"

"Check your PDAs," I said. "Captain Mouse's preliminary report on the Consu auxiliary brains notes that they most resemble Obin brains, not the Consu primary brain. This isn't an accident. This was intentional on the part of the Consu."

"I don't know about this report," Ong said, reaching for his PDA.

"Captain Mouse sent it overnight," I said.

"And you've already read it."

"I couldn't sleep."

"You don't appear to sleep at all," Bava noted.

"I'm a little stressed right now," I admitted.

"The brains," Fris prompted.

"Right," I said. I motioned to Ran. "You are all aware that millennia ago, the Consu uplifted the Obin. They manipulated their genetics to increase their cognitive abilities. This gave them sapience but not consciousness on an individual level."

"We gave them that," Merrin said. "The Colonial Union."

"Yes, we did, and we know that the Consu don't like that we

did," I said, and tapped my PDA. "And now we know why. The Consu uplifted the Obin because they wanted to see what would happen when they did—Kitty says the decision to do it was one of the actual cultural 'cusps' of the Consu—but the choice to *design* the brains to avoid consciousness wasn't an accident. They wanted it for their own purposes."

"They wanted efficient cognitive processors to augment their own abilities," Ran said, to the diplomats and councilors. "They used my species to beta test their technology."

"An entire species, and a beta test that takes hundreds if not thousands of years," Ong said.

"Yes," Ran said, to Ong. "Do not assume the Consu do what they do on the time frames that other species live inside. They are patient and they are deliberate. They are willing to wait."

"That's nice to know," Ong said. "Because the decision to kill every goddamn human on Earth and all of us on this colony feels a little *rushed*."

"It is not," Ran said.

"This colony didn't even exist four years ago," Bava pointed out to Ran. "On the time scales you say the Consu think on, it's a blip."

"But the colony isn't the argument, it's the *tool*," I said, jumping in. "The argument—the 'cusp' the Consu are now on—is how to shepherd us lesser beings toward perfection, and how fast, and by what means. That argument has been going on for centuries, even if we humans have only caught the last part of it. The current fight between Kitty's faction and Bacon's faction is like a single hand in an infinitely long poker game."

"Where the table stakes are *genocide*," Ong said.

"Yes," I said. "Although the Consu would argue this is just how the hand is played."

"You're not convincing me that we shouldn't throw them out into space."

"You don't want to throw them out into space because the only way we all get back, the whole colony, is if I come back successful," I said. "That was the deal. I complete the mission given to me, with proof, and then as its final act before death, Kitty will send the colony back. We need to put that satellite we have with the scientists back together, by the way. We apparently need all of them working. But if you *kill* Kitty"—I pointed to Ong to make the point—"then we all stay here. Because they're not patterning the instructions they're putting in Ran to operate the chain drive. Just the one single skip drive, the one in the command center."

"Which is still information we could use," Merrin pointed out. "The science of skip drive physics is upended. This technology can skip inside of gravity wells and into entirely different universes. That will work even without the chain drive."

"This is the other thing," I said, and turned to Ran. "Tell them."

"The information will be encrypted," Ran said, "forced and patterned in my brain in a way that can only be read by the command center. Any attempt to retrieve it away from the command center will cause it to break down at a synaptic level. Which will kill me."

"They could retrieve it from the command center when you go back," Fris said.

"Kitty thought of that," I said.

"The information can be retrieved twice," Ran said, to everyone in the room. "Once it's retrieved the second time, it breaks down."

There was a pause while everyone processed this information. It was Merrin who got to it first. "But that means . . ."

"Yes," Ran said. "When we return here, I will die."

"Absolutely fucking *not*," I said to Kitty, after it explained the deal.

"Then we will all die here," Kitty said. "My intention is to die here, so it makes no difference to me. I understood you wished to avoid the same fate for this colony."

"Ran's death is unnecessary for what you're asking me to do."

"It is necessary because I say it is necessary."

"Ran's death? Or will any death do?"

Kitty regarded me for a moment. "Are you offering to take its place?"

"Yes," I said.

"That is honorable, and no."

"Why not?"

"I already explained that your brain would not survive the transfer and encoding process for the information," Kitty said. "Even if it could, there is no way to transfer the knowledge to you. Whereas there is for the Obin."

I looked over to Ran. "What does that mean?"

"Kitty means my consciousness harness," Ran said. "It integrates with my brain to process information and to give me a consciousness. It will give them access to my brain."

"A brain that is close enough to some of my own to work for this exercise," Kitty said. "There is irony that in providing the Obin with the abomination of consciousness you have offered me a route to achieve my perfect death."

"And save tens of thousands of people," I reminded Kitty.

"As you say." Kitty motioned to Ran. "The information, once set in the Obin's brain, cannot be overwritten with the tools I have here. It is not acceptable that the information remains in any form. The best option is to have it self-destruct. This Obin will need to have its machinery functioning in order to operate this command module. It will have to remain conscious while it faces its death." Kitty returned its attention to me. "If you would also like to die on your return, I will honor that request. But it will be neither here nor there to what happens to this Obin."

"The answer is no," I said. "You want me to help you in your 'perfect death,' then you need to do it in a way that doesn't end up with my friend dead."

"A less-than-perfect death will still be acceptable," Kitty said. "Besides, it has never been your decision to make."

I looked at Ran. "No," I said.

"I will do it," Ran answered Kitty.

"Ran. *No.*"

Ran looked at me. "In this you are not my boss."

"You can't."

"I can."

"Let me rephrase," I began.

"Gretchen," Ran said, interrupting me. "This is a good deal."

"No it's not!" I yelled at Ran, stunned by the sheer stupidity of what it had just said to me.

Ran shrank back at this, hurt. It might have been the first time I'd yelled at it.

"I'm sorry, Ran," I said, trying to reassure it. "But it's not. Your life is worth more than to be thrown away on a Consu's whim."

Ran cocked its head, considering what to say next. "Long ago, the Obin wanted to know more about those who created us and made us the species that we are today," it said. "The Consu let us ask a precious few questions, and the price of those questions was half of our entire number. We paid it, without hesitation. When your friend Zoë needed our help to save Roanoke Colony, hundreds of us sacrificed ourselves to get the attention of a single Consu."

Ran pointed at Kitty. "This Consu is offering to let us save fifty thousand people. All they want in return for it is a single Obin life. Just one. Just mine. You must understand, Gretchen. In all the time the Obin have known of the Consu, this is the best deal we have ever gotten from them. I would be ashamed to refuse it."

I broke down and hugged Ran, sobbing against its neck. It stood there and let me bawl.

Magdy's door opened and he was there. He smiled when he recognized me. "You again," he said.

"You need to call in sick," I said to him.

"I can't keep doing that," he began, and then stopped because I kissed him. For a while.

"This is a compelling argument," he said, after I stopped to breathe. "But I skipped out yesterday with you."

"You need a better argument?"

"Me? No," Magdy said. "My boss? Maybe."

"I'm leaving," I said.

Magdy frowned. "What?"

"I'm leaving," I repeated.

"You have to explain that to me," Magdy said.

"Can I not? Just for now?"

Magdy opened his mouth to say something snarky, then saw the sadness and exhaustion on my face. "What do you need from me?" he asked.

"First I'm going to need you to hold me while I cry," I said. "Then I'm going to need you to absolutely wear me out with sex. Then I'm going to need you to let me fall asleep on you for a while. When I wake up we'll probably do the first two again."

"All right."

"And I need you to call in sick," I reminded him.

"I will," he said. "I just remembered they can't really fire me."

"That's right," I said. "You have them over a barrel." I kissed him again. "I missed that," I said, when we needed to breathe again.

"I'll be happy to catch you up," Magdy said.

"Good. I like that. I like that a lot."

Magdy looked at me again. "You okay, Gretchen?"

"Ask me that later," I said. "I promise I'll tell you. But right now, just let me in, please."

Magdy let me in.

BOOK THREE

TWENTY

There are very few things in life that are more anticlimactic than a skip.

On paper they look—and are!—amazing. Through the twin miracles of physics and energy, an entire object, usually a ship filled with people and things, punches a hole in its own universe and inserts itself into a different one, almost exactly like the one you just left, at coordinates that are light-years away from where you had been and that would take tens of thousands of years to reach under standard ship drives, by which time you would be dead, which is inconvenient. It's fast travel to literally impossibly distant worlds. It's the most incredible thing thinking minds have ever discovered.

In practice, walking from one room to another is far more exciting. There are no whooshing special effects, no noises or dramatic music to signal the switch from one universe to another. It just . . . *happens,* and if you're not paying attention, you would never know the moment the skip occurs. Even if you *are* paying attention, you can still very easily miss it if you're not the one pressing the button.

The inside of Kitty's command module—the prism, as I had been calling it—was designed to house a single Consu. All the technology of it was designed to route to Kitty's brain, where it would present Kitty with some sort of command overlay the Consu could manipulate through thought or gestures. There were no screens, no outside views, no gauges or monitors or light bars that would indicate *anything*, much less information about whether a skip was successful or not. There wasn't even a hum.

All of the information from the command module that had once gone into Kitty's brain was now going to Ran's. Ran's brain similarity had allowed certain data sets to be deposited via a neural imprinting process that was not explained to me and that I wouldn't understand even if it were, and then the command interface had been loaded into Ran's consciousness harness. The only one of us—me, Bacon and Ran—who knew when the skip had happened was Ran itself.

Which is why Ran was not in the least offended when I asked, "Are we there yet?"

"We are there now," Ran confirmed.

"Exactly where we are supposed to be?"

"Kitty was meticulous in the destination programming."

"Any . . . mishaps on reentry?"

"No."

"You're sure."

"Yes."

"Okay, well, this will be exciting, then." I turned to Bacon, who had not spoken to either Ran or me since it entered the command module. "You understand what happens next," I said to it, through my PDA's translator.

It continued to say nothing to me.

I shrugged. "Look, just . . . try not to kill anyone, all right?" I said. "It will make everything more difficult for all of us."

Still nothing. Bacon and I were never going to be best friends, I could tell. I turned my attention back to Ran. "How are you?"

"I am fine," Ran said.

"The imprinting didn't mess with you? Or the skip?"

"If either did, I can't tell," Ran said. "Although as far as I know there is no way I could tell. Even when we return I will likely not be able to register any problems with my brain function until I am dead. That was phrased poorly. I will not be able to register any problems after I am dead, either."

"No, I understood that," I said. "At this moment I don't need grammatical perfection from you, Ran. I just want you to be okay."

"I am okay," it said. "To the extent I can, I will let you know if I am not."

"Thank you."

"What would you like to do now?" Ran asked.

"No point drawing it out," I replied. "Open us up."

Ran nodded and pressed whatever figurative button it had in its head, and the prism opened up.

Not to the black vacuum of space, which is where most things that skip from one place to another end up, for all sorts of reasons, not the least of which being that aiming at a target moving through space in multiple directions from an entirely different universe is hard.

But I guess if you are the Consu equivalent of Albert Einstein and have created a new understanding of an entire branch of physics you're allowed to show off a little.

Which is why we opened up to the quadrangle of the Colonial Union State Department, on Phoenix, directly in front of Bainburger Tower.

To a quickly assembled phalanx of security guards, with weapons, and behind them, on the pathways of the campus and the stairs of the tower, a bunch of deeply surprised spectators.

This is what I meant when I asked about "mishaps," by the way. Kitty, being a Consu, and by any standard other than a Consu's, a sociopath, did not care if its command module squished any people when it seemingly magically appeared on the State Department's lawn. I, on the other hand, understood that it doing so could lead to complications. So this was one less problem to immediately solve.

Which left me with only one real immediate problem: the line of security guards in front of me, weapons leveled, ready to shoot the hell out of the three of us.

What a tiny part of me wanted to do—all right, why lie, it was most of me—was strike a dramatic pose and say "Take me to your leaders." I would one hundred percent get as far as the dramatic pose before I and Ran and Bacon were pumped full of projectiles. Not the ideal outcome.

So, *disappointingly*, what I did say, loudly and clearly, was "I'm Gretchen Trujillo, head of the Obin desk for the State Department. I am with my assistant Ran, and this Consu, who has full and complete diplomatic immunity. I have returned in advance of a state visit by the Consu and need to see Secretary Mbalenhle and Representative Manfred Trujillo. Please let them know I am back."

The guards did not lower their weapons, but at least they weren't firing them. More than anything else, it was the phrase "full and complete diplomatic immunity" that accomplished that. State Department security didn't usually need to know much, but what it did know, absolutely, is that you do *not* shoot the diplomats. Ever.

Also the word "Consu" had an absolute effect. There was a collective murmuring gasp from the still-assembling crowd, and people began to filter in, at a very cautious distance, to get the first look at a live Consu that nearly all of them had ever had in their life. As they did, I recognized one of them, on the stairs.

"Hector!" I yelled. "Hey! Hector! Hector Barber!"

Hector involuntarily put his hand to his chest, as if to say, *Who, me?*

"Yes, Hector, you," I yelled again. "My cat, Hector! Lucifer! How is my *cat*?"

There were things I was expecting from a high-level mission debriefing. A blubbering, crying father was not one of them.

But there he was, hauling himself up out of his chair the moment I came into the same subterranean Bainburger conference room where I last saw him, to drape himself over me, sobbing.

"I thought you were dead," he said to me, over and over.

"I'm not," I assured him.

"I'm sorry," he said, pulling away to look at me. "I'm so sorry. I should have never asked you to go."

"It's good that you did," I said. "I'm the only one the Consu would willingly talk to. One of them, anyway. Without that we wouldn't have a chance to get everyone back. Well done you, Dad."

"Good, good," Dad said, then hugged me again, fiercely.

"Dad," I said. "You're embarrassing me in front of the bureaucrats."

"Sorry," he said, finally breaking away.

"Also Magdy says hello and says he totally blames you and you suck."

"I believe the first part of that," Dad said.

"I may have embellished," I confessed.

"And how did the two of you get along?" Dad asked.

I smiled at this. "You were right. I wasn't over him."

"I told you."

I lightly smacked him on the shoulder. "Don't get smug about it."

"If we can get started," said Secretary of State Zawadi Mbalenhle, smiling at the both of us. Dad took his seat and I found one for myself. The players in this debriefing looked to be the ones in the meeting I was in before I left. Time truly is a flat circle.

"Where do you want to start?" I asked as I sat.

"You might start with how you managed to appear on the Bainburger Tower lawn with a piece of Consu technology, with an actual Consu inside of it," said Colonel Bridgers, the Colonial Defense Forces representative.

"That's a complicated question," I said. "It involves an entirely newly discovered branch of skip drive physics that took Unity Colony to a wholly different universe, a Consu civil war that was supposed to involve the destruction of Earth by the colony's asteroid"—and here Mateu Jordi, the meeting's representative from Earth, sat straight up in his chair—"and the fact that at least one faction in that civil war is on its way here to come meet me. Which part do you want to dig into first?"

Don't let it be said that I don't know how to get a meeting going.

"Let's do the part where the Consu are coming here," Mbalenhle said, after a moment.

"Yes, let's," said Colonel Bridgers.

"All right," I said. I reached into one of my jacket pockets and produced a small, heavy, metallic disk of cobalt blue. I set it onto the table in front of me with a flat *clunk*.

"What is that?" Dad asked.

"It's the message I'm supposed to deliver."

"What does it say?"

"I was told I didn't need to know at this point."

"And you just accepted that?" asked Jordi.

"If you want to try to argue with a Consu, there's one on the lawn you can give it a shot with," I said to him. "Go with a custodian to pick up the pieces afterward."

"May I see that?" Bridgers asked.

"Sure." I slid the disk over to him.

"God damn it!" Bridgers said, three seconds later, dropping the disk back onto the table.

"The disk is only meant to be touched by me and the Consu I am intended to give it to," I said. "If anyone else touches it, it brutalizes them."

"You could have told me that," Bridgers said.

"Would you have listened?"

"What do you know about the Consu you're delivering this disk to?" asked Mbalenhle.

"Next to nothing," I said. "I know it's the parent of Bacon—"

"Of who?"

"Bacon. Sorry, that's what I call the Consu in the command module out on the lawn."

"You named a Consu 'Bacon,'" Dad said.

I sighed. "Yes, I named one of the Consu 'Bacon' and the

other one 'Kitty,' and maybe the next time *you're* face-to-face with smug, condescending superior intellects who won't tell you their name, maybe *your* oppositional behavior won't make you label them like pets. But right now, this is not the point."

"The Consu is Bacon's parent," Mbalenhle prompted, getting me back on track.

"Yes. Thank you. It's Bacon's parent, and Bacon and Kitty are on opposite sides of the Consu civil war, so it stands to reason the parent is on Bacon's side."

"Which side is . . . Bacon on?" Jordi asked. "The one that wants to murder everyone on Earth, or the other one?"

"Bacon definitely wanted to murder Earth."

Jordi threw up his hands. "Well, *that's* fucking wonderful."

"You're bringing the Consu who want to do that *here*," Bridgers said to me.

"Colonel, if the Consu wanted us dead purely for the sake of us being dead, they would have wiped us—human and alien—off the face of our planets any time they wanted. They don't kill us for sport. They kill us to perfect our species, from their point of view. Even murdering an entire planet with an asteroid"—I glanced at Jordi here—"was going to be done so that the survivors would get back on the path. The Consu aren't sadistic kids frying insects with a magnifying lens. They're gardeners. They'll tear out part of the garden if they think it means the rest of the garden will thrive."

"That's great, if you're not the part of the garden being pruned," Jordi said, wryly.

"My point is that the Consu aren't coming now to kill us," I said. "They're coming because Bacon is one of their own, and they're coming because *this*"—I held up the disk for all of them to see—"is a summons that apparently can't be refused."

"How many Consu are coming?" Bridgers asked.

"I have no idea," I said. "Could be the one. Could be a hundred ships. I don't know how any of this works."

"You understand how this complicates things," Mbalenhle said, not unkindly, to me. "The Consu have done many things to us. To the Colonial Union. To *humans*." She gestured to Jordi, acknowledging his presence and, by extension, the people of Earth. "But this will be the first time a Consu, any Consu, will come to the heart of the Colonial Union itself. It raises all manner of security and diplomatic issues."

"I understand," I concurred. "I also understand that this is the only option I was given to save Unity Colony and everyone on it from a slow death from starvation and loss of resources. I took the chance I had."

There was silence at this, and looks around the room. I wondered what the hell that was about.

"We clearly have a lot to get into here," Mbalenhle said. "We're going to be here a while. We might want to bring in some coffee."

"You need to explain to me what that silence was about," I said to my dad, later, when I was back in my office for the first time since I left. "The one after I said I came back to save the colony."

Dad looked over at Ran, who was also in my office, because it was my assistant and also absolutely itching to tell me how many messages I had, which was almost certainly several hundred. "I shouldn't say in front of Ran," he said.

"I can go," Ran said.

"Or you could stay," I said, and brought my attention back to Dad. "Ran knows what I know, and actually knows more than what I know, since its knowledge of the Consu and its practices were helpful more than once. It's sacrificing more than any other person to bring Unity Colony back, because if everything goes according to plan and we save the colony, its reward is dying. So maybe Ran has earned the right to hear everything you have to say to me."

Dad nodded and turned to Ran. "I am sorry about your circumstances," he said.

"Thank you," Ran said. "Dying is a part of life, but I would have preferred not to get to that part so soon."

Dad didn't know what to say to that—fair—so he came back to me. "We are all immensely relieved that you found Unity Colony and that everyone on it is safe and secure for now. *I am especially relieved, and not just for Magdy's sake.*"

"There's a 'but' coming after that for sure," I said.

Dad nodded. "Yes there is. *But*, as Secretary Mbalenhle said, it complicates things. When Unity Colony went missing, we assumed it had been attacked, and that it had been attacked by the Consu, because no one other species that we know of could have so completely obliterated it like that."

"The Consu did attack it."

"Not in the way we expected," Dad said. "A way that, as awful as this sounds, would have allowed us and Earth and the Conclave a graceful way to end the experiment."

"All right," I said, fury suddenly rising, "you're going to have to explain how the straight-up murder of fifty thousand sentient beings is somehow a *best-case scenario* for you."

Dad held up his hand. "I told you it sounded awful."

"You were fucking *right*, Dad."

"Nobody *wanted* the people of Unity Colony dead," Dad said. "But the fact of the matter is, Unity Colony was failing. Humans and Conclave members weren't integrating the way we all hoped they would. The Conclave species actively shunned humans outside of work assignments and even then segregated themselves away from them whenever possible. And neither the Colonial Union nor Earth humans were making much of an effort to engage either."

I remembered the human wing of the colony hospital sequestered away from the rest of it, and the fact that the only colony administrator who would deal with us at all was Haimi Bava. I nodded to this.

"Everything told us that not only was Unity Colony not working, but it was trending toward conflict. First slowly and then increasingly so. But none of us wanted to be the first to call off the experiment. It would be signaling to the others that larger conflict would be inevitable."

"So if the Consu could be blamed for the colony dying, all of you could save face," I said, disgusted.

"Basically," Dad said.

"This is why you did nothing when the Obin told you the Consu were spotted in the same system as Unity Colony," Ran said, to Dad.

Dad looked at Ran, surprised.

"I told you it knows things," I said to Dad.

"Apparently it does," Dad said. "And no, this is not why we did nothing."

"Why *did* you do nothing, then?"

"What is there to do?" Dad asked. "They're the Consu. They can literally do whatever they want and there is nothing we can do to stop them." He motioned to Ran. "And what Ran may not know is that for more than a decade we've seen the Consu more actively observing us, everywhere we are. Not just this one colony, but everywhere. The Conclave too, although we know that through our own intelligence networks, not through them sharing information."

"That fits with the Consu having an open conflict over the results of the Tripartite Agreement," I said.

"Perhaps," Dad said. "So that's the answer to your question. We didn't do anything about it because for the last decade or more we didn't think it had anything to do with anything. We thought it was the Consu being their usual unknowable selves. And then Unity Colony disappeared. At that point hindsight wasn't helpful."

"I'm sorry you no longer have the pleasant fiction of the Consu destroying the colony," I said, not exactly sincerely.

Dad smiled ruefully. "I suppose I deserve that."

"Yes you do."

"But now we have to see if the present reality is any better," he said. "Because the colony isn't saved yet, and an undetermined number of Consu are coming here, and we don't know what they want or what they intend to do when they arrive."

"Also, I will die," Ran said.

Dad pointed. "Yes. Ran also will die."

"From my point of view this is the most immediate consequence," Ran added.

"If there's anything in that blue disk of yours that has answers, now would be great," Dad said, ignoring Ran's last statement.

I fished out the disk. "I have no idea what's on it," I said. "I have no idea how to access it. I have no idea if it even has information on it. Maybe a disk of blue metal is all it is, and the Consu will know what it means when they see it."

"I'm sort of surprised Bridgers let you leave the meeting with it," Dad said.

"That's why I let him try to take it," I said.

"I'm sure he could have found a pair of tongs or something."

I smiled at this. "I'm guessing that wouldn't be enough," I said.

"Be careful with it," Dad said.

"I can take care of myself, Dad," I assured him.

"And when she cannot, I am here," Ran said. "At least, until I am dead."

"Ran, you can ease up with the mentioning you'll be dead soon," I told it.

"I'm sorry, is it making you uncomfortable?"

"A little. Mostly just sad, though."

Ran opened its arms. "Is it time for a reassuring hug again?"

"Yes," I said. "Give it to my dad."

Ran stomped over to Dad and enveloped him in a hug.

"Are you reassured?" Ran asked Dad, after it was done.

". . . Yes," Dad said. "Thank you, Ran."

"I like reassuring people," Ran said, after Dad left.

"I know you do," I said to it. "You talked to the Obin while I was in my meeting, yes?"

"Yes. I was debriefed as you were debriefed."

"And what do the Obin think?"

"We are thinking many things. Mostly, however, we are waiting."

"For the Consu."

"Yes."

I held up the disk. "Did they have any thoughts about this?"

"They want to meet with you about it."

"I'm glad they only want to meet."

"What do you mean?" Ran asked.

"Something uncharitable that they don't deserve," I said. "But that others might. On that note, I need you to set a meeting for me, Ran," I said.

Ran held up its PDA. "You have many people who wish to have a meeting with you," it said. "Including the Obin."

"We'll get to those," I said. "Let's schedule this one first."

TWENTY-ONE

It took them two days to come for me, and honestly, I thought it would happen much sooner than it did.

Not that the time went by idly. Ran's list of people who wanted to speak to me about the current crisis got longer, not shorter, as time went on; at a certain point it became easier for me to stay in the subterranean conference level at Bainburger and let the confidential meetings come to me rather than the other way around. Diplomats wanted to know the current situation on Unity Colony; the military wanted to do threat assessment for the looming Consu arrival; scientists wanted to quiz me about what I knew about the new understanding of skip drive physics.

I was progressively less helpful for each group, although in each case I did have information and reports from Unity Station's diplomats and scientists themselves, as well as the Obin report on Consu physiology, which the Civil Defense Forces were unsurprisingly thrilled by.

I also had letters and communications from every person on Unity Colony, human and alien alike, who wanted to send messages back home. These I was not allowed to send along. I was informed that sending them to friends and family before the people at Unity Colony were returned to our universe would be cruel if that return didn't happen, and besides, much about Unity Colony was classified. I thought it was more cruel to keep the relatives and loved ones in the dark, and I doubted the Colonial Union had the right to make that call for the folks from the Conclave, but I was overruled.

What I was not overruled on: what to do with the command module we'd landed on the Bainburger lawn, and the Consu who was gloweringly residing inside. Both the State Department and Colonial Defense Forces wanted to move it—the State Department because it was in the way and the CDF because they wanted to take it apart and study it.

I pointed out to the CDF that I would need it to get back, so it had to remain in one piece, and to the State Department that moving it would risk damaging it, and I pointed out to both that anyone who got close to Bacon would probably get turned into very large chunks thanks to its slashing arms. Any retaliation for such behavior would likely end up being seen as a negative by the incoming Consu, who had been summoned by Bacon when we arrived and who would be arriving at an indefinite time in the future but almost certainly very soon. The module, and Bacon, remained where they were.

The rest of the time was a haze of meetings, more meetings, requests for information, requests for clarification of that information, confidential briefings, dodging journalist requests for interviews about how I and an Obin and a Consu somehow showed up on the State Department campus, eating, drinking coffee, reassuring a very pissed-off cat that I would never leave it again, sleeping badly and having a couple of spontaneous sobbing sessions because I was terrified I was somehow going to screw this all up.

Plus, now I missed Magdy, too. That last part was new, or more accurately, newly revived. When I had a spare minute, which wasn't often, I would think back on our last night together, before I left Unity Colony. Magdy did a very good job of not burdening me with his own thoughts and feelings about my leaving him for the second time in our lives. I appreciated that. It didn't mean I didn't know those feelings were there.

I was busy and distracted enough, in other words, that when they did come for me, I didn't notice until it was almost too late.

Maybe that's why they waited. They wanted me to be worn down and focused mostly on getting back to my place and my cat and my pint of ice cream that I had bought the night before to grief-eat but then fell asleep before I could fish it back out of the freezer.

They came for me at the right place for it, at least, the little-traveled street equidistant between the Phoenix City commuter train and my place, the one that was placed at a diagonal from the usual street grid because it used to be a private street and the diagonal was a selling feature of the expensive townhomes built there. Then there were financial shenanigans with the builder, and now Hilbert Street was open to anyone but still mostly unused by anyone who didn't live there and not very well surveilled by Phoenix City's network of cameras.

There were three of them. The first I noticed just before I turned on to Hilbert, a stocky man with earbuds in, talking to some other person on his PDA. They were talking about a plumbing problem the other person had. As I turned onto Hilbert I saw a couple wandering the street, hands clasped, admiring the famous architecture of Hilbert Street's townhomes. Between me and the exit of Hilbert was a delivery van for Geeta's Flaming Pies, an actual specialty pizza place famous for its incredibly spicy offerings and a favorite of a certain tranche of State Department underlings.

Just your usual off-the-street snatch-and-grab, then. If I had to guess, I'd bet the street cameras were offline or image looped, and the car and doorbell cameras on the street were being jammed in some way, and if any actual person was watching, the plan was to have it happen so fast they couldn't do anything about it anyway. The van's logo and license plates would repaint their images the moment they turned off Hilbert anyway. Nice, fast and smart.

So, naturally, I turned around, walked over to the stocky man on his earbuds, and punched him straight in the face.

Or tried to, anyway; he saw the punch coming and went directly to block and counter the hit.

Which made me happy. I'd telegraphed that intended punch pretty hard. If it had connected, then I would have owed some poor innocent dude an actual apology. But no, he went with the block fast enough that I knew that he knew what he was doing, that he had been watching me, and that when I started walking toward him, he was aware his cover had been blown.

The real question was what he would do next and how he would do it. The latter would tell me who he had been trained by. The former would tell me whether I ultimately needed to be dead or alive, and if alive, whether I needed to be undamaged or not. These were all important things in themselves (I would prefer not to be dead, thank you) and also for having some idea of who this jerk was working for.

Four moves later I knew: Colonial Union Diplomatic Security, current or former; I was supposed to be kept alive and undamaged; and the dude was fighting not to control me, but to keep me busy until his friends down the street could arrive.

So I gave him a quick slap on the cheek to surprise him, and to let him know I could, and then backed off. "If you're not going to kill me, then you can tell me who told you to snatch me," I said.

"You know that's not how this works," the guy said, who complimented me by being a little out of breath while he said it.

"It *could* work that way," I said.

"Nah."

"Suit yourself."

By this time the couple had come rushing up. "Is everything all right?" the woman of the couple said to me. "Do you need help?"

"You can drop the act," I said. "Ask your pal here."

"She knows," the dude said.

"How did you fuck this up?" the male of the couple asked my guy.

"It's not his fault," I said. "I'm observant when I want to be."

"Thank you," my guy said, to me.

"We're not friends," I reminded him, and looked back at the couple. "So what now?"

"Now you come with us," the woman said.

"What, in the pizza van?"

The dude from the couple looked at my guy again.

"*I* didn't tell her," he said.

"No, but you planned this. What an absolute shit show."

"You wouldn't have done any better," my guy said, and then the two of them bickered for a moment or two while the woman and I looked at each other with an expression of *Dudes, am I right*. One does not want to offer solidarity to one's attempted kidnapper, but look: We have all *been* there.

Finally, I stepped in. "*Gentlemen*," I said. "We can argue about which of you is more incompetent later. What are we doing now?"

"We're not here to harm you," the woman said to me. "We only want information."

"And you couldn't have scheduled a meeting?"

"It's information you're not willing to give."

"Ah, you mean the disk," I said.

"Yes," the woman said. "We were told we couldn't take it from you and we were told you wouldn't give it to us. So we need you and it together."

"I want to go home and pet my cat and eat ice cream," I said.

The woman nodded. "And you can do that. You just have to come with us first."

"And if I say no?"

The woman sighed. "Ms. Trujillo, we are well aware you know how to defend yourself. You know by now we're equally skilled." She waited for an acknowledgment here and continued, slightly annoyed, when she didn't get it. "If you want to fight all the way to the van, we can do that. But you are going into that van. I am asking you, personally, *please* don't make a fight out of it."

"See," I said to the two men. "*This* is how you do it."

"Whatever," my guy said, and the man of the couple—who were clearly not *actually* a couple—just rolled his eyes.

And then we walked like civilized people to the van, and my guy slid open its side door, and when he did I ducked down because I didn't want to be in the way of the two electrical bolts that were fired out of the van's interior, striking the two members of the not-a-couple and sending them spasming to the street.

My guy had about one second to realize that something had gone sideways before I came up from my crouch, *actually* punched him in the face this time, stunning him, and shoved him into the van, where Diplomatic Security Corps trainees Faiza Vega and Kostantino Karagkounis were waiting to grab and secure him.

"Took you forever to get back here," Vega said to me.

"I wanted to give you time to secure the van," I said.

"We didn't need *that* much time," Karagkounis said, motioning to a downed driver, whom they had subdued and secured. "They were sloppy." He exited the van and hauled in the not-a-couple, closed the sliding door, and then drove us away while Vega and I secured all four of my would-be kidnappers and piled them like cordwood into the back of the van.

While we did that I checked to see if my guy actually had an open circuit to someone else while he was stalking me. He had not. My guy had no PDA on him; his earbuds were unconnected and just for show. None of the kidnappers had a PDA on them. They all carried electrical stun sticks, which we relieved them of. The van, at least superficially, also seemed clean of obvious cameras and non-driving-related surveillance. As far as anyone knew, the job went like it should have.

When we were done and admiring our handiwork, Vega turned to me. "You know, when you came to us the other day and told me someone was going to try to snatch you, and you needed the two of us because we weren't yet in the official security rotation, I thought you were just being paranoid."

"I was paranoid for a couple of days," I said. "And then suddenly I was not."

Vega nodded at this and then motioned with her head to the guy I'd punched. "Look who's back," she said.

I nodded and leaned down next to him. "Hi," I said.

He looked up at me from his prone position. "I don't like you," he said.

"The feeling is mutual," I assured him. "Do you have a name?"

"I'm not telling it to you."

"The last person who said that to me I decided to call 'Bacon,'" I said.

"What the hell are you talking about?"

"Never mind, it's not important," I said. "What is important is that right now, I have you and all your pals secured and in the back of the same van you tried to stuff me in. We can play this a couple of ways. The first is that you can work with me willingly, and you and your pals come out of this embarrassed but otherwise fine. The second is we fight about it, in which case it becomes unpleasant."

"So, the same options we gave you."

"There is some irony there, yes," I agreed. "But there are two added wrinkles. The first is you are secured and I am not, and I have all your stun sticks, so the fighting is not going to go well for you. The second is that while I really *do* try not to lean into nepotism, my dad is extremely well-connected, and when he finds out that you and your friends tried to kidnap me, well, I don't like your odds beating the criminal charges. Which you are definitely going to have unless you tell me what I want to know."

"Maybe your dad sent us."

"Maybe you want one of those stun sticks shoved into your sinus cavity."

"It wasn't Representative Trujillo," the man admitted.

"Thank you for telling me what I already know," I said. "Now tell me what I don't."

The man looked uncomfortable and unhappy.

"Come on," I said to the guy. "We can only drive around so much before we have to go somewhere. It's up to you."

The man sighed. "We were contracted by a man named Mateu Jordi," he said.

"The Mateu Jordi who is part of the diplomatic delegation from Earth," I said.

"I don't know how many Mateu Jordis there are on this planet," the guy said. "But yes, he's from Earth. He wanted to examine that disk you have. He said we couldn't touch it so we'd have to bring you along with it."

I pulled out the disk. "This is it."

"What does it do?" the man asked.

"For your purposes, it will make you feel like your hand is being sawed off."

"It has to do other things."

"I'm sure it does," I said. I put it back in my pocket. "So, Mateu Jordi. Just him, or was there anyone else from Earth?"

"The only person from Earth I worked with was Jordi."

"And you would tell the stun stick the same thing?"

"I would tell the stun stick anything you wanted me to say. But it would still be true that Jordi was the one I worked with from Earth."

"You keep saying 'from Earth.'"

"He's from Earth, what do you want me to say?"

"I want you to tell me that when you say 'he's the only one I worked with from Earth,' that it *doesn't* mean 'and then there are others I worked with too, just not from Earth.'"

"Well, fuck," said my guy, after a minute.

"I have diplomatic immunity," was what Mateu Jordi said when I walked into the hastily called emergency meeting in the Bainburger subterranean conference room with my guy, whose name, it turned out, was Arvik Hasid.

"All right, well, it's good we have that out of the way early," Zawadi Mbalenhle said, and then turned to Colonel Bridgers. "*You*, however, do not have diplomatic immunity, so I'm curious as to what your plan here was."

"What?" Jordi said, looking over at Bridgers, shocked.

Bridgers said nothing for a moment, looking around the room at everyone there, which in this case was me, Hasid, my dad, and Mbalenhle. Then he said, "We've had Jordi under surveillance for a while now—"

"What?!?"

"—and when he contacted Mr. Hasid, we knew about it. We decided to allow Mr. Hasid to try to acquire Ms. Trujillo, and while we have little confidence that he or Jordi would be able to pull any information off that disk, if they did, for security reasons we wanted to know what it was. So after Jordi contracted with Hasid for the job, I was given clearance to contract with Hasid to spy for us and let us know what he knew, and to assist us in securing any information Jordi got off the disk."

Jordi turned to Hasid. "You motherfucker," he said. Hasid shrugged.

"And you weren't concerned at all for Gretchen's well-being," my dad said to Bridgers.

"Jordi emphasized to Hasid that he and his crew needed to take your daughter alive and conscious," Bridgers said to my dad.

"And the fact they were carrying stun sticks to subdue her doesn't bother you at all."

"They have a low incidence of lethality," Bridgers said, and Dad had a physical response to that which I suspect was not clinically good for his health. "We cleared their use because the attempt had to have a chance of succeeding." Bridgers looked at me. "But we were also aware Ms. Trujillo was likely to have been able to deal with it. As she did."

"I had help," I said.

"Yes, well done there," Bridgers said. "We missed that one. We were expecting you to use your Obin friend."

"It's one reason why I didn't."

"And what if the kidnapping attempt had succeeded?" Mbalenhle asked Bridgers.

"Once any information was retrieved from the disk, we would have come in and arrested everyone involved, and confiscated the information before Jordi and his people could have received it."

"What would you have done with the information?"

"Studied it, obviously."

"And shared it with the rest of the Colonial Union government?"

"Obviously."

"Liar," Mbalenhle said.

"The point is moot," Bridgers said. "Jordi's plot failed."

"It's *not* moot," I said. "And you could have stopped the kidnapping attempt, but you chose to allow it to happen." I turned to Hasid. "Yes?"

"Yes," Hasid said. "I didn't mind. I was getting paid twice and I didn't have to kill anyone."

I nodded and turned back to Bridgers. "Even if Jordi started it, you decided to go through with it. You are responsible. So you can tell us what you wanted the information for."

Bridgers calmly tried to stare me down for a moment, which was not particularly successful. Then he did a little shrug. "This new understanding of skip physics is important. On the positive side, its ability to transport ships and large space stations to universes where none of us exist solves the fundamental problem of why we all fight each other at all. There now exists the potential for infinite real estate. Not just for us. Not just for Earth. But every species."

He motioned to Jordi. "But then there is the fact that the very first thing the Consu thought to do with it was to make a weapon out of it. Jordi isn't wrong about wanting to know more about how this all works, and if it can be stopped or defended against. This isn't just a weapon. It is *the* weapon. A planet-killer. A civilization destroyer. An existential threat on a scale that none of us have seen before."

Bridgers learned forward, setting his arms on the table, and pointed to me. "So, yes. We weren't the ones to initiate this plan to pull information off the disk, if there is any information on the disk to pull. But once it was in motion, there was no reason to stop it, and lots of reasons to do it. Right now, apparently only one Consu knows and understands the entire scope of this new physics. What a coup if we can have that same knowledge, before the rest of the Consu do. What a prize if we can use it to keep humanity safe from their interference forever."

"By leaving this universe or by ending the Consu?" Dad asked.

"Right now, I have a definite preference," Jordi said.

"I don't share his preference," Bridgers said, of Jordi. "But I understand it. More than that, I can sympathize with it. The goal of the Colonial Defense Forces is and always has been to make space in the universe for humanity. The Consu, or some part of it, has tried to wipe billions of us from existence, for their own religious purposes. If the Consu are going to continue down this road, and make it them or us, then I want the weapons to give us a fighting chance." Bridgers looked back to me. "And that was worth a little light kidnapping, Ms. Trujillo."

I narrowed my eyes at Bridgers and then looked back at Hasid, who looked horrified at all of this. "Didn't know what you were getting yourself into, did you?" I asked.

"Look, I have child support," Hasid said. "I was just trying to get paid."

Before I could say anything to that the PDAs of Mbalenhle, Bridgers and Dad all went off with a strident blare, which could not have been good. Also not good: the fact that when each of them was done reading what was on their PDA, they all looked at me.

"Let me guess," I said. "The Consu are here."

"Yes," Dad said.

"How many of them are there?"

Bridgers looked at his PDA again. "Apparently, all of them."

TWENTY-TWO

When the counting was done there were seven hundred thirty-two Consu ships that appeared in Phoenix space, which seemed overkill to me—I was there to meet a single Consu, there only had to be one—but I was not consulted, and the Consu never were subtle about anything.

Seven hundred and thirty-two was more ships, by a couple hundred, than all the other ships, Colonial Union or otherwise, currently in Phoenix space. Both the Colonial Union's civil and military leadership put a stop order into place for new ships coming to Phoenix. They were hopeful the Consu were not there to pick a fight, but they didn't need anyone coming into the system, freaking out, and opening fire.

Within an hour of arrival, the Consu violated Phoenix territorial space, brought a ship down to Phoenix City, and without permission or explanation took Bacon and the command center it was in back up into space. As it became clear where their retrieval ship was heading, a citywide alert was flashed on every PDA, and the State Department specifically ordered any staff still at work or on the night shift to go inside and head to designated shelter zones.

I ignored this, as did Ran, both of us heading from my office, where I had gone after the emergency meeting broke up, back to the quad. We were stopped by security who were blocking off the quad to keep people like me from getting in the way.

From where I was, I could see the command module being hoisted into the retrieval ship, and the retrieval ship then lifting up toward the sky.

"God damn it, I needed that thing!" I yelled to the retreating ship.

"I don't think they can hear you," Ran said.

"Thank you, Ran, I was aware of that," I said to it.

My PDA made a noise and let me know I was getting a call from Diplomatic Security.

"Yes?"

"Ms. Trujillo, this is Agent Weir. There is a Consu here on the steps of the Bainburger asking for you by name."

Did they leave Bacon behind? I thought to myself. "I'm being blocked by security," I told Weir.

"Give me a second and I'll have you let through."

"Me and my assistant both," I said, and disconnected. I looked over to Ran. "Things are getting complicated."

"Things were already complicated," Ran replied.

We were let through and made our way to the steps of the Bainburger, where, indeed, a lone Consu was standing at the foot of the steps, flanked by Diplomatic Security.

One of them broke off and came up to me and introduced himself as Weir. "What would you like us to do?" he asked.

"I want you to back your people way the hell up and let me talk to this Consu as privately as possible."

"Is that going to be safe for you?"

"If it's not there's not much you're going to be able to do about it," I said. "But I don't think that's what this Consu is here for."

"What is it here for?"

"It's a messenger," Ran said.

The security moved back to a cautious distance, and I approached the Consu. It wasn't Bacon—I could see that much. It looked older and more distressed, and very little about it radiated the condescending superiority one usually got from the Consu.

I knew what this was about. "You're a criminal," I said, to the Consu.

"I am a criminal," the Consu intoned. "I have disgraced myself before all Consu and therefore lower myself to speak to you."

I knew that from this point there would be a lot of intonation about how it was unworthy and we lower species were unworthy and it was speaking my unworthy language so we could have a conversation because we were unworthy together, but I didn't have time for that. "I don't want to minimize your plight," I said, interrupting its spiel, "but I have to tell you I have already spoken to noncriminal Consu. Two of them. And apparently I am supposed to speak to another."

"It is for that reason I am here," the Consu said. "I ask you now to show me the—" And here was a bone-rattler of a noise.

"That is the disk," Ran said to me, helpfully.

"Have you been able to speak Consu this whole time?" I asked it.

"I know a little," Ran said. "We Obin all know a little."

I shelved this side conversation, reached into my pocket, retrieved the disk and presented it to the Consu.

It shrieked and ran up on me, coming close to examine it with its own eyes. I tried mightily not to flinch and may have failed.

"Here," I said. "Take it."

The Consu shrieked again and drew back. "I cannot," it said. "I am not worthy to hold it. You are not worthy, and yet you hold it. This is forbidden. A heresy. And yet you hold it."

"Yes, I hold it and I am unworthy and unclean and all of that," I said. "I get it."

"Do not mock this," the Consu said. "You do not understand the thing you hold."

"No, I don't," I admitted. "So why don't you tell me."

"It is not my role to tell you," the Consu said. "I was sent only to confirm you held it and it accepted you as its bearer."

"All right, you confirmed it. Now what?"

"You will be summoned." The Consu glanced toward Ran, and then back toward me, and I wondered what that glance was about. "You will be summoned," it repeated.

"When?"

"When it serves the purposes of those who are summoning you," the Consu said. "You will travel to your Phoenix Station to wait until then. You must be ready to answer the summons when it comes, and we will not pollute ourselves to visit this planet again."

"Rude," I said.

"We do not visit your planets other than to purify them," the Consu said. "If we land here again, that will be our intention."

"Got it," I said. "Phoenix Station it is."

The Consu looked back to Ran and said something in Consu to it, with a noise like metal crashing. I didn't have my PDA with me, because by habit I left it in my office, so I had no idea what they said to Ran. Ran responded, in Obin, and again I was in the dark. I didn't like that at all.

The Consu returned its attention to me. "I have completed my task. No more is required of me."

"What now?" I asked it.

"Now I move on," the Consu said, stepped farther back from me, and erupted into flames that burned with the intensity of white phosphorus. Ran grabbed me and turned me away from the pyre that used to be a living creature, possibly saving my vision in the process. I blinked hard, eyes watering, hoping the afterimages glaring in my retinas didn't become permanent.

When I finally got my vision back there was nothing left of the Consu but a pile of ash and what was likely a permanent stain at the foot of the Bainburger Tower steps.

"Christ," I muttered to myself, backing away and waving off the security people who were coming to check on me. "Why do they have to do everything in the most dramatic way possible?"

"It is their nature," Ran said.

"They could use a better nature."

"They understand that," Ran said. "That is why they made us."

"That's one way of looking at it," I said. "What did the Consu say to you?"

"It said that the Consu could not tolerate that I had access to their work and that I had been marked for death."

"You said something back to that."

"I said that I had already been given a death sentence by another Consu, so they would have to get in line."

I blinked, this time in amazement. "You actually said that?"

"Was it not the correct thing to say?"

"No, it's factually accurate," I said. "It's that it's also, so . . . *sassy*."

"I am sassier in my own tongue," Ran said, very seriously.

I fished out the disk. "You knew what this was all the time," I said. "You knew their name for it."

"We know the name for it," Ran said. "We know little else about it. Us knowing the name for it is like knowing the word 'cat.' It speaks nothing to the character of the individual animal."

"You keep not telling me things, Ran."

"I did not mean to hide that from you. And I told you as soon as it was relevant."

"I'm not sure I like this 'when it's relevant' metric."

"You also don't like when I keep going on about things that have no relevance," Ran pointed out.

"You have me there," I admitted.

"If you like I can tell you random Consu facts at irregular intervals."

I laughed at this.

"I did not mean that as a joke," Ran said.

"I'm well aware of that, Ran," I said. "That's why it's funny."

"I do promise to tell you things when you need to know them," Ran said to me.

"Thank you, Ran," I said. "What do I need to know now?"

"How and when you are going to get to Phoenix Station."

That part, at least, was not difficult. I traveled to Phoenix Station on a military transport arranged by Colonel Bridgers, who would never be accused of kidnapping me because it was all an official surveillance mission, which I did not love but did not have time to think about right now, and I was put up in the Phoenix Station Grand Hotel by the State Department, because we didn't know how long it would take for me to be summoned or what that summoning would look like, and I couldn't camp out on station benches until then.

Don't be fooled by the name; the Grand was the oldest and most run-down of all the Phoenix Station civilian hotels, and my room was cramped and small and smelled vaguely of cheese, which couldn't have been good. Government service was doing us all proud.

"You remember the first time we were here," Dad said to me. We were in the Grand's lobby bar, with our respective drinks. He had accompanied me to the station and would be there for a few days, attending to business of his own. Ran, who had also traveled with us, was off running its own errands. "The station, not this bar."

"I knew what you meant," I said to Dad. "When we arrived to head off to Roanoke. Although *you* had been here before."

"Many times," Dad said. He'd been a representative for Erie in the Colonial Union government, and Phoenix Station was where every ship arrived. "It was still different when we had a colony of our own, though. And it was interesting to see Phoenix Station through your eyes."

"Then you'll remember that my eyes thought it was boring as hell," I said. "If I hadn't met Zoë when I did I probably would have gotten arrested for minor vandalism just to have something to do."

"You never had the same appreciation for all of this that I do," Dad said.

"No, Dad, I don't," I confessed. "And at this point I wonder why you do."

Dad frowned. "What does that mean?"

"What I mean, Dad, is that you have been directly involved in the formation of two colonies, Roanoke and Unity, and both of them have been disasters to one degree or another."

"Oh, well, I wouldn't say that's true," Dad said.

I looked at him levelly.

"They weren't disasters because of me," Dad amended.

"Maybe not, but no offense, Dad, that doesn't mean all that much," I said. "Roanoke was almost wiped off the face of the universe, twice, and while we're here in the bar with our drinks"—I jiggled my glass, causing the ice in it to tinkle against the sides—"the people of Unity Colony are on the verge of starvation or worse."

"You're saying I should give up the colonizing business."

"I'm saying I wonder why it matters so much to you at all."

Dad looked into his glass for a couple of moments, possibly trying to see if the words he wanted to say were in there. "With Roanoke, it was ego," he said, eventually. "I liked the idea of bucking the established order of things, of saying that we needed to form colonies with our own people instead of farming Earth for them. I was right about that"—Dad looked over at me significantly for this—"but I was right for the wrong reasons. I didn't actually care much about what we were doing to Earth. It was monstrous, but it was beside the point for me. I was doing it because it gave me a cause, and attention and some little bit of power. And there was also the idea that I might be remembered for founding a colony and being the father of an entire new planet."

"You're not kidding about the ego," I said.

"You're not actually surprised, are you?" Dad asked.

"Not at *all*," I said, and Dad smiled at this. "I just didn't know if you would ever admit it to yourself."

"Enough time has passed," Dad said. "And Roanoke is still there."

"Not that you're thought of as the founder."

"That fucking movie," Dad groused, and took a sip of his drink.

"So that's Roanoke," I said. "What about Unity?"

"That wasn't about ego," Dad said, and then caught my look. "Don't give me that side-eye. The Tripartite Agreement has given us détente and trade, but it hasn't given us real peace.

We're on a collision course with the Conclave, and they're bigger, and everyone knows it. We need to find a way to live with them before they roll over us. We're mean, but there are more of them."

"Did you think Unity was going to work?" I asked.

Dad shrugged. "Maybe? I wanted it to, and everyone else was at least willing to give it a try. If nothing else, it kicked the problem a few more years down the road."

"Until the Consu got involved."

"Yes. Until the Consu got involved." Dad raised his glass. "To the Consu. Always making a mess where they're not wanted."

"Why, Dad," I admonished. "They're only doing it to perfect us."

"I'm perfect already," Dad said.

"There's that ego again."

"Nah. Just truth." Dad took another sip, and then looked up and behind me. I craned my head back and saw Ran.

"You're doing that lurking thing again, Ran," I said.

"I'm not lurking," it said. "I have come to collect you. It's time."

"Right now?"

"A shuttle was seen leaving one of the larger Consu ships. It's heading here."

"Any notifications or directions from the Consu at all?"

"No."

"Of course not," I said. "That would be polite. How long until the shuttle arrives?"

"It will be here in less than ten minutes."

I held up my glass. "But I just got a drink."

"Chug it," Ran said.

TWENTY-THREE

The shuttle was clean and sparse and had nothing in it other than a space for me to stand in, and once I entered it, it immediately closed behind me, not allowing Ran or anyone else to follow. This shuttle was meant, clearly, for me and for me alone. I stared back at Ran and Dad, and then the station doors closed behind me as well, sealing them off from the vacuum of space as my shuttle disengaged from the station and headed toward the Consu ship.

The Consu ship the shuttle aimed itself toward was unremarkable in construction; it could have been the ship of any intelligent race. I suppose when you're the superior beings in this neck of the galaxy, you can move around in a cardboard box if you want. You don't need to impress anyone.

The shuttle moved toward the ship and a portal irised open, allowing the shuttle inside, irising closed behind it. The shuttle landed on the floor of the bay, and the doors opened to let me out. This was clearly my stop.

I exited out of my clean and sparse shuttle to an equally spare and clean bay with only one other thing in it aside from my shuttle: Kitty's command module, unsealed and open to entry. I began walking toward it and stopped when a door opened and two Consu came toward me. When they got to me, one of them unfolded and reached out one of its inner hands, motioning as if telling me, *Give me.*

I understood what it meant and offered it the cobalt blue disk. It took the disk without any visible pain, which meant it was the Consu I had been meant to meet. It then immediately left with the disk, which surprised me. As I went to follow, the other Consu stepped in front of me and unfolded slightly, clearly warning me to stay where I was.

I stood, unhappily, for roughly a half hour, and then the door opened once more and what looked like the same Consu returned and came up to me. "You are Gretchen Trujillo," it said, in an exceedingly pleasant speaking voice.

"I am," I said. "May I ask your name?"

"It is"—and here was a screech that could have made a banshee envious—"but I doubt you will be able to vocalize it. I understand that you gave my child and its former partner names in your own language, did you not?"

"I did."

"Not . . . very serious names."

"No," I said, because why lie at this point in the game? "They both irritated me by not offering their names, so I gave them stupid names that reflected my irritation."

"Very well," the Consu said. "You may also give me a stupid name."

"Oh," I said. "I would rather not."

"Why not?"

"You haven't irritated me yet."

"I promise you that I will, in time."

"I would rather not."

"Please."

"*Fine*," I said. "Your name is Fluffy."

"That is a very unserious name."

"I *know*. That's what you asked for."

"So I did." Fluffy held up the blue disk. "Do you understand what this is?"

"Not a bit," I said. "I know it's important enough that you had to receive me to get it, and now that you have it, it's important enough that you have denigrated yourself to speak my language and treat me without contempt, which is more than either... Kitty or Bacon did. But what it is and what it means, I have no idea."

"The closest thing your culture might have to what this is would be a will," Fluffy said. "Instructions for the disposition of one's legal affairs and physical objects. That is correct?"

"That's what a will is, yes."

"You will forgive me if I am not exact. I only just now subsumed the contextual map for humans between the time you gave me this"—it motioned with the disk, slightly—"and now. There will still be gaps and misunderstandings as it settles in."

"That's fine," I said. "And also, I have no idea what you're talking about."

"It doesn't matter at the moment, other than it is what allows us to have this conversation and for me to treat you with the respect accorded to you."

"Thank you," I said.

"So." Fluffy wiggled the disk again. "Like a will. Except that your concept of 'will' is only a fraction of what this represents. What is recorded here is a life command and demand, which can only be offered once, when the individual making it has abandoned all plans for its own future and everything it ever was or intended to be. The obligations it presents cannot, by our laws and customs, be ignored or left unfulfilled by those it encompasses."

"Can't or won't?" I asked.

"I understand how that is a reasonable question for you," Fluffy said. "For us, it is not. The horror of leaving such a command unfulfilled when one has the capability to honor it is existential for us. It is a compulsion unto death."

"So our friend Kitty has left you an unrefusable command."

"In short, yes. You understand that Kitty was, indeed, my friend at one time?"

"I do."

"And, like 'will' being less than a perfect analogue, so is 'friend' here. It's better to say that our lives were formally bonded together in a way that transcends mere acquaintance and companionship."

"I thought Kitty was Bacon's partner."

"Yes. Again the concepts are not quite the same and difficult to make approximations to. If your brain were more advanced we could graft a contextual map onto it and then in a few moments you would understand perfectly. But we have to make do with words because your brain is not nearly advanced enough. No offense."

"None taken," I said, although I did in fact take more than a little offense.

"Suffice to say Kitty and I were very close, and even with the rupture of our relationship it would make sense that they would burden me with these responsibilities." Fluffy wiggled the disk, and then offered it to me. I took it. "But it was not only me to whom responsibilities were given."

"What do you mean?" I asked.

Fluffy motioned to the other Consu in the bay, the one who had stopped me from following Fluffy when it first left. "My colleague here. Who also has a name you cannot pronounce, but you must call it something, so I will suggest the name 'Goober.' Is that sufficiently unserious?"

"Absolutely unserious," I assured it.

"Thank you. Do you know why Goober is here?"

"It stopped me from following you when you took the disk," I said. "So I assume it is your security detachment."

"Goober was here to kill you."

"Excuse me?" I said, looking at Goober, who, because apparently it had not downloaded a context map or whatever, was not following the conversation and probably had no idea it was being discussed.

"No one who is not a Consu has ever been given the responsibility of that 'disk,' as you call it. The idea that one had is an insult to our species. If there had not been instructions otherwise, once I had read it and committed myself to its dictates, Goober here would have taken your head."

"It could have tried," I said. "That wouldn't have ended well for it."

"I am aware that you have fought and killed Consu before," Fluffy said. "Ones who I knew, I will have you know, as I assigned them to retrieve Kitty once its location became known to us again. The circumstances then were very different to now. We would not have allowed you time to respond."

"Well," I said, after a moment. "This certainly puts a damper on our relationship."

"You are safe now," Fluffy said.

"Because of what was said on this," I said, holding up the disk.

"Precisely so. Kitty did not share with you what it placed on there?"

"It said nothing to me other than I had to deliver a message to you, and then gave me the disk. I assumed all that was on it was a message to you. There was never any mention of something for me. What I'm supposed to get out of it is bringing Unity Colony back here."

"And that was all Kitty shared with you."

"That was the deal we made, yes."

"Interesting," Fluffy said. It turned to Goober and offered metal screeches. Goober made a movement that I translated as expressing surprise, and then both of them looked at me in a way that could have been either curious or predatory, depending.

"You two are freaking me out a little," I said.

"You do not need to be afraid," Fluffy said to me.

"You said that before, and yet here we are with me being afraid."

"Let me put it another way," Fluffy said. "You do not need to be afraid of us because we do not without purpose kill one of our own."

"That's great," I said. "The problem is, I'm not one of you."

Fluffy pointed to the disk in my hand. "That's not what this says."

I narrowed my eyes at the Consu. "Fucking what?"

"Kitty has commanded that everything they have and are is yours now and has specifically bequeathed to you its identity and burdens. This is its right and its responsibility, a thing that is not obligated as a dying directive, but once made, cannot be ignored. You are now its"—here was an untranslatable screech—"which you may understand to be 'heir,' but which means something significantly more, because it incorporates Kitty's legal and existential identity. In a very real sense to us, you are now Kitty. And as you are, you are now also Consu."

I stared. "Bullshit."

"If it were bullshit, as you say, you would already be dead."

"I'm *not* Consu," I said.

"I would not have given you the honor myself," Fluffy said. "And yet Kitty did, and its choice in the matter is not to be gainsaid. You are Consu."

I held out my hands. "Do you see any slashing arms here? Do you see a carapace? You can check my DNA if you like. We are nowhere near the same species."

Fluffy regarded me. "What do you think 'Consu' means?" it said.

I waved at the two Consu in front of me. "Obviously."

"Consu does not refer to our *species*," Fluffy said, and made a noise that might have sounded like "Consu" if it had been scraped out by colliding shuttles. "That is our word for it. It means 'those who understand.' It can signify any who are far enough on the road to perfection to earn the title. Our species are Consu. But others could be as well. Others should be. That is why we set ourselves upon other species. So they can be perfected, and in being perfected, become Consu."

I rubbed my temples and squatted. "My head hurts."

"You are learning a lot suddenly and your intellect is small, so this is understandable."

"Thanks for that," I said, sarcastically.

"I don't mean to belittle you," Fluffy said. "I am trying to be sympathetic to your plight."

"I believe you," I said. "Thank you. Sincerely."

"For what it is worth, this is both exceptional and unfair to you," Fluffy said. "Exceptional in that a Consu extending its imprimatur onto someone outside of our own species has never happened before. Unfair because—and again, this is no offense to you—this is a status you are not in the least prepared for, or deserving of."

"Well, you're not wrong about that," I said. "I think I might throw up."

"It is permitted," Fluffy said.

I didn't vomit. I (eventually) stood up instead. "Look, I appreciate that you honor this fiction enough that you haven't ordered Goober here to slice me up into steaks. And I accept that Kitty made me its heir for some reason. To the extent that it helps me get my people home, I will take it, and gladly. But you have to believe me when I tell you that Kitty treated me with nothing more than polite contempt at best. It didn't like me. It tolerated me only a little more than Bacon did, and *Bacon* hated my guts and would have killed me if it could have. Kitty only tolerated me because I was useful. Nothing more or less."

"I believe this," Fluffy said.

"Good. Then you'll believe me when I say that there is no universe, this one or the one my people are currently in, where this *boon* was offered to me as a kindness. So, please, tell me why Kitty would do this to me."

"Did Kitty explain the great philosophical argument roiling all of the Consu?"

"The one where you're debating whether to kill us all fast or slow? Yes, I know about that one. And I know you are the architect of the 'kill us all fast' plan."

"I wouldn't characterize it like that."

"I don't know, murdering a whole planet of people by chucking an asteroid at it that also has people on it seems like you're in a hurry, if you ask me."

Fluffy took this interruption with grace. "As you say. Kitty and I have found ourselves on opposite sides of this argument, even though, for the longest time they pretended to be on our side. Our child Bacon suggests that was so we would use our resources to develop Kitty's skip physics designs, and I would agree with that."

"All right, and?"

"The philosophical argument among the Consu will likely continue for some time, but Kitty has proposed the practical argument between the two of us come to an end. As Kitty's heir, you bear the burden of their proposal and their argument. If you win it, then all the designs for equipment that accommodate their new understanding of skip physics become yours, to dispose of how you will. If I win the argument, then all of Kitty's work and notes on the new skip drive are mine. They are encoded on the disk for me to access in this eventuality."

"And just how do we settle this argument?" I asked, although I had a sinking feeling I already knew.

"We fight each other to the death, obviously," Fluffy said.

I nodded. "Of course."

"You have fought our kind before."

"It doesn't mean I was itching to do it again anytime soon."

"You are obligated as heir."

"Am I? You said it yourself: I am nowhere close to being perfected. I'm not under the same compulsion to take on this fight."

"So you would forfeit?"

"What if I did?" I asked. "What would happen then?"

"It has literally never happened."

I made a *ta-da* motion. "I have literally never happened before either, so here we are."

"I would argue—and I will argue—that if you forfeit then it is the same as if I won. I would have access to the new physics understanding, and my philosophical position would be bolstered among other Consu."

"So, all in on the 'kill you all faster' theory of perfection."

"Yes. There would be the problem that you would need to be dead for me to access the data."

I glanced over at Goober. "So if we fight, then I might die. If I forfeit, I will definitely die."

"Yes."

"Unless I run and you never find me."

"That would be unfortunate for humans," Fluffy said, and let that hang in the air for a good long while.

"Well, *fuck*," I said, finally.

"Will you forfeit?" Fluffy asked.

"Clearly I won't."

"I did not think you would," Fluffy said. "A Consu never would."

"I'm not doing it for the reasons a Consu would," I said.

"For a Consu, what you do is more important than why you do it," Fluffy said. "Take Kitty as an example. The fact it is attempting a full closure to its life experience is more important than the fact that it is using you to do so."

"Well, you were right about one thing," I said. "You really have irritated the shit out of me."

"It was inevitable as soon as I understood the scope of Kitty's demands. If you were not now Consu, it wouldn't matter. But you are, and so it does. And for that, I am sorry."

The construction of this particular apology made me want to break things, so I changed the subject. "How do we do this? I've never fought a duel before."

"This is a Consu matter; it should take place among Consu," Fluffy said.

I looked around. "So, here."

"If you wish."

"And what do we do for weapons?"

Fluffy raised its slashing arms. "Traditionally we fight with these," it said. "We will provide you weapons to offer you a matching capability. You will be able to choose from any weapon we have available."

"When?"

"You are the one with a timetable," Fluffy said. "How long can your friends at Unity Colony survive without your intercession?"

"That was low."

"I did not mean to be disrespectful," Fluffy said.

"I'll need a couple of days to prepare," I said.

"Signal us when you are ready. You are Consu. We will respond."

I nodded and started walking back to the shuttle, to go back to Phoenix Station. Halfway there, I turned. "You don't seem upset," I said to Fluffy.

"About what?"

"The idea that in a couple of days you will have to fight to the death with me."

"Your species and mine think about death very differently," Fluffy said. "We do not fear death. We fear a death with disorder. Kitty's demands offer me a death with meaning. A death with order. A death that brings me closer to perfection. I am not unmoved that Kitty would offer me such a death."

"Yes, well," I said. "I think about it a little differently."

"I know you do," Fluffy said. "Give yourself time to make your peace with it. Then come back here. I will give you an honorable death, Gretchen Trujillo."

There was nothing I could say to that, so I left.

TWENTY-FOUR

"You had to name it Fluffy," Dad said to me in the debriefing when I returned to Phoenix Station.

"It fucking *made* me do it, okay," I said. "I didn't *want* to."

"What I'm hearing from this is that the information we wanted to find on the disk was there," Colonel Bridgers said. "All the math and information for the new understanding of skip drives."

"One, the information would have been inaccessible to you because the format it's encoded in isn't like anything we have," I said. "Fluffy talked about 'context webs,' which sounded like all the information presented to the brain at once. You need a Consu brain to unlock it. That's nothing like we do."

"Don't be too sure about that," Bridgers said. "Our Special Forces have something similar. We call it 'unpacking.'"

"Two," I continued, "the information is keyed to Fluffy specifically. I couldn't access it. I couldn't access anything, and apparently that disk is keyed to me directly." Bridgers opened his mouth to respond to this, so I rushed in. "Three, why are you here talking at all? You tried to have me kidnapped. Fuck off."

"It's a little late to change horses here," Bridgers said, to me.

I turned to Zawadi Mbalenhle, who had made the journey up to Phoenix Station for the debriefing. "He goes or I go," I said.

"Thank you, Colonel Bridgers, that will be all," Mbalenhle said. Bridgers sat there for a moment, disbelieving, and then got up and left, wordlessly. "He'll still want a report," Mbalenhle said to me after he left.

"Give him a report," I said. "If he comes near me again, I'll break his nose."

"He's CDF," Mbalenhle reminded me.

"Yeah, but I'm *really* pissed right now."

"You're confident that we couldn't have gotten anything off the disk," Dad said.

"Not unless you're Fluffy," I said. "And not unless I'm dead."

"Will you be able to get anything off the disk if you kill Fluffy?" Mbalenhle asked.

"That wasn't the deal I had with Kitty, and even if the disk unlocked any information for me, I don't know how we access it. Do we even have tools for that?"

"The person who could answer that was Colonel Bridgers," Mbalenhle observed.

"When we got the technology from the Consu on Roanoke to fight the Conclave it was already packaged for us," Dad said. "And as far as I know every other time we got tech from them it was the same way, or we stole it from another species, and they had it already translated for them."

"What about your Obin friend?" Mbalenhle asked. "It was given direct access to Consu technology."

"Extremely limited access," I said. "The equivalent of being given a two-use key to press a button. And then the key explodes after the second use."

"Ran is taking the prospect of its death very well," Dad said.

"Ran is Obin," I said. "They don't fear death unless they have their consciousness turned on, and even then it doesn't bother them much. It doesn't bother the Consu either, or at least they pretend that it doesn't. I think at this point only we really get worked up about it."

"What do they know we don't?" Dad asked.

"Our problem is we know too much," I said.

"And what about you?" Mbalenhle asked. "You're going to be fighting for your life soon, without any real choice in the matter."

I looked at her and then at Dad, who I know was being far more stoic about it than he actually felt. "You know what, ask me that one later," I said.

"All right," Mbalenhle said. "Then a practical question. What can we do to help you prepare?"

"Find me a gym here on the station that I can use," I said. "One with lots of padding."

Ran slammed me down onto the mat, again. "You're dead," it said, again.

"Christ," I said, picking myself back up. "I liked it better when you took it easy on me, before I knew you could kick my ass any time you wanted to."

"I did that to keep you motivated," Ran said. "You don't need that motivation now."

"No," I agreed. "The threat of dying and stranding fifty thousand people in a hostile universe is motivation enough."

"Then let's begin again," Ran said. "Remember that I am using my arms to slash as the Consu will. You will need to find a way inside the arms to get at its brain."

"That's not how I did it last time," I said.

"The Consu are unlikely to turn off the gravity to give you an advantage," Ran said, and motioned for me to get up. "Again."

Twenty seconds later I was on the ground once more. "You are dead," Ran said. "Would you like to try again?"

"Let me be dead for a little while first," I said, breathing hard.

Ran collapsed onto the floor next to me.

"Thank you for that," I said.

"For what?" Ran asked.

"For pretending that you are tired out, too."

"I am tired," Ran said. "It has been a while since we have had one of these matches."

"Well, you know," I said to Ran. "We've been busy hopping between universes and fighting Consu and trying to find lost colonies and then finding ways to bring them back."

"We have been active," Ran agreed.

I laughed at the understatement and turned to face my assistant and bodyguard. "Thank you, Ran," I said.

"You're welcome," Ran said. "What are you thanking me for?"

"For all of it," I said. "For being my assistant. For being my bodyguard. For being socially awkward in funny ways. For being the one person I can always rely on, even if you don't tell me things until it occurs to you that they might be useful."

"Ah," Ran said. "And I thank you for being an interesting boss. For helping me understand emotions. For telling me kindly when I am too much. And for not being angry when I don't tell you everything yet."

I reached out and put my hand on its arm. "You're welcome, Ran." I withdrew my hand and sat up. "All right, come on. If this is the last time we ever do this, I want to win at least one round."

"You'll win your fight and we'll do this again when we get back," Ran said, picking itself up off the mat.

I looked up at it. "What?"

"What?"

"That thing you just said," I said. "Say it again."

"You'll win your fight."

"Yes, and *then* you said what again?"

"That we'll do this . . . oh," Ran said. "I hear what I did there."

I stood up. "That wasn't just a slip of the tongue, was it?"

Ran stood there quietly for a moment, and then said, "Remember that you just said you like me even when I don't tell you things," it said.

I gave Ran a hug so hard it squeaked. "Now," I said, after I released the hug. "Tell me what the hell you meant by that, or I'll kill you myself."

"Please do not be angry with Ran," Deputy Ambassador Clock said to me, in a secure conference room on Phoenix Station. Clock had come up immediately once Ran had its slipup. Ran begged me to wait for a full explanation until Clock could arrive. "Ran was under my orders not to reveal this information to anyone outside of the Obin embassy."

I looked over at Ran and then back at Clock. "Why is that?" I asked. "Am I not trusted?"

"*You* are trusted," Clock said. "Others you have met with are not."

I thought of Colonel Bridgers and nodded at this. "Go on," I said.

"The Consu you have named Kitty reordered a significant section of Ran's brain in order to use it in conjunction with the Consu's command module—what you were calling the prism. It was able to do this because of the resemblance between the Obin brain and the supplementary brains that the Consu have now incorporated into their bodies."

"Yes," I said. "I know this part."

"I understand it was your initiative that allowed us to finally learn more about the Consu brains," Clock said.

"I was pushy," I agreed.

"Thank you for that."

"You're welcome, but get to the parts that I don't know, please."

"In order to program Ran's brain, the Consu needed an interface to access it," Clock continued.

"Yes," I said. "The consciousness harness."

"We believe the Consu considered the harness relatively rudimentary, and also we suspect that it was focused on the very specific task of sending you back here to engage in your fight with the Consu you've named Fluffy. In doing so, Kitty the Consu made an error."

"What was the error?"

"Ignorance," Ran said. "Or arrogance."

"The Consu was either unaware or didn't care that while it was using the consciousness harness as an interface, the harness was also storing all of its action into a cache," Clock said. "This cache is one Obin use to store events and emotions of their day, so they may come back to them at a later time for more detailed processing."

I turned to Ran. "You store up your favorite bits of a day?"

"From time to time, yes," Ran said. "Or the parts where I made mistakes and I replay them so I don't make the same mistake again."

"On one hand, helpful; on the other hand, I wouldn't want to relive my embarrassing moments."

"I've recorded some of yours that I have been around for," Ran said. "They were useful to remind me that even people experienced with emotions still embarrass themselves."

"Well," I said. "Glad to be useful."

"You truly are," Ran said, much too cheerfully for me to be happy about.

"Please continue," I said to Clock.

"When Ran realized his cache had stored the Consu's actions, it sequestered the cache and turned off new caching to keep it from being overwritten. When it returned to this universe, we downloaded the cache and examined it to see if the programming was operable from within the consciousness harness itself. It was."

I looked at Ran. "You can run the return trip from your harness?"

"Yes."

"So this means your brain won't explode when we go back?"

"It was never going to explode," Ran said. "The neural pathways in my brain would denature and become inactive."

"Ran."

"I understand, however, that you are speaking metaphorically," Ran continued. "So in that context, no. My brain will no longer explode."

I burst into tears. Clock looked over at Ran.

"Crying can also mean happiness," Ran said to Clock. "It does not mean she is upset that my brain won't explode."

"Thank you for the clarification."

"Crying is tricky," Ran informed Clock.

"I'm sorry," I said, trying to put myself back together, and not quite managing.

"You care for Ran," Clock said, after watching me sob for a few minutes.

"Of course I do," I said, wiping away my tears. "It's my friend. It has cared for me and protected me and fought with me. I'm as close to Ran now as anyone I know."

"Except your cat," Ran said.

"Fine, except for my cat," I allowed.

"And your father," Ran continued. "And also now Magdy, whom you have resumed having sex with."

"Ran!"

"I'm sorry, that was not germane to the discussion," Ran said.

"It's not, and also how did you know?" I asked.

"You smile when you think of him," Ran said. "You're not aware that you do it, but I notice. See, like that," Ran said, pointing.

"You're not wrong," I said, and had an emotionally confusing moment of smiling for one person I cared for, and weeping with relief for another. "The point is, yes. I care for Ran. Very much."

"If you like we can pause so you may weep more," Clock said.

"I'm fine. Please continue."

"Once we realized that Ran did not have to endanger itself for the return journey, we resolved that it made sense not to share that information. You, Ms. Trujillo, were to be told only at the last minute, because your cooperation would be required to continue the subterfuge that Ran was dead."

"You didn't want Kitty to know you bypassed the brain programming."

"Correct. Ran would feign death, be securely placed in a morgue or other holding area, and when Unity Colony was returned and Kitty allowed to continue its death journey, Ran would return to duty to you, unharmed."

"And that's it," I said.

"Yes."

"But . . . that's *not* it, is it?"

"I don't understand," Clock said.

"Yes, you do," I said. "You downloaded the cache or programming. You have Ran's brain, intact. You have a basic working model of the physics involved to revolutionize skip drives in this universe. You have the key that the Consu themselves don't have."

"Unless you die," Ran said.

"Yes, thank you, Ran, that was a qualification I was hoping was implied."

"You are training to battle this Consu you are calling 'Fluffy'?" Clock asked.

"I am. With Ran, in fact."

"How is she doing?" Clock asked Ran.

"Badly," Ran said.

"That is unfortunate," Clock replied. "The sect this Fluffy belongs to will use this information to spark a war."

"And what will *you* do with it?" I asked Clock.

"We don't wish a war with anyone," Clock said.

"You say that now," I said. "But anyone who has it will eventually be tempted. Colonel Bridgers went right to it in one of our meetings. Mateu Jordi from Earth was thinking about it, too. That's two for two for humans going directly for weaponization."

"We are not humans," Clock said.

"No, but your history isn't any better than ours," I said. "Obin are merciless in battle. You wage total war. Your history is complete with absolute atrocities that you've performed because you've lacked consciousness and mercy. You have consciousness now, but you can turn that shit off any time you like. Don't pretend this technology is any safer with you than it is with humans. Don't pretend it's safe with anyone. We're all too fond of war and real estate."

"What do you propose?" Clock said.

"First of all, I need not to lose my duel to the death with Fluffy," I said, and grabbed my head. "Oh, God, *why* did I start naming them such stupid names?"

"I will do all I can to train you," Ran said. "I will do everything I can to help you win."

"Thank you, Ran," I said. "I know you will."

"This is what you do," Ran said. "You surprise your opponents. You don't give them time to think. You don't play fair. I've seen you do it. I've helped you do it."

"Yes, you have," I said, and thought about it for a moment. Ran and Clock waited for me while I thought. "Ran," I said, eventually.

"Yes?"

"I have a question for you."

"The answer is yes."

"You don't know what the question is," I said.

"I know my answer is yes nevertheless," Ran said. "But please tell me the question."

"I just wanted to know if you'd be my date to my duel."

"I would be honored," Ran said.

"Good," I said. I turned to Clock. "And now I have a question for you, and I'm hoping that you are going to say yes, too."

TWENTY-FIVE

Two more days of training and planning with Ran, and then I was as prepared as I was going to be. As a Consu, courtesy or otherwise, I was allowed to bring Ran with me as my support staff and coach. I was allowed to bring no one else, which meant that once again I was leaving my father at the shuttle gate. He gave me a fierce hug and a kiss on the cheek, said "So proud," and then walked away without turning back. Ran and I stepped into the shuttle, let the doors close behind us, and then stood companionably next to each other for the entire trip to the Consu ship.

The ship swallowed our shuttle, the doors opened again when we landed, and Ran and I stepped out into the bay. In the bay stood Fluffy, with its child Bacon as its support, and, I would guess, a large number of the crew of this Consu ship as witnesses and spectators. Aside from the shuttle and the crowd, the bay was nearly as bare as the last time I saw it, with only Kitty's command center, and a rack of bladed weapons, to break up the monotony.

"Welcome back, Gretchen Trujillo," Fluffy said to me, and motioned to its side. "You remember my child, whom you call Bacon."

"Of course," I said, and motioned to Ran. "This is Ran. Bacon and Ran have met before."

"I have heard. I understand that if you are successful today, the return trip will cost Ran its life."

"That is how Kitty planned it, yes," I said.

"Then I honor its sacrifice, should the duel go poorly for me."

"Thank you," I said. Ran said nothing; Ran knew that it was not meant to be heard from here.

"I see you are wearing a Colonial Defense Forces combat unitard," Fluffy said to me.

"Yes," I said. The Colonial Union combat unitard looked like fitness apparel and was close to the toughest armor humans had ever made. It could take a shotgun blast at near-point-blank range and keep the person inside of it alive. The catch: It could do it once. In this case the unitard could probably protect me from the first several slashes that Fluffy might make on my body. I was not counting on it to take too many more after that. "I hope you don't mind that I chose to wear it."

"It is your right to choose how you come to our duel," Fluffy said. "I will note to you that this bay has a sapper field active in it. If you brought a projectile weapon, it will do you no good."

"I brought no weapons," I said. "You said that I could choose any weapon here. I trusted that you would not leave me without options."

Fluffy motioned to the rack and its impressive set of bladed weapons. "These are the finest weapons we have. As is customary, any weapon you choose is yours to keep, if you can indeed keep it."

"Thank you," I said. I went to the rack, and it was no lie: The weapons there were absolutely beautiful to look at. If I picked one up I had no doubt it would be impeccably balanced, devastatingly sharp, and able to deal a terrifying amount of damage—that is, if I could land the blow. "You honor me with the selection of weapons you've provided."

"You are Consu," Fluffy said. "You deserve no less."

I looked at the assembled crowd. "Your ship's crew?"

"All but a few who are tending to the ship's maintenance. This battle is also being presented to the other Consu ships in Phoenix space. There are those who support Kitty's side of this philosophical argument. There are those who support mine.

Some are yet to decide. The outcome of this duel will be instructive for the last of these."

"I hope it will be," I said.

"Then choose your weapon, Gretchen Trujillo, and let's begin."

I nodded and stepped away from the rack of weapons. "I'm ready," I said.

"You haven't chosen a weapon," Fluffy said.

"No, I have."

"You're going to fight me unarmed," Fluffy said, skeptically.

"I'm fully armed," I said.

"You're either brave or stupid, human."

"And you're stalling, Fluffy."

"As you wish," Fluffy said. "With respect and with your permission, I ask for my child to have the honor of signaling the beginning of the duel."

"I will permit it," I said.

"Thank you," Fluffy said, and screeched something at Bacon. Bacon took a step back, and looked at Fluffy and then at me. It screeched something that, according to the information I had on Consu dueling, meant we each were to take our positions. I chose my position, somewhat away from the shuttle, and Ran took up a position behind me. Fluffy chose its position based on mine.

A second screech, and Fluffy unfolded itself, extending the horrifying slashing arms of the Consu, which could and would take the head off a human as easily as a human could pluck a grape off a vine. I stood comfortably, arms to my side, not presenting a combat stance. Bacon looked over to me, as if to say, *Really?* I gave it a look as if to say, *Yeah, really.*

Bacon looked back toward its parent, gave what I assume was the Consu version of a shrug, and then gave the final screech that signaled the duel had begun.

"You've lost," I said, to Fluffy. "You're dead."

Fluffy did exactly what I wanted it to do; it stopped dead in its tracks. "I beg your pardon," it said, to me.

"You've lost," I repeated. "You're dead."

"If your plan is to confuse me, it's working," Fluffy said, and then extended its slashing arms. "But it won't work for long."

"Let me explain," I said, and walked back toward Ran, and then we both walked back toward Kitty's command center. I touched its hull. "You see this?"

"Yes," Fluffy said.

"This is my weapon," I said. "And as it happens, I intend to keep it."

And with that, Ran and I slipped inside the command center just as sirens began to blare, alerting the crew that something was seriously wrong with their ship.

The last thing I saw before the command module sealed itself was Fluffy bellowing and rushing toward us, all pretense of civility gone, pure animal rage, nothing understanding in its demeanor at all.

And then the command module was sealed and we were gone.

"Let's see how we did," I said to Ran. "Open her up, please."

Ran opened up the command module. On the other side of the opening were some of the crew of an Obin starship, and Deputy Ambassador Clock.

"Welcome back," Clock said, to me and Ran.

"Thank you," I said. "Were we missed?"

"There are currently the beginnings of confusion," Clock said.

"Then we should make things clear."

Clock motioned. "Follow me, Ms. Trujillo."

A few minutes later Ran and I were on the bridge of an Obin ship, and a communication channel was opened on a general band that the Obin knew the Consu used.

"This is Gretchen Trujillo," I said. "As you know, I and the Consu"—and here I tapped my PDA, which had the actual name of Fluffy in ready to go in the Consu language—"were joined in a duel, sanctified by the rites of"—another PDA press, this one using the word for the disk I still had in my effects back on Phoenix Station. "I have won this duel by sending"—Consu name on the PDA—"and their entire ship into a universe uninhabited by the Consu or any other species of which we are familiar. There is no way back for them. They will die there, alone and defeated. This avenue of argument is now settled. I am Consu and I am victorious and as such I invite all of you to leave this space. Do it now, before you really piss me off." I cut off the communication.

"I am not sure about that last part," Ran said to me.

"I guess we'll find out," I said, and we watched, with the tactical screens of the Obin ship's bridge showing the hundreds of Consu ships in Phoenix space, waiting to see if any of them would begin to move.

And they did. A few at first, and then more, then dozens, and then hundreds, moving away from Phoenix and toward—well, honestly, I didn't care where they were going, as long as they were going away. It would take them days to clear the system, because they didn't have the next generation of skip drive, but that was their problem. They were on their way. And then I was on my way, to a room reserved for me on the Obin ship, where I could take a nap, because I had had a really stressful day.

When I woke up, Ran was hovering over me. "I really wish you wouldn't do that," I said.

"You have messages," Ran said to me, holding its PDA.

"I bet I do."

"Where do you want to begin?"

"Is my dad in the message queue?"

"Yes he is."

"Then let's start there."

It's amazing what you can do in ten days, when you're motivated, have friends in high places, and also a machine that bends the known laws of physics like a pretzel. But ten days is still not a lot, and it was all the time we had. At the end of those ten days, Unity Station would be dangerously low on food and supplies. There would be no more margin. We would have to go back.

Dad was not happy about any of this. "*You* don't have to go back," he said to me for roughly the one hundredth time since I'd told him I was returning to Unity Station and why. "You've done enough. You could let someone else do this part."

"Who else, Dad?" I asked.

"There's Ran," he suggested.

I laughed at this. "No, Dad. Ran is good, and one day, Ran will be great. But this is something only I can do."

Dad looked grumpy at this but didn't argue any further. After a hundred and one times, I suppose, I had worn him down. I gave him a long hug and a quick kiss and told him I loved him, and then left him to complete a task he had given me weeks, and a lifetime, ago.

A day later I and Ran sealed ourselves up again in the command module, for what was going to be the last time. "You ready?" I asked Ran.

"I am ready," Ran said.

"Hit it," I said, and then just like that we were back in the Unity Station cargo bay. Skip drives are emotionally unsatisfying this way.

I unsealed the command module and exited it to find Kitty sitting there, serene as could be. "You've returned," it said to me.

"I have," I agreed.

"And your task?"

"Before I get to that, I want to tell you that turning me into a Consu was a dirty trick," I said.

"You are the first human so honored," Kitty said. "And I daresay you will be the last, for a very long time to come. Several of your millennia at least."

"But not because I wanted or deserved it," I said. "Just so you could be sure of a perfect death."

"It wasn't sure," Kitty said. "You could have failed. But it seems you didn't."

I reached into my pocket and retrieved the cobalt blue disk. "This is yours," I said.

"It is not," Kitty said. "When I gave it to you, it became yours. You may keep it. A souvenir of your victory. How was your battle?"

"Quick," I said.

"That seems unlikely," Kitty said. "Your opponent, in addition to being a brilliant mind, was an adept warrior. I have to say I did not expect you to succeed."

"And yet you sent me anyway."

"A more perfect death was worth the risk," Kitty said. "How did you defeat it?"

"I fought unfairly."

"That tells me nothing," Kitty said.

"All right," I said. "I used the command module to send them and their entire ship to another universe and stranded them there."

Kitty made a noise. "If you had done that you could not have returned here," they said.

"Uh-huh," I said, and then turned toward the command module. "Ran!" I yelled.

Ran popped out of the module and came over to me. Kitty watched silently as it did so.

"I would like to know how you did that," it said, finally.

"Oh, I bet you would," I said. "Now. Our deal."

"Is unfulfilled," Kitty said.

"How is that?" I asked.

"You said you stranded your opponent—"

"Fluffy."

"—in another universe. Stranded is not dead."

"It's not dead but it is defeated," I said. "Its influence is gone. The conversation among the Consu has changed. This cusp is going your way. And anyway, the mission you gave me was to deliver a message."

"The message included a duel. The duel was to end with a death."

"It did. Or will, in time."

"I am unsatisfied," Kitty said. "I hold that you did not live up to your end of the bargain. I am not obliged to live up to mine."

I smiled. "You know what, I'm not at all surprised to hear you say all of this."

"I am disappointed," Ran said.

"Disappointed, sure," I said. "Surprised, no. *Anyway*." I motioned back to the command module. "You're going to want to get into that in the next couple of minutes if you don't want to spoil your perfect death."

"What does that mean?" Kitty said.

"It means that in about one hundred and twenty seconds all the air is going to be purged out of this cargo hold and they're going to open it up to the vacuum of space because we have some things to bring in here, and you and that module are going to be in the way. We're going to chuck you both over the side. You can be in it or not, your choice."

"Also I have disabled its ability to skip," Ran said. "You can try to fix it if you choose, but any attempt to do so will disable its life support. You would suffocate quickly."

"Which won't be great for your perfect death," I added. "Okay, bye." Ran and I walked away, me hoping Kitty would be too confused and distracted to get angry and try to kill us. It wouldn't succeed—sharpshooters had already sighted in Kitty from the doorways before we skipped over—but that didn't mean I wanted it to make the attempt.

It didn't. Behind us we heard silence and then a scurrying as Kitty ran toward the disabled command module. As we reached the end of the cargo hold we heard it sealing up behind us.

"You *did* remember to disable the skip drive on it," I said.

"Yes," Ran said. "I did not run it through the life support, however. That was just to keep Kitty busy for a while."

"What happens if it tries to reenable the skip drive?"

"It won't explode," Ran said. "But the math for what will happen is exotic. Kitty's final moment won't be very happy at all."

"What a perfect death," I said.

Ran and I had not skipped directly from Phoenix to Unity Colony's cargo hold. We skipped from a large Obin cargo ship, jammed to its internal rafters with food and supplies, that we dragged along with us when we skipped from our universe to this one. The ship had enough supplies to restock the colony for weeks, which was good, because when we arrived the food stocks for some species were down to their final two or three days. We could not have arrived any later than we did without horror.

We were welcomed as heroes.

That lasted three days.

That was because, on the fourth day, there was some unwelcome news to be delivered to the colony at large.

And, of course, *I* was the one who had to give it.

It was only fair. It had been my plan.

"We can't go back," I said from the colony's council chambers, in a statement sent across the colony's video feed to every colonist and translated into every language they spoke and listened to. "The technology that brought us here was intended to be used to destroy not only this colony but an entire planet of people. It was only through the intercession of a single individual, for reasons unrelated to the potential deaths of billions, that this fate was avoided.

"All the people who understand this technology are now here," I said, and this was true: The Obin who worked with Ran had come with the last cargo transport, along with Deputy Ambassador Clock, who was made leader of the Obin over here. "All the other people who were involved with it are dead or on their way to being so. We can't pretend that one day this technology won't again find its way into the hands of those who want to perpetrate a holocaust. But by staying here, we can delay it. By years, by decades or longer. We stay here to keep everyone else we know and love safe."

"In return, we are given something we need. Something that will allow us to live, and not just live, but to thrive, today and for generations to come. Now, with the help of my Obin associate Ran, let me show you what I mean."

I nodded to Ran, sitting next to me. As I did so, the chain of skip drive satellites circling Unity Colony came to life. They did not need Kitty's command module to do it; the Obin had modeled a bare-bones version of the technology needed to make it happen. It was just enough to work. Kitty's module had indeed been shoved unceremoniously into the dark to make room for the supplies from the Obin ship. We didn't bother to track it. Fuck Kitty.

"It's done," Ran said. I nodded and opened up a video feed to outside of the colony, which was broadcast to everyone inside of it.

On the video feed was a world, blue and green and brown and white, land and oceans and clouds and ice.

"This is what we are given," I said. "A whole world. A world with space enough for all of us, of every species. A world we can all make our own, with effort and courage and a little bit of luck. It has everything we need; all we have to do is go get it."

"The people we've left behind did not forget us," I continued. "In orbit around this planet are dozens of cargo ships, like the one that is supplying us now, that have all the things we need to build a life here. All we have to do is go get them. We can stay here on Unity Colony while we prepare. But over months and years, we will go to the planet and make it ours.

"Unity Colony was an experiment to see if all our people could work and live together. The experiment is over. Now we *have* to live together. All of us, building together, living together, supporting each other through everything this world gives us, every challenge it throws at us, every struggle it brings our way. There is no Unity Colony anymore. There is simply Unity. There is simply us."

"You give a pretty speech," Magdy said to me. "It's almost like you're the daughter of a politician."

"Shut up," I said, fondly. The two of us were walking in the colony's hydroponic farm, which, as Magdy had predicted a couple weeks earlier, had largely been stripped of everything edible. Now that the restocking had meant everyone could eat more than short rations, the plants here would have a chance to grow back. It would take a while. But now there was time.

"How did you get all those cargo ships here in such a short amount of time?" Magdy asked.

"Ran didn't get a lot of sleep," I said. "It had to navigate the control module onto those cargo ships, send them here, and then come back, dozens of times."

"Yes, but how did you find those cargo ships' worth of material in the first place?"

"When the Colonial Union and the Conclave paused colonizing, they had cargo ships' worth of colonizing equipment stockpiled," I said. "We grabbed those. And then for the food and seed stocks and everything else, whatever was coming into Phoenix was fair game. We nationalized a lot of things quickly."

"That must have made you popular."

"I'm pretty sure everyone got paid. My only worry is that in the rush to grab things we made some mistakes. There might be entire cargo containers full of stuffed animals. We'll find out."

"I suppose we will," Magdy said, and then suddenly got uncharacteristically quiet.

"What is it?" I asked him.

"I didn't expect you to come back," he said. "You were gone on a long-shot mission to save us and . . ."

"And you expected me to fail."

"I didn't expect you to fail," Magdy said. "I expected everything to fail *you*."

"There were moments of failure all around," I said. "But I had a reason to get back."

"Well, thank you," Magdy said.

"I wasn't talking about you," I said. "I was thinking about shoving that stupid Consu out of the cargo bay."

Magdy, bless his easily bruised heart, looked genuinely wounded for a moment. I reassured him by giving him a kiss.

"You're mean," he said, when I stopped kissing him.

"This is not a surprise to you," I pointed out.

"No it's not," he agreed, smiling. Then he got serious again. "Do you think it will work?"

"Will what work?"

"This," Magdy said, motioning around us. "All of it. Everything. Unity Colony wasn't exactly an unqualified success, you know. We could all barely stand each other. And now we're stuck with each other forever."

"It could fail," I said. "I made a nice speech and suggested we were all in it together. But if people decide they would rather hate each other than help each other out, then it's easy to have it all fall apart. But there is one thing that makes me optimistic."

"What's that?"

"That we are absolutely one hundred percent alone out here," I said. "There is no Colonial Union. There is no Conclave. As far as we know in this universe there is no intelligent life in this neck of the galaxy. It's just us. Anyone wants to go it alone here, they are truly alone."

"Until they grab that special skip drive and go back," Magdy said.

I shook my head. "The command module is gone," I said. "The colony asteroid is in a stable orbit, but as soon as we're all on the planet, we'll skip it into the sun to make sure it doesn't accidentally fall into the planet. Then the only skip drives we'll have are the boring normal ones that don't play well with gravity wells and only take us to the universes that are just like ours."

"You sound confident you've stuffed that genie back into the bottle."

"I'm not," I said. "I am confident that it's another universe's problem, however. That's good enough for now."

"If you say so."

"I do say so. Stop arguing with me and tell me I'm smart."

"You are smart, Gretchen. Also sexy and funny and an enormous pain in the ass."

"I am the whole package."

"You're never boring," Magdy said.

"No I'm not."

"And you're confident this planet is going to work for us?" he said.

"You're complaining about the planet now," I said.

"I'm not complaining," Magdy said. "But you've brought us here and you tell us that it's perfect, and sure, it looks nice from the video feed, but you and I both remember living on a planet that looked nice on a video feed but smelled like rancid socks and had werewolves on it. So, yes, I'd like to know you checked this planet out before you brought us here."

I stepped back and looked at Magdy. "You really don't know," I said.

"Know what?"

"Let me see your PDA."

"Where is your PDA?"

"It's back in my room."

"You have to stop doing that."

"It's keeping Lucifer company," I said. "I put bird videos on for him to keep him busy. He's a little jumpy from the move. Bird videos make cats happy."

"Very Gretchen to prioritize a cat over everyone else."

"I have no regrets. Just get it out and pull up the video feed of the planet."

Magdy got out his PDA and pulled up the video feed. "Yup, it's a planet," he said to me.

"Does it look familiar at all?"

"Should it?"

"Maybe a little. Look again."

Magdy looked again. "Yeah, coming up with nothing."

"I can't believe I'm in a relationship with an ignoramus."

"I like the first part, less the second."

"Think how I feel."

"Look, just tell me."

"You *absolutely* impossible man," I said. "That's Earth, my love. That's home."

ACKNOWLEDGMENTS

For a change I am going to keep the acknowledgments short. Sorry acknowledgment junkies, maybe I'll write longer next time.

First, thank you to Patrick Nielsen Hayden and Mal Frazier, who didn't crawl through the computer lines to strangle me as I slipped two months past my deadline. I have no excuse. I am a bad man.

Thank you also to the production people who worked on this book, including but not limited to: Deanna Hoak, Tania Bissell, Jessica Warren, Jeff LaSala, Rafal Gibek, Heather Saunders, Jim Kapp, and quite obviously, the legendary John Harris for yet another magnificent Old Man's War cover. I feel genuinely blessed to have his art on my books.

Thank you in addition to everyone in Tor marketing and publicity, starting with Alexis Saarela, my publicist, and adding Sarah Reidy and Lucille Rettino. Over at Tor UK, Bella Pagan and Michael Beale are the best. And so are Katie Stuart, Steve Feldberg and Esther Bochner at Audible. Ethan Ellenberg, Joel Gotler and Matt Sugarman are the fabulous Team Scalzi.

There are people I am missing here, and I'm skipping friends who offered no end of encouragement because I said I wanted to keep this short. Just know that you are all the best and I will thank you in person, possibly with chocolates.

Two people I will not skip, however, are Kristine and Athena Scalzi. I love them both across this and any other conceivable universe.

Now I'm going to bed.

—John Scalzi,
January 21, 2025

ABOUT THE AUTHOR

JOHN SCALZI is one of the most popular science fiction authors of his generation. His novels, which include the enduring Old Man's War series, have won numerous accolades, including the Hugo and Locus Awards. He lives in Ohio, and also online at scalzi.com.